MAN ON FIRE

MAN ON FIRE

Humphrey Hawksley

SEVERN
HOUSE

First world edition published in Great Britain and the USA in 2021
by Severn House, an imprint of Canongate Books Ltd,
14 High Street, Edinburgh EH1 1TE.

Trade paperback edition first published in Great Britain and the USA in 2022
by Severn House, an imprint of Canongate Books Ltd.

severnhouse.com

British Library Cataloguing-in-Publication Data
A CIP catalogue record for this title is available from the British Library.

ISBN-13: 978-0-7278-9034-4 (cased)
ISBN-13: 978-1-78029-790-3 (trade paper)
ISBN-13: 978-1-4483-0529-2 (e-book)

All Severn House titles are printed on acid-free paper.

MIX
Paper from
responsible sources
FSC
www.fsc.org   FSC® C013056

Typeset by Palimpsest Book Production Ltd.,
Falkirk, Stirlingshire, Scotland.
Printed and bound in Great Britain by
TJ Books, Padstow, Cornwall.

To Jonie and Christopher

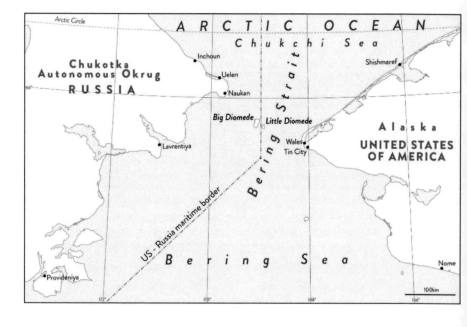

ONE

Bering Strait, Alaska

Rake Ozenna eased the throttle of his fourteen-foot aluminum fishing dinghy and scanned the dense fog that slid fast across the still water. Visibility shifted, sometimes down to a hundred feet or less, sometimes clear to show dark granite rock protruding from the treeless wind-battered landscape of Big Diomede, an island the Russians called Ratmanova. It covered eleven square miles and rose fifteen hundred feet from the sea. No civilians lived there. This was Russia's easternmost military base and along its ridge stood a line of military watch posts facing America.

Behind Rake was Little Diomede, three square miles and as high as the Empire State Building, the smaller, pyramid-shaped island where he had been born and raised, his home community of fewer than a hundred souls.

Rake listened for the sound of an outboard motor, careful to keep his own dinghy inside American waters. Technically, he was on leave after a Syria deployment. But because of where he lived, and his familiarity with the environment, he had been asked to handle a speed-boat crossing from Russia. The boat should be leaving from the small helicopter base around the western side of Big Diomede, taking only minutes to reach the American border. His instructions were to guide the power boat to the other side of Little Diomede, where a bigger vessel, a disguised trawler, would take its occupants on board. He did not know who they were or how many. Rake had been told the crossing was part of a joint US-Russian intelligence-gathering exercise of which the base commander was completely aware.

The border was closed and unmarked. There were no national flags on either island, no buoys in the water, nothing to indicate that this was the frontier between two antagonistic world powers. There was no government security of any kind on Little Diomede, no police, no military, no US Customs and Border people. Border defense against air and sea threats was run by the North American Aerospace Defense Command out of the Elmendorf-Richardson base outside of the Alaskan city of Anchorage, 650 miles to the southeast.

The Diomedes were two dots in the many remote island clusters that ran down from the Arctic into the Pacific Ocean. Since 1867, when the United States bought Alaska from Russia, there had been an understanding that Moscow and Washington should keep this border quiet. Direct confrontation should be unthinkable. The region was too sparsely populated for war, the environment too hostile, and military supply lines would be a nightmare. Far better to settle differences in proxy conflicts elsewhere. During the Cold War, the border had been referred to as the Ice Curtain. Apart from a few tense days some years earlier, when a rogue Russian commander had tried to take the American island, the understanding had held well.

There was the occasional splash of water against the side of the dinghy. Sunlight splayed through the fog. With him was Mikki Wekstatt, whom Rake saw as an older brother. As often happened in remote parts of Alaska, babies were born, families broke up and parents vanished. Both Rake and Mikki had been abandoned by their parents and raised by a couple on the island. Mikki, ten years older, had convinced Rake to join the army, first the Alaska National Guard and from there a series of secondments to special forces units, mainly to Afghanistan, Iraq and Syria.

Mikki got out tackle. If they had a three-hour wait, they might as well do some fishing. Mikki was tall, slim and wide-shouldered, and a decorated army marksman. He had stayed sergeant, while Rake had broken through to officer class. Now Mikki was a detective with the Alaska State Troopers and trying to persuade Rake to quit the military and join him. Mikki wanted Rake home, where he belonged, leading their tiny community. There was talk of the government shutting down Little Diomede and moving people out as they had done on the Russian side. Rake and Mikki were the new tribal leaders. They had to keep the community alive. Rake listened but wasn't convinced. Sure, he wanted one foot in his community, but he also wanted the outside world, which was why he had brought a longtime on-again off-again girlfriend back to the island with him.

Carrie Walker and Rake had once been engaged to be married That was five years ago and it hadn't worked out. As a trauma surgeon, Carrie worked war zones and they had met in Afghanistan. But, after that, they were barely together. Rake was constantly on deployment. Now, Carrie was trying to settle down at a big hospital in Washington, DC, but that was proving a challenge. She was too restless for an institution. She fought with management to get patients better treatment. A relationship with another doctor had hit the rocks. Rake had suggested Carrie join him for a week or so on Little Diomede, which had no doctor of its own. She was staying in Rake's house, a government-built stilted cabin on the island's hillside, in a separate room, which was fine with Rake who was decompressing from a tough three months in Syria. Over the past few days, she had been giving the islanders a free check-up. Carrie was the only woman he had been unable to shake from his mind. One time she had said she needed to know what he was feeling and what he wanted. Rake didn't have an answer. Those things had never been much part of his world.

Maybe she was that other world he wanted to keep. Maybe he did want to end up changing, becoming someone else. Didn't everyone? Maybe he and Carrie would end up in bed again. Maybe not.

Rake focused on the blue-gray water occasionally rippling with a light breeze between the two islands. At this time of summer, the sun barely dipped below the horizon, leaving the islands and sea perpetually bathed in light.

'So, we wait?' asked Mikki.

'We do.' Rake wore an earpiece with a line open to Washington, DC, from where the operation was being run. There was drone surveillance – Rake did not know exactly what – and the long-range radar station at Tin City was monitoring. Rake's orders were to report only the successful meeting-up and then the safe delivery to the trawler.

Through gaps in the fog, Rake spotted circling birds which flew out of hillsides with the sound of engines. At one time, the Diomede islands had more than six million birds between them.

Now, Rake wasn't so sure. Climate change had skewed fish stocks, which had damaged bird life. Halibut were way down. Cod and pollock were coming up from hundreds of miles south as the waters there got too warm. Rake was seeing more and more seabirds too emaciated and weak to fly because their staple diet of smelts was vanishing.

'So, what's with you and Carrie?' Mikki stretched out a line and speared its fishhook with bait made up of crab meat and walrus blubber. Mikki and Carrie got on well, but he never liked the pull she had on Rake.

'She's trying to settle in DC.' Rake didn't move his gaze from the water. 'Finding it bumpy.'

'Thought they wanted you to do something at West Point.'

'They call it a mid-career officer's course.' Rake read the fog, how it worked with water, sun and temperature, dense and slow moving. With so little wind it would stretch for a mile, probably more.

'You need to give Carrie space to find someone,' Mikki was saying. 'She's at that stage of life. They'll go white picket fence, all that crap you can't stand . . .' He broke off and raised his hand. 'Fuck! Was that a .50 cal?'

They both heard gunfire, a single burst, six rapid rounds that could have come from a Russian heavy machine gun. A .50 caliber was an American designation. The Russian equivalent was slightly larger, at .57 caliber, with a range of more than two miles. They heard an engine. Rake eased up the throttle. Mikki glanced curiously at him. 'You said that us and them know what's going on?'

'That's what I was told.' Rake quietened the engine and guided the dinghy to keep as out of sight as possible within the fog cloud. There was another burst, ten rounds.

Mikki dropped the fishing tackle, unzipped a waterproof rifle case and brought out an M40 he had kept after an Afghan tour.

TWO

'Two o'clock.' Rake pointed to his right.

Mikki sighted the weapon through thick fog.

Rake saw a blur, texture changing in the mist. Sound was clearer. The high, incoming pitch of an engine travelling at a speed. On normal days, if a Little Diomede fishing dinghy came too close, the Russians would use a massive public address system to yell at them to keep back. Today, they stayed silent.

The approaching engine missed a beat and picked up again, increasing power. From behind came a siren, not the usual one, more screaming like an emergency vehicle.

'Two vessels.' Mikki's right eye was on the rifle's scope.

Rake moved the dinghy forward. The GPS said they were a hundred and fifty meters inside American territory. They were not permitted to cross into Russia. They could touch the line. A red flare went up, its glow scattering through mist cloud. Rake identified the outboard as the sort used on a fast, long-range river craft. Somewhere nearby he heard the second vessel, the familiar inboard hum of a Russian military patrol boat.

'Ten o'clock,' said Mikki.

To their left, an inflatable ribbed craft came into sight, going fast and erratically. Someone was either leaning or collapsed over the wheel. A flash of white yellow blazed from behind, followed by a streak of tracer and the roar of machine-gun fire that tore into the inflatable, shredding fiberglass and rubber. The vessel tilted back, weighed down by the outboard. The person in it clawed at the sides, failing to get a grip, tearing at frayed rubber.

'Go back, Americans.' A patrol boat voice in broken English. 'This is Russian territory.'

The GPS put the sinking inflatable thirty feet inside Russia, moving east toward the American line. Rake eased back his throttle. The patrol boat had used a weapon he recognized as the 7.62-mm general-purpose machine gun, standard issue on Russian coastal vessels. The more powerful heavy machine gun would have been from the Russian island itself, two weapons deployed simultaneously on a border where guns were usually quiet.

The command again: 'Go back, Americans, or we will open fire on you.'

They would not shoot him, thought Rake. Not here, not with the way the American President was cozying up to Russia.

'Distract them,' Rake instructed Mikki. He clipped a rope to his belt, took out his earpiece, sheathed his fishing knife and slipped into the sea. Cold water rushed around him, pumping his heart. He swam, barely breaking a ripple. Mikki turned on a recording they used to irritate Russian border guards, a mix of speeches by Stalin, Gorbachev, Putin, military music, a local Alaska radio talk show, people yelling at each other about Arctic drilling, all jumbled together, speakers turned up full volume.

Rake reached the inflatable. A limp hand, a woman's, hung over the side. He pushed himself up. The rubber tore more, and the craft dipped. Water poured in. She toppled over him, her fingers gripping his, and fell dead-weight into the sea, taking Rake under with her. He surfaced and hooked his arms under hers, lifeguard style. He kicked his way back to the dinghy, using the belt rope to guide him. Blood trailed from her. The sea-water temperature was low enough to kill within minutes. She grasped him, feeling for his hand. She was alive, with energy. Mikki pulled in the rope. Rake swam hard toward the dinghy.

Mikki stretched down, taking her weight from Rake, who let go just as a fist struck the right side of his head, glancing across the temple. Arms wrapped around his neck and dragged him backward. Water flooded into his mouth, catching in his throat, choking him. A second blow smashed into the left side of his head, blurring his concentration.

There were two swimmers, in wetsuits, goggles, oxygen tanks, flippers, the works. One had an arm locked skillfully around his neck. The other had the woman. Water swept over him, the swell from the patrol boat coming toward them, men on deck, shouting instructions.

Rake let himself be taken. They could have killed him. They hadn't, but that didn't apply to the woman. They had shot her with intention to kill. Rake would try to get away once he'd worked out how to neutralize both swimmers simultaneously.

The Russian plan must be to bring back all three of them. They would portray it as a rescue operation for a fishing dinghy in trouble. They would cite the International Convention on Maritime Search and Rescue under which Russia and America operated. There was cooperation in the Bering Strait, which made what was unfolding so strange and out of place.

A Russian search lamp, bouncing through the fog, succeeded only in splaying light into a glare. The second swimmer let go of the woman. She floated free, probably unconscious, left to die. The swimmer had two hands clasped to the bow of the dinghy to stop Mikki going into the water after her. The patrol boat was close, water splashing through from its propellers. Mikki drew his state-trooper-issue Glock 22.

Unexpectedly, Rake's swimmer turned to look back, his arm loosening enough for Rake to unsheathe his knife. The swimmer saw the glint of steel, lit by the search lamp. Rake's blade moved through the water. Instead of blocking it, the Russian pushed himself back.

'Udachi,' he shouted through the mouthpiece. *Good luck.*

On the dinghy, Mikki had his pistol poised to fire. But his swimmer let go of the bow, ducking under the water and away, two military frogmen following a sudden reversal of orders to leave. Rake guessed what was happening: forget about the Americans, too much trouble. Deal with the woman, floating between Rake and the dinghy. Her leg kicked. A Russian frogman broke surface inches from her, a knife in his right hand, raised to strike and kill her.

Mikki shot him, three decisive cracks of gunfire from the Glock, one missed, one to the face, one somewhere else that Rake didn't see. He kicked himself forward and rolled onto his back in time to see the second swimmer's knife plunge down against him. Rake caught his wrist and twisted back the knife hand to cut the oxygen connection. The swimmer gasped. His grip weakened. Rake kicked him away. '*Idti!*' he shouted in Russian. *Go.*

Even with his buddy dead, mouthpiece torn away, the Russian didn't go, predictable for a soldier whose mission was un-accomplished. His concentration was skewed enough for Rake to bound forward, wrap his legs around him and pull him in close. He slashed the hand that held the knife and rammed his elbow hard between the man's eyes. His enemy floundered. Rake pushed him away and, looming like a phantom, the Russian boat appeared through the fog, its bow bearing straight down on him.

Mikki fired his rifle in deliberate, steady controlled pairs, winging one crewman on deck and shattering the wheelhouse glass. Rake had seen Mikki hit a polar bear at three hundred yards from a dinghy in winter seas. This target was bigger and closer. The machine gun could have torn through Mikki and the dinghy in moments. But it stayed quiet. Rake pushed himself back out of the turbulence of the wake.

Why?

Russia and America were trying to be allies, not shoot at each other on their quiet, shared border. They had attacked, withdrawn, attacked again, as if the crew was following a stream of conflicting orders. They were not returning Mikki's fire. Clearing water from his eyes, Rake saw the woman, trying to swim, knowing the direction she needed to go. The remnants of the patrol boat's wake splashed around him. Mikki guided the dinghy toward her.

Rake held her, keeping her head above the surface, careful not to grasp too hard, not knowing where she had been shot. Mikki lifted her gently under the shoulders, sliding her over and laying her on a blanket. He hauled Rake in, then opened full throttle. The thrust of the engine put the bow in the air and the stern further down in the water. The Russians didn't fire again. Nor did they cross into American territory. Mikki swung toward Little Diomede island, bringing back the throttle to ease the bumps. Rake checked the woman's vital signs. There was a pulse. She was shivering. There was a wound in the lower right leg. Judging from rips in the clothing, she had been hit by at least two rounds in the torso. Her breathing was light and erratic.

'Look at me.' Rake gently pressed his hand against her cheek. 'Stay with us. You're going to be fine. We'll have you dry and warm in a few minutes.'

Her eyes opened, expressionless, and closed.

'What's your name?' *Keep her engaged. Keep hope. Keep her alive.* 'Look at me.'

She was in her mid-thirties, Asiatic features, with short dark hair and a rounded face with a sharp chin. She wore a one-piece green waterproof, its top shredded. Underneath, her clothes were wrong for the environment, as if she had bought them from an expensive city camping store.

She opened her eyes again, bloodshot with salt water.

'We've got you.' He gently held her hand.

Her eyes moved jaggedly left to right, until they focused on Rake. Something seemed to ripple through her, something she understood. Her voice was faint, barely audible.

'You are safe,' said Rake.

'No. Not safe.' She had enough strength to squeeze his hand. 'Not safe,' she repeated.

THREE

The island of Little Diomede was covered in a thin haze that swirled around small houses built on stilts up the steep hillside. Islanders stood with a stretcher on the rocky beach encircled with large dark boulders in a tiny bay which kept the water calm. The aluminum hull jolted and scraped on pebbles as Mikki brought the dinghy ashore. Strong hands pulled it in.

'This is America,' Rake told the injured woman. 'You made it. We're going to get you—'

'Not safe,' she said again, her voice quivering.

Rake was about to give the signal to transfer from the boat to the stretcher when he heard Carrie's voice from the hillside. 'Wait.' Blonde hair tied in a bun, dressed in a green smock, a large medical rucksack slung over her shoulder, she ran down narrow concrete paths, along rough ground toward the jetty, jumped onto a boulder and then to the beach. 'Wait,' she repeated. 'I need to check her injuries.'

The islanders stepped aside. The woman lay across the middle seat of the dinghy, her back straight, her feet down, her breathing shallow, her face blotched with pinks and reds, wrinkled from cold salt water. Her eyes stayed fixed upwards at the sky. A black bang of hair tufted across to the left of her forehead, stuck in congealed blood gashed from her ear.

Carrie barely acknowledged Rake and the others. Her concentration focused on the wounded woman. 'What happened?' she asked while checking her pulse.

'Gunshot wounds,' said Rake. 'Right leg. And somewhere in the torso.'

Carrie's expression was unfazed, face sharp, skin drawn tight across prominent cheek bones. She unzipped her rucksack, pulled out a metallic bandage pack containing a combat gauze impregnated with a clotting agent to stop bleeding. She unraveled the gauze, laid it across the upper right leg and gave it a second to start soaking up blood. Joan Ahkaluk, the island nurse, took over holding it. The woman winced. Her eyes squeezed shut.

'We're going to lift you,' Carrie told her. 'It will hurt.'

There was no response. Rake gave the count – one, two, three, lift. In a second, she was on the stretcher. Joan laid a pillow under her head, rested her left fingers on the pulse and held down the gauze with her right hand. Treading smoothly over the rocky ground, they carried the woman to the school, a large modern building on the edge of the settlement. Mikki slipped his rifle into the case and asked, 'Who the hell is she?'

'I don't know.' Rake's phone vibrated through its waterproof case. The caller was Harry Lucas, the government defense contractor running the mission. 'We have her,' said Rake. 'She's badly hit. There's been a firefight.'

'We picked up that much.' Lucas voice was clipped. 'What happened?'

'They tried to kill her. They backed off. Then they tried again. We got her out.'

'But why?' Lucas asked testily, as if Rake would know. 'We're meant to be working with the Russians on this.'

'You tell me, Harry. It's your op.' Rake stayed on the right side of anger. Lucas was responsible, but Rake doubted it was his fault. He was too thorough for that, and security operations could somersault at any time.

'Is she conscious?' Lucas asked.

'In and out. What do you need?'

'She should have a thumb drive.'

'If it's there, I'll get it. What's on it?'

'A cryptographic code.'

'Code for what?'

Lucas didn't answer. Rake pressed, 'What do I ask her, Harry? She's conscious now. In five minutes, she might be dead. So, what do we ask her?'

'The drive contains details of a new weapon that's out there.' Lucas drew a breath. 'We don't know what, except it's a game-changer.'

'So why are the Russians giving it to us?'

'Best guess is that the Russian military wants it. The Kremlin doesn't, especially now with its new détente with us, which is why they're sharing.'

'You need to know what the weapon is?'

'Correct, and get her identity and the drive that she's carrying.'

Inside the school, on Carrie's instructions, they lay the woman on a stainless-steel dining table fixed to the floor with benches each side. Behind was a kitchen. Her wounded right leg sprang out and recoiled, an unconscious reaction to a nerve message. Joan's husband, Henry, held it and scissored through her pants. Mikki prepared a tourniquet. Joan rested her hand on the patient's neck, speaking to her softly.

Carrie saw Rake on the phone and said, 'We need an air ambulance. Now.'

Rake repeated to Lucas, who had anticipated it, 'Thirty minutes out.'

Joan held the woman's hand. She and Henry had raised Rake from the age of seven. His mother left when he was five. His father stayed another two years, then vanished too. There was a rumor he had gone to Russia.

The woman's eyes opened unsteadily, trying to focus on the ceiling. Her breathing was steady. The way her head tilted emphasized her Asiatic features. She was slight and fit. Her hair was black, her eyes green-blue, her height around five foot eight. Her clothes – warm, tough, designed for travel – would have been all right for a fast, secure crossing, but not for going into near-freezing sea water with no wetsuit, only a protective green one-piece which was torn at the top, a zip pocket sliced through, fabric hanging loose. This was where she would likely have secured the drive, zipped and waterproof. Rake felt inside and found nothing.

Carrie shone a flashlight into her eyes which were half-open but unresponsive. She raised the woman's head to examine the back. Blood ran from the ear around the temple to the base of the skull. She moved the flashlight to the ear. 'Torso,' she said.

Joan cut open the shirt and vest. There was a raw blood mark where a single round had penetrated below the ribcage. It looked slight, even harmless. But a single bullet could rip through muscle, bone, organs and blood vessels, and the damage would be near invisible.

'Legs.'

From the amount of blood on the clothing, Rake thought an artery might be severed. But her life had been saved by Carrie's clotting agent and Mikki's tourniquet. The patient shifted, seemed to want to push herself up.

Carrie put her arm under her shoulders, taking her weight. 'My name is Dr Carrie Walker. We're going to get you well. You're in America. You are safe.'

Rake was at Carrie's side and said, 'Where is the drive—'

'Not now,' Carrie snapped.

Rake kept going. He crouched so he was close to her face. 'What is the weapon?'

Her eyes opened, trembled, closed again. Carrie lowered her back.

'The drive?' Rake pressed. 'Where is the drive?'

Carrie's gripped Rake's shoulder, trying to pull him away. Joan arranged a pillow under the patient's head.

'The code?' Rake sensed Carrie's growing hostility. The survival of her patient was pitted against retrieving the information she carried.

'Not safe.' Barely a whisper, breath from her lips. She lost her strength.

'The Kremlin?' tried Rake, hoping one of his questions would prompt a response.

Carrie stepped away and asked Joan in a low voice: 'Do you have propofol or pentobarbital?'

'Our barbiturate sedative is thiopental,' answered Joan.

Carrie said, 'If we sedate her and induce a coma, we lessen the demand for oxygenated blood and reduce pressure on the brain, which will cut the risk of long-term damage.'

'We need to keep her conscious.' Rake would lose any chance of speaking to her if they induced a coma.

'We're trying to save her life.' Carrie's face creased in a way Rake had seen many times before, tense, pushing her tongue against her lower lip, brooking no opposition.

'I need to find out—' Rake attempted.

'When exactly do you need to find out, Rake?' It was less a question, more Carrie ramming home her point. 'An induced coma will buy a couple of hours to get medical treatment. The tourniquet will hold. We may need a thoracotomy, surgery underneath the ribcage to stop internal bleeding. If we do, we can't save her because we can't do it here. The head wound shows contusion over her ear and temple to the back of the skull. She could go into shock at any minute because of bleeding on the brain.'

'OK.' Rake nodded, seeing that Carrie was right. Whatever the patient muttered now would be uncorroborated or downright wrong. Once she was in the coma, they could do a full search for the drive.

'Thiopental will do,' Carrie said to Joan. 'In fact, better because it's faster. We'll go for seven milligrams.'

Carrie administered it with a syringe. With the first intake, the patient tried to push herself up again. She arched, trembling, and her head jerked round toward Rake. Her eyes were sharp and open. She lifted a hand enough to beckon him, trying to speak. Rake stepped over, his ear to her mouth. She whispered. He couldn't make it out. She spluttered, spraying saliva over him, and gripped his arm. Her body shook with huge strength from young muscles. Her eyes darted around. Then her muscles relaxed, and she collapsed back onto the table.

Carrie shone the flashlight into her eyes, touching two fingers against her carotid artery in the neck, keeping them there. 'She's settling.'

Joan covered her blood-smeared chest with a blanket and wiped vomit from her face. Rake checked the rest of her pockets, running the sodden seams through his fingers in case the driver had been sewn in. He found nothing. She had no papers either, no money, nothing personal. He lifted her fingers. They had been scarred above the upper joints, the skin smooth, rubbed down with alcohol leaving fingerprints unreadable.

'Anything?' asked Carrie.

Rake shook his head, rested his hand on Carrie's arm. 'Thanks, and well done.'

'Go put some dry clothes on.' Carrie gave him a short smile. 'And get my stuff while you're up there. I'll be leaving with her.'

Rake pushed open the door and stepped outside into sunlight and wind. He walked around the veranda to call Harry Lucas. The fog had cleared. The summer sun was rising in the sky it had never left. Across toward Big Diomede, there was no sign of the patrol boat, no trace of the killing, quiet, a border at peace with itself, a normal day.

'Helicopter's fifteen minutes out.' Lucas came across the line.

'Carrie's put her into a coma. If she had a drive, it got ripped out.'

'OK.' Lucas's tone was flat, accepting of the worst possible news.

'She scarred her fingers, looks like in the past week. She carried nothing.'

'We need to keep a lid on it,' said Lucas.

'Understood.' The islanders were suspicious of all government agencies. They would keep quiet.

Lucas continued, 'An air ambulance will be in Wales to take you all to DC.' Wales was a mainland settlement about thirty miles from Little Diomede.

'Carrie says she may need surgery under the ribcage to stop internal bleeding.'

'Then she'll go to Nome,' replied Lucas calmly. 'I need you and Mikki Wekstatt in DC. Carrie should stay with her.'

You couldn't drag her away, thought Rake, ending the call and signaling to Mikki through the window. The small school dining area resembled a makeshift emergency room. A dozen islanders gathered around the table, giving space to Joan, Henry and Carrie. Mikki was on a stool by the door, keeping watch as if they were in enemy territory. Rake told him they were going to DC and the helicopter would be here in ten minutes. They left the school and took the boarded walkway toward their homes, passing an old dirty dark green Alaska National Guard post that had been abandoned in the early nineties. Mikki's house was bigger and had the skull of a polar bear he had shot on a post outside the door. Seal skins were stretched taut to dry on wires on the other side of the path. Rake's smaller house, no more than a one-bedroom cabin, was next door. His cold-weather gear hung on hooks inside the door, with an old green Soviet army cap which he had worn as a kid when he lived there with his father. Rake kept the place neat, like in an army camp, when you had to know where everything was in the dark. There were photographs on the wall of people he thought were family, faded color and black and white. Most would be dead now. Some had ended up on the other side when the border closed in the Cold War. His father had gone over there chasing some woman. He kept his photograph in the middle of the wall, standing on a rock with a rifle, gazing across the strait toward Big Diomede. Rake left a gap for his mother, an empty frame with a smiling emoji face in it, in the hope that one day he might know what she looked like.

Above the pictures, in a decorative cradle, was the long penis bone from a walrus he had shot as a teenager, and underneath that a seal-skin drum from his school days when they had learned native dances. He moved the drum to unlock a wooden trunk where he kept his weapons, some licensed, some not.

He brought out his SIG Sauer P226 pistol and shoulder holster and a waterproof bag of six fifteen-round magazines and his SIG 938 with an ankle holster and three ten-round magazines. He had used his Ontario Mark 3 six-inch double-edged stainless-steel combat knife on the Russian frogman. He laid it on a chair and brought out the slimmer seven-inch Fairbairn-Sykes given to him in Syria by a corporal in the British Special Air Services whose life he had saved. Next to that he put a small knife that he had taken from an Islamic State fighter near the Syrian–Turkish border. Its fixed blade had a black ceramic coating to prevent light reflection.

He stripped off and showered for a minute while stomping salt water out of his wet clothes. He put on loose travel gear and threw a change into a bag. Having given the small bedroom to Carrie, he was sleeping on the floor. Straight after deployment, Rake preferred the floor.

Carrie was messy. Some of her stuff was strewn over the unmade bed. Some stayed in her rucksack. A bra was hung on a mirror hook which Rake had decorated with a small American flag. She had placed a photo of her mom and dad on the bedside table. Her mother, a nurse, was Russian, and her father a coronary surgeon from Estonia, where Carrie had been born. When the Soviet Union collapsed, Estonia filled with anti-Russian senti-ment. Her parents took their two daughters to India where they found work in a hospital. They ended up living in Brooklyn. While Carrie's little sister, Angie, became an ear, nose and throat specialist, married with children, Carrie had been unable to settle.

Once she had told Rake that she envied him because at least he knew where home was. After his Syrian mission, he was summoned to the Pentagon for a debrief. Carrie was working at a big hospital near the State Department. He had called suggesting coffee. She was in a vulnerable mood that Rake recognized and he suggested, half-joking, that she come to Little Diomede and give everyone a medical.

'Don't hit on me, OK?' she had replied. Carrie was like that – decisive, flexible, fearless. It turned out that at the hospital she had saved a patient's life by breaking an operating room protocol. It was what made her a good trauma surgeon, but bad at fitting in to institutions. She had also split up with a new boyfriend she'd been planning to move in with. Carrie seemed to hold up her sister, Angie, as the role model she should be. Angie had once told Rake she felt the same about Carrie.

Rake didn't do such complications. A lot of the time he gave no thought to what he felt about anything. Carrie had been on a low; he had offered sanctuary. There had been a fight on the border, a woman got hurt, and he was now going to DC. It was about what was needed and getting the job done.

He packed Carrie's rucksack, collected her toiletries from the bathroom, gathered his wet clothes, opened the door, locked it, hung the clothes on a line near the seal skins. Mikki stepped out of his house. The helicopter was approaching. It was the old Bell chopper from Nome. On its engine sound, birds flew out from the hillside. Henry stood on the helipad to guide it in. Carrie and Joan walked on either side of the stretcher as it was brought down from the school.

Helicopter downdraft scattered scree, splashing sea water onto the chipped concrete of the helipad. Carrie signaled for the stretcher to stay back while the skids touched down and settled. The woman lay flat, eyes closed, face pale, bloodstains on bandages, but tranquil in her induced coma.

As Carrie signaled for the stretcher to move onto the helipad, the woman shook and let out a short, tight scream. Her whole body convulsed.

'Cardiac arrest,' shouted Carrie. 'Put her down.'

The edge of the downdraft blew across.

Carrie pumped the chest fast, the heel of her hand on the

breastbone. A crewman jumped down from the helicopter with a defibrillator. Carrie took the electrode pads and placed them diagonally above and below the heart. She set the defibrillator to near maximum charge, and pressed the buttons.

The soft thud of electricity forging through a human body was drowned out by helicopter noise. The patient didn't respond. Her convulsions had stopped. She lay without sign of life. Carrie tried chest compressions again. Nothing. 'We need to turn her over,' she instructed.

'She's gone,' said Joan.

Carrie said, 'One from the back.'

Rake and Mikki lifted her enough for Joan to get a paddle under her shirt midway down her back. Carrie waited for the connection reading, then administered the charge. Nothing again.

'It's over,' said Rake.

'She's gone.' Joan gently rubbed Carrie's shoulder.

The helicopter rotor blades ticked round. Birds swirled above it, waiting for it to take off. From the veranda of the school, and on the scree above the beach, islanders watched silently. The woman whom Rake and Mikki had pulled from the water barely an hour ago was dead.

Carrie kicked stones toward the sea. 'She didn't make it,' she shouted to no one in particular.

'You did good,' said Mikki.

'She fucking died! What good is that?' countered Carrie. 'She was our age, Rake. She was our fucking age. She didn't deserve . . .' She kicked more stones and wound her hair into a tighter knot.

'She died. But you didn't shoot her.' Rake pointed across to Big Diomede. 'They did. They killed her.'

FOUR

Harry Lucas ran a private contracting company with a control center in his apartment near Dupont Circle and offices five miles south in Crystal City. He owned a laboratory there for forensic examination and a small mortuary for precisely the type of situation that had arisen.

From Andrews Air Force Base, southwest of Washington, Mikki Wekstatt and Carrie Walker had gone to Crystal City, Wekstatt to oversee forensics and Carrie the autopsy. Rake headed to Dupont Circle. All communication was being slated Top Secret, the highest level of US intelligence classification, which matched Lucas's own security clearance of DV, or Developed Vetting.

Lucas had served with the US Marines in the early stages of the Afghan and Iraq wars and then won a seat in the House of Representatives where he became chair of the House Intelligence Committee. He had been a rising star, married to an equally high-flying politician across the Atlantic, who had handled the long-distance relationship, competing careers and inevitable divorce better than he had. Stephanie Lucas moved on to become Ambassador to both Washington and Moscow, and was now the British Foreign Secretary. Lucas had gone off the rails, losing his seat and hitting bottom before pulling himself back up to do what he was doing now.

He had chosen Crystal City for his business because it was close to the Pentagon and colleagues in the expanding private security industry. But since President Peter Merrow had won a second term in November, Lucas found himself more often in the White House than the Pentagon, the CIA headquarters in Langley, or the historic Anacostia neighborhood in southeast Washington where Homeland Security was based.

Merrow was keen to retarget the intelligence community toward China's expansion. He was encountering resistance, particularly from those whose careers had been made from Middle East and North African conflicts, and who now sat in positions of authority. He had concluded that rather than take on two global powers at once, he should bring Moscow alongside against Beijing in a reversal of Richard Nixon's 1970s China initiative.

This Bering Strait operation was meant to underline the two governments working together on the most classified of issues. Lucas only knew that the thumb drive carried by the agent contained intelligence about a new weapon. The scant communication referred to overwhelming destruction. The information was to be a gift from the Kremlin to the White House. Lucas also had no idea why it was to be delivered across the sea border and not to an embassy or somewhere more straightforward.

The initiative had been Russia's, a phone call from the commander of the Eastern Military District to the commander of the US Indo-Pacific Command in Hawaii. The two men had met a year earlier at a security summit in Singapore. From there the operation had appeared to move smoothly into shape, except it sounded like a departmental turf fight had broken out, taking it down to the wire. Ozenna had told Lucas that the Russian troops must have been getting contradictory orders, first attacking, then withdrawing.

Lucas's surveillance showed the Lincoln Town car carrying Rake was rounding Logan Circle into Church Street and would soon arrive at his apartment. As the vehicle pulled up, he opened the door and showed Rake into a large open-plan living room, simply furnished with tough gray carpet and a rectangular, stainless-steel coffee table with dark leather chairs and sofas around it. On a ledge under a bookshelf stood a coffee machine that scented the room.

Rake was unshaven, wearing the thick blue denim shirt and jeans he had grabbed before leaving Little Diomede. He put his small rucksack on the floor, helped himself to coffee, and asked, 'Who was she?'

'She was a courier with backing right up to the Kremlin, or so we thought. That's it, Major.' Though Lucas and Rake had worked several operations before, and respected each other, they were not close. Lucas often referred to Rake simply as Major.

'And this weapon? This code?' Rake had told Lucas that the woman had said nothing before she died.

'We don't know.'

'The Russians know.'

'The Kremlin is distancing itself. They say you opened fire on a civilian ribbed craft. When their patrol boat came to help, you fired on it. They have two dead, one wounded, murdered by Americans.' Lucas's sharp blue eyes carried no message, no accusation, no guilt, not even stress.

'They opened fire first.' Rake sipped his coffee. 'The patrol boat was already there. Its guns tore open the ribbed inflatable.'

'Your instructions were to pick her up only once she had crossed.'

'She was shot by the Russians when in American territory. We tried to save her.' Rake put the coffee cup on a ledge. His tone was soft, unemotional, firm. 'Mikki and I will not be the fall guys. This mission did not go wrong because two trigger-happy Eskimos screwed up.'

'I know.' Lucas stepped to a door to the right of the bookcase, flipped open a keypad on the wall, gave himself a fingerprint and iris scan, then punched in a six-digit code. The door slid open. 'I haven't asked you here for a debrief, Major. I've asked you to help me find out what the hell is going on.'

The windowless, high-ceilinged room was the same size as his living area, its walls banked with electronic equipment and screens which flickered on as they stepped in. Lucas closed the door behind them. On one screen were dozens of images resembling the woman who had died.

Although her features were mostly Asiatic, in some images she seemed more south European. Her skin complexion was olive and Mediterranean. She was lively, with an engaging expression with other people, focused when alone, whether walking along a street, or driving a car, both hands on the wheel, concentrating on the road. She was an energetic dancer, smiled at hotel porters, hugged friends, locked a persuasive gaze on wait staff when ordering at restaurants. Her hair was short and dark, stylishly cut, exactly as Rake had seen her, except in a couple of shots where she wore a long blonde wig that bounced on her shoulders.

'My facial recognition software has been working overtime,' said Lucas. 'According to best matches, her name is Katia Codic, aged thirty-four, on the books of the FSB 2010 to 2016. After that, no known affiliation.' Lucas zoomed in on one specific shot. 'Except for this, Major, which is another reason you're here.'

Katia was at a corner table, captioned as being in the Lotte Hotel, Seoul, South Korea. She wore a navy-blue business suit with a neatly knotted maroon scarf. A small matching handbag lay on the table. The man with her was Caucasian, well over six foot, with tidily cropped brown hair. He leaned back in his chair, head tilted, with a fraction of his face in shot. He wore a dark blazer, beige pants and slip-on black leather shoes, the stock outfit for a successful mid-career businessman.

Lucas flipped to a shot of him leaving, turning so he was fully recognizable. Rake moved closer to the screen to confirm what he was seeing. He looked abruptly at Lucas who said, 'Yes. It's him.'

'He's involved?'

'I don't know, but he knows our Katia Codic.'

Rake leant against the wall, arms folded, studying the man on the screen. Colonel Ruslan Yumatov and Rake had crossed paths twice before. Yumatov had been the second in command of a failed operation to take Little Diomede. Russian troops were on the island for barely a couple of days. Rake helped end their occupation by crossing the ice to Big Diomedes and taking the base there. Yumatov appeared again, masterminding an operation to attack a US-Russian presidential summit in Norway. It had almost cost Carrie her life. Rake could have let Yumatov die when his vehicle broke through river ice and plunged into freezing water. Instead Rake had pulled him out. That was the last time he and Lucas had worked together. Colonel Ruslan Yumatov should have been incarcerated somewhere, interrogated and forgotten, even executed. According to official Russian records, Yumatov was dead. His attempted assassination of both the US and Russian presidents had never leaked.

Rake pulled an energy bar from his pocket and tore it open with his teeth. 'So where is Yumatov?' He pulled up a chair next to Lucas, controlling his reaction. He chewed on the bar, tasting honey, walnut, ginger, whatever else was in there.

'He's being held as an enemy combatant, like a Guantanamo detainee except not in Guantanamo. He hasn't spoken a word.' Lucas curled thumb and forefinger into a zero. 'Zilch. Nothing to any interrogator – the soft guys, the hard guys, the sleep-deprivation guys, the waterboarding guys, the truth-serum guys. His psychological rigor is astounding. We even tried SP-117.'

SP-117 was a Russian-made truth serum, stronger than most in the way it manipulated the nervous system. Serums worked as depressants, slowing the transmission of information to the brain and blurring concentration, making it easier to tell the truth than lie. SP-117 acted like a sniper's shot: hard, targeted, powerful.

'The only sound he makes is twice-daily voice exercises to stop his laryngeal muscles atrophying. Russian liturgical chants are his favorites.'

A tiny green lamp went on over Lucas's screens, accompanied by a low beep. Lucas drummed his fingers on the workstation. A screen settled with newly computed results of facial imaging. Lucas pulled in Russian and Chinese formulae, technically illegal in the United States. He worked contacts on the dark web where stolen surveillance footage was traded, keeping himself ahead of the game. There were four images, each of Yumatov and the woman they now identified as Katia Codic. The first showed them in the Navigator Club Lounge at Moscow's Domodedovo Airport, booked on BA 232, the afternoon flight to London.

A month later they were on the steps of an elegant white five-story town house in Davies Street, London, owned by a private security company called Chatham Mayfair. Such companies had mushroomed. Anyone with a military or intelligence background was setting one up. Several had asked Rake to join, offering a high salary, which he saw as a slow death to nowhere. At the ground-floor window of the London house stood a barely distinguishable figure, arm half-raised as if in a farewell wave.

'It's too vague for facial recognition,' said Lucas. 'I've opened back channels to the company for an identification.'

Six weeks after that, Yumatov and Katia were in the Winter Garden of the Tokyo American Club, facing each other in pale green armchairs, travel laptops open on a low table between them.

The fourth image, dated two days later, placed them with two men, casually but expensively dressed, one Asian, one Caucasian, both around forty, at a Japanese restaurant called Shiko Two in Dresden. Unlike with the London photograph, the two men had no identities.

Rake wasn't big on regrets, but the firefight over Katia Codic was too fresh to avoid thinking they might all be in a better place if he had ended Yumatov's life when he'd had the chance. Lucas phone lit up. 'It's Detective Wekstatt. I'll put him on speaker.'

FIVE

'First the ballistic,' said Mikki. 'Then we've got some interesting stuff from the fibers of the ribbed inflatable.'

'Go ahead, Detective,' said Lucas.

'She took two nine-millimeter slugs in the right leg, AS Val subsonic rounds. The third, in her ribcage, was .338 Lapua Magnum from an Orsis T-5000 rifle. Ballistics reckon it was a ricochet from the inflatable or it would have killed her outright. Must have been from the wheelhouse.'

'The one you took out?' said Rake.

'Probably.'

'None of that is standard issue on Big Diomede.'

'Exactly.'

Standard issue was the AK-12, a modern version of the globally acclaimed AK-47 or Kalashnikov. The AS Val was a covert operations weapon used by special forces units, with ammunition designed to give off no sound-barrier crack. Troops in the Big Diomede watch towers used the 7.62-mm Dragunov, a sniper rifle that had been around since the 1960s, which was what Rake would have expected from the patrol boat. The Orsis T-5000 only came into service in 2011. He had come across it in Syria where it had been a game-changer because of its longer range, 2,000 meters against the Dragunov's 800. Both were favored weapons of a Russian unit known as Zaslon, or Screen. Drawn from the best special forces, Zaslon was tasked with protecting civilian government personnel and establishments, like embassies. It reported to the Russian Foreign Intelligence Service, the equivalent of the CIA.

'And the inflatable?' Lucas asked.

'Fibers from under her fingernails must have got there as she was clawing to stay above the surface. They are a polyethylene rubber called Hypalon. Except the Russian military don't use much Hypalon in their inflatables. It's too expensive. And here's the twist. We've tracked this to Japan.'

'Japan?' questioned Lucas, glancing at Rake to share his curiosity.

'A factory in the district of Kobe owned by the Ariga Corporation, a medium-sized conglomerate; not Toyota or Sony, but not mom and pop either. The chemical structure matches Ariga's patent filing,' said Mikki.

'Meaning this is commercial, not government,' deliberated Lucas.

'There's no record of the sale of an Ariga inflatable to Russia or to China,' said Mikki.

'Why buy a Japanese one?' said Rake. 'The Russians make very good inflatables, and they get some from China.'

'We'll run it through PSIA,' said Lucas. PSIA was Japan's national intelligence agency, which had recently become part of the Five Eyes intelligence-gathering arrangement with Australia, Canada, New Zealand, the United Kingdom and the US. It was now known as the Six Eyes.

'But there's more,' said Mikki. 'Mixed with the fibers were sand, silt, broken shells, all the shit of the sea and coastline where the inflatable had been dragged into the water. We've narrowed it to a stretch of about a hundred miles on Russia's Chukotka Peninsula that runs from Naukan to Enurmino. They get similar sediment on our side from Wales up to Estenberg, but these samples contain traces from the Yukon River.'

'She set off from Big Diomede,' said Rake.

'Exactly, which is a rock and doesn't carry Yukon River beach sediment,' agreed Mikki. 'The two closest mainland settlements with matching sediment are Naukan, fifty miles from Big Diomede, and Uelen which is about seventy. Naukan is a ghost place. The Soviets moved everyone out in '58. So, it has to be Uelen.'

Rake knew Uelen, a remote and exposed narrow strip of land with the sea on one side, a lagoon on the other and a few lines of huts with dog sleds and snowmobiles. The Alaskan Eskimos and Russian Chukchi and Yupiks were all Bering Strait natives, many from families separated by the Cold War. During the political thaw, Henry had arranged for a group to go to Uelen to look for lost relatives. He had brought along ten-year-old Rake in the hope he would find his father. He hadn't.

Lucas asked, 'Could there be a tactical reason for using Uelen for this mission?'

'Can't see one,' said Rake decisively. The Bering Strait connected the Pacific and Arctic Oceans and carried ferocious currents, like the strength of fifty Mississippi Rivers, flowing north. The sea was low in salt because of melting glaciers. The river flowed from Chukotka and Alaska, making its waters susceptible to higher winds and hostile weather. Such a long journey in a rigid inflatable power boat, going against the current, was possible, but would surely be the last choice?

As the call ended, Rake said, 'We need to get long-range radar flight tracking, find out what aircraft went in and out of Uelen in the past few days.'

'Let's take a break and work this one out.' Lucas clicked open the door. Rake took a last bite from his energy bar and dropped the maroon wrapper into the bin under the workstation. As they stepped out, a jab of pain ran through his right shoulder. It settled into a throbbing ache, reminding him that the knocks taken in the water on the border were only hours ago. Lucas put on some jazz vocal bluesy music, hotel lobby stuff, familiar but difficult to place. He fixed himself another coffee, sat in an armchair, and took up a pad and pen. Rake stayed on his feet, drank from a bottle of water, and said, 'You were told that Katia's crossing was authorized by the Kremlin.'

'Correct.' Lucas was making a list on the pad.

'Katia worked with Ruslan Yumatov for a couple of years before we took him in.'

'Seems so.'

'When will we get the identities of the men in the Dresden restaurant?'

'Any moment.'

'Katia was stopped by weapons that are not standard issue on Big Diomede, but are used by Russian special forces, including Zaslon.'

'Correct.'

'Ruslan Yumatov was a member of Zaslon, last active in Syria.'

'Correct. But Yumatov has been off the circuit for more than two years.'

Rake continued, 'Katia's inflatable had been in the Russian settlement of Uelen, but she set off from Big Diomede.'

'We need to dig deeper on that.'

Rake took another sip of water. 'A special forces unit overrode the authority of the base commander?'

'I agree.' Lucas stopped writing and put the pad on the arm of his chair. 'And it became a firefight because of opposing factions in the Russian government. One wanted us to have the information Katia carried. One wanted it stopped.'

'The Kremlin would know. The White House can ask outright.' Rake glanced at Lucas's pad and saw how his jottings ran parallel to Rake's own conclusions, the White House, the Pentagon, the intelligence agencies. Along chains of command, even in the field, Rake had never come across anyone as adept as Lucas at handling contradictory pressures. Lucas was about to pick up the pad again, when his phone lit and he said, 'Some identities are in.' He went through the iris and fingerprint scans and keypad code to open the door to his work area.

On the screen was the Dresden Japanese restaurant where Katia and Yumatov sat in a booth opposite two men who had now been identified. The Asian was Japanese businessman Michio Kato, aged 41, rigid, unsmiling, formal in a dark suit and yellow-patterned tie, and a badge carrying his company logo. Yumatov was talking, Kato listening. He was son of Jacob Kato, chairman and founder of the Ariga Corporation, registered in Kobe, Japan.

Lucas drummed his fingers on the workstation. Rake leaned on the ledge. This was the company that made Katia's inflatable. Lucas called up a search on the father, Jacob Kato, who appeared in photo-ops with dignitaries and government leaders. He ordered a full search on Ariga.

The Caucasian was Gavril Nevrosky, aged 46, a German businessman from Dresden. He had a boyish, energetic face, and his eyes were on Katia who, smilingly, seemed to be offering him salad in a pair of chopsticks. Lucas called up a summary of Nevrosky. They read it in silence. The family was originally from Ukraine but had moved to Germany when the Russian empire collapsed in 1917. Based in the eastern province of Saxony, it followed and exploited precarious European political winds. They had helped Jews escape in 1930s Germany. When the Nazis took full power, the family supplied transport to take Jews to the camps. They were a key part of the repressive communist East German regime. Later they used the chaos that came with the fall of the Berlin Wall to take a lead in black market and organized crime which was when Gavril Nevrosky was coming of age. He took over the family empire and expanded its influence throughout the old Soviet bloc. He went on to embrace the European Union, using it as a mechanism to launder money and convert businesses toward legitimacy.

'Where's this from?' asked Rake.

'National Security Council.' Lucas flipped to the source. 'Briefing for a presidential Executive Order 13581 on organized crime, 25 July 2011. The Nevrosky report fed into evidence on the Russian networks.'

Rake read the bottom line where crime networks were listed. There were four: Russian, Italian, Mexican and Japanese. Lucas scrolled through a separate column.

'Is Ariga named?' asked Rake.

'It's not.'

Rake read aloud from the Executive Order. 'These are organizations that constitute an unusual and extraordinary threat to the national security, foreign policy, and economy of the United States.'

Lucas put the grainy shot from the London town house on the screen with the tall figure behind the window. 'We're still waiting on who he is.'

Both fell quiet, arranging their thoughts, until Lucas asked, 'What could Katia Codic have been working on with Ruslan Yumatov?'

'Katia's dead and Yumatov won't speak,' said Rake. 'So, the White House needs to ask the Kremlin direct what this threat is – cyber, space, WMD, exactly what – and if the Ariga Corporation or Gavril Nevrosky have anything to do with what went down on the border.'

SIX

Moscow, Russia

Sergey Grizlov, the polished and immaculately dressed foreign minister of the Russian Federation, read through a file on the German businessman Gavril Nevrosky. Grizlov knew of Nevrosky. His last deal had been an investment into Russia's Siberian energy projects, buying a stake off the French. Word had it that he manipulated a handful of central and east European governments but kept the lowest of profiles.

From the back seat of his state-issued black Sollers limousine, Grizlov looked through the rain-streaked window as traffic crawled along the freshly painted maroon Kremlin wall. The windscreen wipers fought a losing battle against a morning summer downpour, the rain made filthy as it fell through Moscow's polluted air.

Grizlov had no government escort to clear stalled traffic. He carried the title of Foreign Minister but had been kept out of the Kremlin loop for almost two years now. This morning, he found himself summoned to meet the German gangster Nevrosky, whose reach into the Russian and European underworld gave Grizlov an idea of the direction he feared his government might be heading.

Grizlov's wealth, education and urbanity did not fit the current yearning for nationalism and grit. He hadn't minded being eased to the sidelines. He had been working non-stop, it seemed, since God knows when, since the first chunks of the Berlin Wall hit the ground all those decades ago. He had made millions from disintegrating state-run companies and gone on to navigate Russia's political quagmire, accumulating wealth and contacts in equal measure. He enjoyed his current high status without any real power and his travel, letting himself be rolled out to meet foreign leaders. Grizlov spoke many languages and had a good way with people that could often close a difficult deal.

The limousine turned through the Borovitsky Gate on the southwest corner, with its narrow, white-lined arch and clock face overhead. Grizlov had a deep love for the Kremlin, which literally meant 'a fortress inside a city' and had been a site of Russian Slavic power since the second century. Its walls and towers dated back to the fifteenth century, and the white and pastel-yellow façade of the Senate Building, where he was heading, to the eighteenth. The Kremlin marked the history of Russia and how she used her power. One of Lagutov's staff led him up the short flight of concrete steps and through to the President's private office. It was empty. The door was closed. Grizlov was left alone.

On the left side of the room, against the wall behind the desk, the national white, blue and red Russian flag hung from a stand. Another flag with the Russian Federation's coat of arms, the double-headed golden eagle, was to the right. The room displayed elegance without ostentation. There were tall windows with dark yellow drapes and a chandelier over the President's dark wood desk, with a table and two upright tapestried chairs on the other side for visitors. The desk itself was tidy. There was a writing surface, a keyboard, a large screen to the left and holders for three phones.

Lenin, Stalin and Putin had all used the Senate Building. They had decorated, rebuilt, torn things down and renovated to their tastes. The self-effacing President Viktor Lagutov had simply moved in, changed nothing and got down to work. He had begun as an interim ruler, a technocratic pair of hands to guide the nation to its next stage of revival. It had been assumed another charismatic strongman would take over the reins. Yet Lagutov had seen off three American presidents and countless European leaders. He projected diffidence, appeared to lack enthusiasm for the job and faced no serious challengers.

Grizlov had expected Lagutov to come in through a side door from the rest room or another area of his office. But the main doors opened, and the Russian President walked in, deep in conversation with Gavril Nevrosky, ignoring Grizlov until they reached the center of the office.

Lagutov's face was pale, his walk slightly stooped, and he wore a much-lived-in dark pinstriped suit and a badly knotted red tie. He looked more like the academic he had once been than the leader of one of the world's most powerful nations. Nevrosky, on the other hand, appeared to be taking the lead. He had a rounded youthful face and flushed red cheeks. His eyes and expression embraced all around him. He wore a dark blazer, a blue shirt with gold cufflinks but no tie, pressed cream linen pants and well-polished brown loafers. For his part, Grizlov resembled a late-middle-aged fashion icon, like a fading film star hired for an expensive watch commercial.

Nevrosky stretched out both hands, 'Sergey Grizlov,' he exclaimed. 'I am your greatest fan. What you have achieved for Russia, indeed the whole of Europe, has been magnificent.' He ignored pandemic protocol and clasped Grizlov's right hand with both of his, giving him more of a massage than a handshake. 'The President has been filling me in and we're so glad you're here.' Nevrosky unclasped Grizlov's hand and turned to Lagutov. 'Aren't we, Viktor? Here we have the man who can rescue us from our mess.'

Grizlov stayed quiet. Lagutov stepped around to his desk, sat down and placed a phone in front of him with such quiet decisiveness that Nevrosky's ebullience drained. Grizlov took a faded yellow tapestried chair to the left, Nevrosky to the right.

Lagutov let the silence build for many seconds, then said, 'There's been a border shoot-out in the Bering Strait.' He turned the phone around and around on the desk. 'I was betrayed. A former FSB agent, a young woman called Katia Codic, tried to make a crossing with the help of the Eastern Military Command. She carried information pivotal to our national security. Mr Nevrosky alerted us, for which Russia will always be grateful.' Lagutov inclined his head in respect to Nevrosky. 'We were almost too late. We may or may not have stopped Katia Codic. She may be dead. Or she may be wounded and alive and with the Americans. We don't know. But we have to assume the worst, which is why I have asked you here.'

Grizlov had not survived Moscow's labyrinths by asking questions when none was welcome. What had happened, he wondered? What information was Katia Codic carrying, and how could an institution like the Eastern Military District set about betraying the President of the Russian Federation? He stayed quiet.

Lagutov said, 'You do not need to know what Katia's information is, Sergey, but you do need to be aware of the context and, as I speak, I want you to know that Mr Nevrosky is a trusted and good friend of Russia.'

The German gave a nod of appreciation. He kept his eyes on the President. Grizlov wondered what else beside the Siberian energy contract Nevrosky had been given, at what price and why.

'We are losing Europe, Sergey,' said Lagutov.

Grizlov allowed curiosity to stretch across his face.

'And if we lose Europe, we lose Russia again, and I cannot allow that to happen,' continued Lagutov. 'Mr Nevrosky will explain.'

Nevrosky cleared his throat and faced Grizlov. 'Europe's fragmentation, which benefited us so much, has ended. Britain breaking away, the weakening of America, nationalism, civil unrest in France, separatism in Spain, bankruptcy in Greece, countries kicking against the super-state, all of which was on the media day in and day out – we thought it would continue, allowing us to move into vacuums here and there. But it's stopped.'

The file Grizlov had read in the car referred to Nevrosky's influence specifically in Bulgaria, Poland and Hungary, as well as in his native Germany, where he funded extremist movements on both the right and the left.

'We had spread the message that the European Union was no better than the Soviet Union, that democracy was making people powerless, that they were being lectured on how to think. I don't need to tell you, Sergey, because you know it so well.' Nevrosky paused and rubbed his hands together. 'People are not thinking like that anymore. This wave of populism has ended. There's a company I've hired for many years which harvests personnel data to help us win elections, not just national elections but the small grass-roots elections to soccer clubs, business groups, local government, because this is where influence lives.'

Nevrosky now pressed both hands against his cheeks. 'The owner of this company, to whom I have paid tens of millions over the past few years, is shutting down on me. He will not do the work anymore. I asked why. I thought he did not like my politics.' Nevrosky clasped Grizlov's arm. 'No, Sergey. It was not political. He withdrew because he could no longer guarantee me a win, and that would risk his reputation.'

Nevrosky let go, leant back and folded his arms. 'The indus-trialists who had been buying into our vision have seen the polls and are withdrawing.' He became more agitated. 'And an end to their funding means an end to their loyalty.' He was stating common knowledge. Despite upheaval, Europe had not fallen apart, but consolidated. Its mission now was to become more of a self-contained global force, which meant pushing back against interference from Russia. The much-discussed rise of right-wing nationalism had lost momentum.

Lagutov raised his hand to indicate that Nevrosky should stop speaking. 'We do not have the luxury of time,' he said. 'Next week is the European Defense Summit in Bonn.'

Grizlov understood perfectly. After years of wrangling and muddle, more than thirty European governments were about to sign a common security treaty. The treaty's purpose was to act as a unified European front, against extremism and hostile powers like Russia and China. To prepare, over the previous months, various militaries had publicly exposed and expelled right-wing and neo-Nazi factions from their ranks.

In crises, Lagutov did not get angry. He became perplexed, then irritated at himself for not seeing a way through. Grizlov would only hear what Lagutov wanted him to know, which would not be details of fights at home, however lethal, but dealings with America, smoothing ruffled feathers and getting information.

Lagutov said, 'Katia Codic had information that will jeopardize our Europe policy. We need to know if she is alive or dead, and what she has revealed to the Americans.'

Grizlov studied the disquiet that creased the President's face and asked his first question. 'How can I help, sir?'

SEVEN

Washington, DC

C arrie Walker rode the elevator up to her eighth-floor apartment on Virginia Avenue NW, allowing the day's tension to drain away. What was meant to have been a relaxed morning of routine medical checks on Little Diomede had ended in a private mortuary in Crystal City with the corpse of a woman about her own age who had been shot up and bled to death. The pathologist told Carrie that her chances of survival had been next to none. Internal bleeding meant she had needed a thoracotomy, surgery between the ribs. There was no way Carrie could have done that in the school kitchen. This truth did not help Carrie feel any better. She hated losing a patient, loathed it more than anything in the world.

She had driven back with Mikki Wekstatt, dropped him at the Holiday Inn on Rhode Island Avenue where he and Rake were staying, and had taken the car on a couple more miles southwest to her place in Foggy Bottom.

Carrie loved the little apartment, compact with a walk-in wardrobe, large bathroom and L-shaped living, dining and sleeping area, with a large bed that came down from the wall. She had a view over the Watergate complex with its sense of history; a reminder – she told friends – that governments mess things up all the time. She decorated it randomly with stuff from her travels, tried to make it look like a home. She liked the busyness of city life. She liked time alone. This little place in the heart of Washington, DC had been a great landing zone as she tried to change lives, from travel and conflict to settled routine. Her younger sister Angie drew energy from her children, dogs, husband and work. Carrie needed to learn how to do the same.

She had been doing so well. She had a good job at the big teaching hospital ten minutes' walk away. She was dating a doctor there, younger than her but a high-flier who understood the system. They had talked of moving in together. Then she had saved a knife victim's life by breaking a rule about blood protocols, written to protect the hospital, not its patients. Her lover lectured her about hospital procedures and trauma medicine when he had never even been near a makeshift basement clinic operating by flashlight without anesthetic. Carrie was now facing a disciplinary panel which was when Rake had called and offered her a few days' sanctuary on Little Diomede.

'And the rest is history,' she muttered to herself, as she opened the apartment door to see the same clothes strewn over the same furniture as when she had left what seemed a lifetime ago.

It had been Angie who'd first said that if Carrie wanted any chance of a normal life she needed to get Rake out of her mind. He was too dangerous to be with. A therapist at one of her mandatory Post Traumatic Stress Disorder assessments concluded that Carrie associated Rake with violence because they had met in a hostile environment. This was the polar opposite to the type of life she said she wanted, which was why getting engaged to Rake hadn't worked and it was best kept that way.

Carrie put her medical rucksack on the floor, threw her jacket over a dining-table chair and was about to take a shower when Rake called. He needed to see her now.

'It's almost midnight,' she protested.

'It's not social,' he said. 'And I'm not going to hit on you.'

They sat cross-legged on the brown-gray Alaskan caribou-hide rug Rake had given her years ago. He drank black coffee and told her what he knew about Katia Codic, which wasn't much, except that she had worked with Ruslan Yumatov, who was still alive. If there was one man that injected a shiver through Carrie's whole body, it was Yumatov. Psychopath was too kind a diagnosis; he was way worse than that.

'You OK to talk about the time you spent with him?' asked Rake.

'That's why you're here. And don't make it sound voluntary. I was his fucking prisoner.' Carrie looked away, plucking at the short rough hairs on the animal skin.

'Can you remember anything that might give us a hint of what he was doing with Katia?'

During the day or two she was with Ruslan Yumatov, he had one moment killed someone in front of her, the next tried to win her over by spinning crap about them being 'fellow Slavs', then killed again. He had been charming, caring and cruel, all the time executing a plan that would have killed hundreds, including his own president.

'Big mistake,' she whispered.

'Big mistake, what?'

'We could have killed him, you and I. But we didn't, and the world is a worse place for it.'

'Don't dwell on it,' said Rake.

She noticed a cut on his forehead and a thin scar above his eye. The cut was new, the scar a month or so old. Rake's dark hair wasn't quite buzzcut, but it was short and neat. His eyelids were heavy, making it difficult to see his eyes, which was how Rake got when he was tired and concentrating. His skin, leathered by a lifetime of hostile weather, was stretched across his high forehead and rounded cheekbones. She leaned forward and touched a bloodstain smeared across the shoulder of his green denim jacket. There was a tear halfway up its right sleeve and a white stain of dried salt water on the cuff. 'You're not dressed to mix with the great and the good, are you?'

Rake smiled, put his cup on the floor next to the rug. 'Anything, Carrie? Anything come to mind?'

He gave her time. Rake hadn't been fazed by Yumatov. He seemed to forget about him and moved onto the next job. Carrie hadn't been able to. One evening she had told Rake, and he had tried to talk it through with her. But he wasn't a therapist and, being a soldier, he understood a lot of what Yumatov was doing and why. Psychopath was a lazy description, he told her. To Yumatov, killing was another weapon, one which ignited anger that worked in his favor. Rake was clumsy in explaining and didn't tread carefully around Carrie's emotions. But she liked his rawness, and his caring has left her loving him even more. The sex that night had been comforting, slow, wonderful. Carrie had felt totally protected which, from time to time, everyone needed.

He was the toughest guy she had ever met by far, and an unpredictable and delightful lover, and she trusted him. But . . . something, some pebble in her shoe, came with it. Before and after Rake, her lovers had mostly been doctors, and for some reason the fussy type. The one she had just split up with was a good kisser. The sex was OK, certainly not the worst, but before anything happened he needed everything just so, lights dimmed, teeth brushed, no dishes in the sink, alarm set and the rest of it. Passion got postponed for clothes being neatly folded. Once, by contrast, when Rake was in Istanbul and heading to Syria, Carrie flew in from Baghdad and arrived at his hotel-room door coated with Iraqi dust. He pulled her inside, held her hard, like he was crushing her, kissing her, on her breasts, her back, her ass, all over her filthy hair and sweat-dried skin, After their encounters, her mood would dip, and she never knew whether it was from having been with him or not being with him. Why can't we make it work, she thought? Or is it that I can't, so I end up with fastidious creeps?

'I don't remember him ever talking about Katia Codic,' she said, steering her concentration back to Ruslan Yumatov. 'There was plenty of angry-visions stuff. He saw himself as someone special. He wanted to rip the system apart and substitute a new one, which we now know he was planning. He had a fury about what happened to his family, all that old record about the collapse of communism.'

'Weaknesses?'

'His wife and kids. He wanted them to be proud of him. He was a poor boy from the factory and she's an academic, I forget her name . . .'

'Anna.'

'That's right, Anna, from St Petersburg. An economist. He needed her to respect him and understand what he was doing.' She looked up suddenly, a thought darting through her mind. 'And you, Rake. And me, when I think about it.'

'In what way?'

'You were the enemy soldier who needed to be defeated. The way he talked, it was like – if he could get you, everything would fall into place. He wanted to convince me that he was right to do what he did because we were both Russian, children of the same generation.' She shrugged. 'Well, I'm half Russian and half Estonian, but to him that didn't matter. I am a fellow Slav. And he failed. Come to think of it, he failed on all the fronts we know of.'

'But no Katia?' he asked again, in case something had unlocked in her memory.

'No.'

Rake pressed his phone keypad, and Carrie's phone pinged. 'Have a look through these interrogation reports. See if you can find something we could leverage.'

Carrie pushed herself to her feet, stamped her right foot to get her blood flowing. 'Wanna fix us something to eat?' She glanced at her narrow little kitchenette. 'See what you can find. There should be pasta.'

She pulled out a chair from the dining table, sat down at her laptop and loaded Rake's files. First came a couple of photographs of where Yumatov was being held, a government-owned farmhouse in Virginia, about an hour's drive from Washington. There were no images of the exterior, only of his cell, if that's what it was, a basement area with a narrow window running wall-to-wall just below the ceiling. There was a stainless-steel desk and chair, bolted to the floor. Yumatov lay on his back, hands behind his head, his right leg hooked over his left knee, staring upward. Or were his eyes closed? Carrie couldn't quite see. He wore a blue-gray jumpsuit, more like loose-fitting gym wear than prison uniform. His hair was closely cropped, prison-style. He looked relaxed and in good shape, a man more at ease with himself, no sign of struggling with demons.

Carrie heard the flare of the gas range as Rake rummaged through her kitchen. The reports were compiled by a unit called the High-Value Detainee Interrogation Group, a collaboration of the FBI, CIA and Pentagon. Yumatov had been held for two years and seven months. During that time, he had not spoken once to his interrogators. He had asked for nothing. He had shown no violence. He had not tried to escape. There were no mood swings, no yelling, no hunger strikes. A range of techniques – from waterboarding to truth serums to sleep deprivation to simply leaving him alone – had failed. His health was good, his blood pressure, cholesterol, liver and kidney functions normal. He was allowed his own callisthenic routine which he carried out for three hours a day. After the first six months, they stepped things up and brought in equipment to check on blood flow through the brain into the specific cerebral cortexes prone to anger, attraction, lying and the truth. They conducted eye tracking, which matched a fluctuating pupil size to emotional response, cognitive processing and arousal, including sexual arousal. They monitored thermal imaging, blood flow to the face during stress. They detected no emotional fluctuation. They experimented with a technique known as switch framing, which matched the interrogator's response to Yumatov's. It ended with both sides sitting in silence. Only five per cent of interrogation subjects used silence as their weapon. One session lasted for six hours, with no food, no water, and not a word said. Interrogators reported they had never experienced a case as determined and prolonged as this.

She heard the rapid cut of a knife and went to the kitchen, where Rake was arranging a line of finely chopped parsley next to a pile of red pepper flakes and a lemon cut in two. Water bubbled around linguine in the pot. He turned and held up a tired-looking head of garlic, making her laugh.

'It'll do,' she said.

'Find anything?' he asked.

'I'll take a shower and think about it.'

'Food's ready in ten.'

She randomly flipped on a playlist which turned out to be chamber music by Alexander Borodin, her father's favorite composer, even though Borodin was Russian, and her Estonian father publicly loathed everything Russian. Her mother was an exception, and even that was far from straightforward. One of Carrie's resolutions was to start learning piano again. She had stopped ten years earlier when she started doing trauma medicine in war zones. Those days were over. The piano could resume. She had a dream of playing, with Angie on cello, to her parents, nieces, nephews, even the dogs, at Angie's house in Brooklyn.

What the hell was she doing? she thought, walking to the bathroom through the narrow corridor that doubled as a wardrobe. Rake cooking a midnight supper? Carrie showering, putting on music. What the hell? No. No. No. She took off the clothes she had worn from Little Diomede, releasing smells of sea water, aircraft fuel and mortuary chemicals. She turned the water on powerful at medium temperature. She washed away the day's grime and thought of Ruslan Yumatov.

Yumatov was a working-class steel-town boy who had made

good. He'd married well. He'd mixed and worked with the most influential people in Russia. What was his weakness? Was it that he couldn't shake off his bitterness about his father being defrauded in the sharp practices of the 1990s? Was it that he had never been accepted by his wife's people? Did he think the Moscow and St Petersburg elite looked down on him? Squeezing shampoo through her hair, Carrie thought back on those terrifying hours she had been with him, searching for a tell. His refusal to cooperate with his interrogators gave him power. If he were holding secrets, there was less chance of him making a mistake. Because he had not resisted, he felt no sense of failure, at least not during his detention. Carrie had studied behavior and violence. There were people who enjoyed being cruel because it released into the bloodstream neurotransmitters of well-being – dopamine, serotonin and oxytocin. These were sadists. Then there were those for whom cruelty released adrenaline and cortisol, creating fear and revulsion. These were the majority. And there were those, like military commanders, who used cruelty as a mechanism to achieve a goal. Was this Yumatov, happy to use extreme violence to get what he needed?

She got out, dried and, to ensure her own discipline against a weakness for Rake, she put on day clothes, jeans, buttoned shirt. She left her hair loose and wet on her shoulders.

Rake had found cutlery, place mats and water glasses. She had seen him cook up a storm from scraps in the middle of nowhere before. He worked from instinct, having grown up hunting, killing and cooking along the Alaska coastline, then at remote outposts on deployment. The pasta was good. He had put out a bottle of Italian Primitivo from her rack in case either wanted it, which they didn't.

'Any thoughts?' Rake squeezed lemon on to his linguine.

Carrie had her mouth full. She swallowed and sipped water. 'You've got a couple of surveillance photographs of Yumatov with Katia. He may have nothing to do with her getting shot.'

'That's right. But if it is connected . . .' He stopped abruptly as his phone flashed with a message. 'Sergey Grizlov, Russian foreign minister, has called your friend Stephanie Lucas and wants a meeting.'

Carrie and Stephanie Lucas had been friends on and off for

fifteen years or more, not close, but good for a night out of bitching and sharing when they ended up in the same city. Stephanie was now Baroness Lucas of Clapham, the British Foreign Secretary and Grizlov's counterpart.

A second line of message lit, and Rake read, 'Gavril Nevrosky has been with Grizlov in the Kremlin.'

That did change things, thought Carrie. Nevrosky was in the photograph with Katia and Yumatov. She stopped eating. 'Things build up in the mind of someone who doesn't speak for two years,' she said. 'Injustices, hatreds, love, legacy; they can become mountains because there's no one to weigh them against.' She let her fork dangle in her right hand. 'In all the stuff I read, Yumatov has been confronted only by professional interrogators, never by someone he knows.'

'The wife and kids are in London.' Rake looked up from his phone. 'They think he's dead.'

'OK, so you and I go. He's an hour away, we can go now, go tomorrow. They have all those behavioral monitors – we can see how he reacts. If there are signs that he'll talk, we can bring Anna across from London.'

Rake called Lucas, repeating exactly as Carrie had said it. As she ate she felt the pasta doing its work. She swept the linguine round the plate to soak up juices. She listened to the Borodin piano and thought about opening the Primitivo. Rake spoke quietly to Lucas, stepping away by the kitchen, head lowered, voice quiet.

He finished, came back and said, 'We work good together, you and I.'

'Are we on?'

A minute earlier, she'd been about to ask Rake if he wanted to stay over. But he was lifting his jacket off the back of his chair. 'Harry has to run it through the White House,' he said. 'Plan is to go tomorrow around midday.'

EIGHT

Lamps snapped on in the corridor leading to Ruslan Yumatov's cell. Four guards appeared, wheeling a pale blue chair made of reinforced plastic, which meant he was being taken upstairs for an interrogation session.

Yumatov was carrying out his exercise routine – as he did every day – while reminding himself who he was and where he came from, and those he loved. He performed press-ups, and repeated to himself, 'I am Ruslan Maximilian Yumatov. I am forty-seven years old. I was born in the southern Urals. My father was foreman at the Magnitogorsk Iron and Steel Works and a member of the Communist Party of the Soviet Union.'

He shifted to stretches and concentrated on his family. 'My wife is Anna Elisabeth. She is forty-three years old, beautiful and loyal. Our children are Maximilian who turned ten on the eighth of May and Natasha who will be eight on the eleventh of November. I made sure my family was safe. I love them. They are my cause. I am a good man.'

He ended with thirty minutes' jogging on the spot, which he used to process his failure and his captivity, painful but necessary. Only by facing up to mistakes could he put himself on the path to success. His goal remained the restoration of the fairness of the society he had grown up in. His plans to achieve this had been based on the need to disrupt and rebuild, tearing down a tired old system and replacing it with another brimming with energy and ambition. He had learned in the Chechen wars that the skilful use of violence deep within families and communities was the fastest way to get results. As a soldier, Yumatov planned through a military prism, allowing room for mistakes and bad luck.

He had been detained now because an American soldier, Rake Ozenna, had both jeopardized his plan and saved his life. As he pounded the floor, sweat soaking into his T-shirt and dripping from his forehead, Yumatov invented in his mind a meeting with

Ozenna, the conversation they would have, the death he would inflict.

In the early days of captivity, he had measured personal success as recreating the life he and Anna had in Moscow, their shared belief in Russia's future, their love for their children. But, as months passed, he realized how complicated reunion would be. Anna, Max and Natasha went to London. The children would be in a school with new friends. Believing her husband dead, Anna might have taken a new lover, a new father to his children. Such a personal dream could become a trap. Anna had supported him, but he had never been sure about her, whether – with her high education and elite St Petersburg society upbringing – she might have looked down him, an uneducated soldier from the Urals. He found himself fighting outbursts of rage, imagining himself unwanted by his own family, a stranger to his own children, lost in an alien Western city, trying to fit in when, in truth, there was no place for him there.

In this last high-intensity session of his exercise routine, Yumatov sculpted a different personal goal, away from the family, away from love and reunion. It was so simple, so uncomplicated, that Yumatov had imagined Rake Ozenna's death multiple times, honing it, perfecting it, forcing the American's emotionless face and eyes to show humanity as he realized that he was about to die and that, as a soldier, he was not as good as Yumatov. When all else blurred, when doubt ransacked hope, it was this image more than any other that propelled him forward.

Yumatov toweled sweat off his face and shoulders and stepped to the corner of the room to look directly up into a surveillance camera. Eyes unblinking, he stared as deeply into the lens as he could, challenging them to read into him whatever they liked because they would see nothing. The guards were waiting outside. He was relaying that he had almost finished his exercises and was ready for yet more questioning – his schedule, not theirs.

Over the months, they had asked Yumatov about his network, who was running him in Russia, how many people, which nationalities, where the money came from. From their questions and their frustration at his silence, he pieced together snatches of insight. These people still believed power lay with governments. They had no concept of how much had changed.

The sessions had fallen into routine. For more than a year, the same team had been in place, with no rotation to freshen them. Yumatov detected boredom and a drop in energy levels. Their excitement at having a new prisoner had matured into irritation at a bad career choice.

His living area measured thirty-two feet by fifteen, a good size, like a studio apartment. His food was served through a hatch in the door made of thickened glass. He was watched around the clock, even when crapping. His cell looked onto a blank white-washed wall across the corridor outside.

Truth serum was the most difficult to handle, particularly SP-117, made by his own government and brutal in the way it hammered the brain, leaving him drained, depressed and woolly headed. He recovered by increasing his calisthenics and testing his memory. How many women had he made love to? How many men had he killed? How many children?

He had not uttered one word to his captors. His silence showed his strength and ensured he gave them nothing. They had never told him where he was. They wanted him to think he was being held in a black rendition site in Thailand. From the window at the top of his cell he could see down into a yard with signs in the Siamese alphabet and vehicles with Thai number plates. They had never let him out into the fresh air. But Yumatov knew Asian air conditioning, and it didn't feel or smell like this.

This was his 946th day in captivity. The guards in the corridor outside wore black uniforms with Thai military insignia. Three stood back while one opened the door. Two pushed the chair inside and Yumatov, compliant as always, sat in it. They shackled his wrists to the chair's arms and his ankles to its legs. They secured straps from a headrest around his forehead and his chin.

They wheeled him along the corridor and took him up one floor in the lift into a large Asian-decorated room with gold ceiling cornices, gray pastel wallpaper lightly patterned with mountains, a thick deep-blue carpet emblazoned with birds, and matching drapes drawn across the windows. In one corner stood a shrine with unlit joss sticks, five oranges in a bowl and a statue of the Buddha.

Waiting for him was the interrogator Yumatov knew best, Paul

Sikelsky, a thin, jumpy FBI agent, who did not hide his anger and frustration at Yumatov's silence.

'We got some big cheeses coming to see you this afternoon,' said Sikelsky, leaning in so close that Yumatov could smell his stale breath and cheap deodorant. 'I've been here seventeen of your thirty-one months, and you've given me nothing. These new people think they can just turn up and make you talk.'

The guards secured Yumatov's chair to the floor.

'So, I'm asking you a favor, Colonel Yumatov,' Sikelsky said. 'Before they come, give me one name, one bank account, give me *something*, for Christ's sake. At least fucking speak, so I'm not put out to grass.'

Sikelsky's drawn, thin face reminded Yumatov of middle-aged men in his hometown, driven crazy by fear of losing their jobs, hope sucked away, age against them. Yumatov decided to grant the wretched Sikelsky his favor. He used to be in the youth choir at his father's factory, motivating workers with songs about the Soviet vision. He had such a strong, clear tenor voice that his mother had wanted him to become a professional opera singer. His father had said it would be impossible, and he was right. Perhaps if the old system had survived.

With the Soviet vision gone, Yumatov exercised his voice with Orthodox liturgical chants which demanded greater flexibility of pitch, staggered breathing and, when unaccompanied, a voice needed to hold a note, which he could. Neither Yumatov nor Anna were religious, but liturgical chants portrayed Russian spirituality and national identity and gave Yumatov a feeling of pride. Before she left for London, Yumatov had installed 'The Resurrection', a chant from Kiev that began with a tolling bell, as the ringtone on Anna's phone.

Yumatov sang, imagining musicians and fellow singers with him, ensuring he followed the melody and key exactly, without wavering. Surprise washed through Sikelsky. He grinned and stepped toward Yumatov, shaking his head in disbelief, then abruptly turned away as if to look toward the window. A round from a high-powered weapon tore through his skull. The room filled with exploding ammunition and bullets ripped through bodies and into the walls, shattering the Buddhist shrine, shredding upholstery and killing Sikelsky, the four guards and a fifth in the doorway.

There was gunfire in the corridor and outside. Six attackers ran into the room, wearing black jumpsuits and black gloves, their identities hidden by face covers. Two unshackled Yumatov's ankles and cut the straps holding his head. A package was dropped into his lap. Inside was a neatly folded light gray summer suit with a blue cotton shirt and comfortable leather shoes.

'Put them on,' he was instructed in Russian. 'One minute.'

Yumatov dressed, saying nothing. He was escorted out. No one held him. He was alive. Outside, two guards lay dead in the corridor, another at the top of the staircase leading to his cell. Through an open door to the room opposite, Yumatov saw the bodies of two agents, Sikelsky's colleagues, men he had come to know. At the front door, he was given a Heckler and Koch MP7 machine pistol, made for close-quarters combat. They *were* on his side. Warm, humid, still air enveloped him. He drew it deep into his lungs, the first natural air he had breathed in 946 days.

The house, Yumatov saw, was an old country mansion two stories high, with tall windows and a second-floor balcony with white wooden railings. There were garish signs and banners in Thai and Chinese strapped around the courtyard, and a Mercedes sedan and an armored car. Three more bodies lay dead. Four black Cherokee SUVs stood outside the front door like a VIP convoy at a five-star hotel. The man who gave him the machine pistol opened the back door of the front vehicle, and Yumatov climbed in. The driver took them out through an arched gateway and looped round across the lawn to where a helicopter was touching down on sloping grassland. It was a Bell 206B JetRanger, used for business executive transport. Two men jumped out, also dressed in black, faces hidden. They took Yumatov's arms, ran him to the aircraft and helped him up. Within seconds, they were in the air. The machine pistol was taken from him, and he was handed a beige canvas pouch. Yumatov unzipped it and saw German and Russian passports, money, euros and dollars, a German driving license and other documents attached to his temporary new identity as Angus Frederick Olsen. He wanted a headset to ask what was going on. There was none.

The helicopter stopped climbing and headed south, flying low and fast across slightly rolling agricultural land. He saw neat houses and paved roads, and an intersection sign: *Highway 7 to Washington, DC*. Not Thailand. This was America. Within minutes, the helicopter was descending over a small airfield for private business aircraft. He looked into the dark eyes of the man who gave him the pouch. He was unresponsive, the type of soldier Yumatov liked to have around him, the grit of the earth. The man's hand was on the cabin door. He opened it on a green light and pointed across the apron to a business aircraft, a Learjet 45XR. The steps were down. The pilot gave a thumbs-up from the cockpit. Yumatov walked on board into a smell of new leather and electronics. No one was there. He buckled himself into a gray window seat. The pilot came from the cockpit and pulled shut the door. Barely ten minutes had passed since he was broken out.

NINE

The property where Ruslan Yumatov had been held carried the name Langston Farm crafted in thin green lettering above its twelve-foot-high gate, which was open. Two whitewashed brick guardhouses stood on either side of the driveway, streaked by drizzle from the gray sky. A high fence ran around the edge of the property, behind a line of pine trees, making it near impossible to see in from the road. The security at Langston Farm was not unusual among big properties close to the capital, which was why it did not stand out as a US federal government detention and interrogation center for unlawful combatants.

From their helicopter, Rake and Harry Lucas absorbed the scene of death below them. Then Lucas instructed the pilot to land. They jumped out. There was a body in each guardhouse, one slumped over a narrow wooden work shelf, the other awkwardly lopsided on the floor, each with a bullet to the chest and head. There was blood, but no smashed glass, splintered wood or marks of skidding tires. The men seemed to have died without a struggle. This was smooth, lethal work, carried out with professional precision.

The helicopter took them the short half-mile to the house. They circled the two-story mansion, flew over a carriage driveway where Rake counted five fire trucks, then over a courtyard ringed by outbuildings with three corpses on the gravel and two Virginia State Trooper vehicles at the entrance. There were also two FBI vans and an FBI sedan with people milling around.

Lucas had been alerted after the county sheriff's office in Loudon, Virginia, received a call from a local farmer about unusual helicopter activity at Langston Farm, the early hour, the fast in-and-out low-level flying, danger to power lines and the rest. The sheriff had a special government status marked against Langston Farm, which required any issue to be kicked up to the Virginia State Police, who had standing instructions to kick it further up to the joint CIA, FBI, DOD High-Value Detainee Interrogation Group which had been dealing with Yumatov. Harry Lucas, a private contractor, was finally identified as the handler. State troopers had secured the property and reported twelve bodies, all male, all with gunshot wounds. Lucas had insisted that any wounded be attended to but everything else should stay as it was. There were no wounded and Yumatov was gone.

They landed on rough grass, which Rake noticed was marked with skids that must be from the helicopter that had flown Yumatov out. He and Lucas jogged into the courtyard. There was a body in the driver's seat of an armored vehicle with the door hanging open, and a line of bullet marks across the armored windscreen which had not shattered. The corpse looked like he had been shot point-blank, with barely a face. Two bullet holes scarred one of the Thai signs. The doors to a Mercedes sedan were also open, being used as cover for the two men who had been shot dead there. Lucas asked the troopers if anyone was inside the house. There was not: the property was clear. Even so, Rake drew his pistol, prompting Lucas to do the same. In the hallway were three bodies, and blood smears on the wall, but no furniture out of place, no chipped wood on the polished floor, no scratches or bullet marks on the walls. The executions must have happened up close and fast, with the element of surprise. It was different in two rooms running off the corridor. Two men, civilian clothes, had died there, one sitting in a comfortable leather chair, a death so swift that his fingers still clenched a carboard cup with spilt coffee on his sleeves and pants. Another was sprawled on the floor by a bank of telephones and keyboards. The larger room opposite was a mess, shot up everywhere, cartridge cases on the floor, six dead and a cloying smell of blood. The chair used to interrogate Yumatov was secured to the floor, but the shackles hung loose, not broken or severed, but unlocked and unstrapped. His detention overalls lay nearby.

They went down to the floor where Yumatov had been kept, where there had been a tougher firefight. Reinforcements had come in but died as they entered. They stepped over the body of a guard at the foot of the stairs. Another lay halfway down the corridor leading to Yumatov's cell, where the thick glass door was open. On the back wall, beneath a streak of blood, was the seventh guard, but also one of the attackers. From the blood soaked into his jumpsuit it looked like he had taken several shots to his chest and legs.

Rake counted fifteen guards and one attacker, making it one hell of an assault. Lucas made a phone call. Rake peeled off the face cover of the dead gunman – Caucasian, mid-thirties, a rough, thin, scarred face – and took pictures. Lucas, talking on his phone, beckoned Rake to follow him and headed upstairs, asking abrupt questions about the helicopter, where Yumatov was. They were in the courtyard outside by the time he finished the call.

'The helicopter took him to Leesburg Airport, nine miles south,' said Lucas. 'He got straight onto a Learjet with a flight plan to Baltimore, half an hour's flight. By the time it landed, we still had no idea he was gone. The pilot said his passenger was a businessman named Angus Olsen.'

Rake glanced around the carnage in the courtyard. There was nothing to say. He called Carrie, woke her up and told her they wouldn't be heading out to meet Yumatov and why.

'What the hell!' she exclaimed sleepily. 'Some fucking coincidence!'

'Your party will be on the line, Colonel, once we have switched.' An hour out of Baltimore International Airport, the lone stewardess, in a beige uniform with short, neatly styled dark hair, handed Yumatov a black headset and microphone connected to an encrypted satellite feed from a private Gulfstream 650.

Yumatov allowed himself to be carried along. This operation to get him out of the United States had obviously been planned down to the finest detail. He knew he had no choice. He was beholden to those organizing his escape which unsettled him. In captivity, he was master of his domain. Now he had lost control and he needed to force himself to trust. They had given him a weapon, one on the property and one now. A gun gave a man a sense of control, but it could be deceptive. Yumatov needed to sharpen his instincts.

He was on his third aircraft in barely an hour. The flight to Baltimore had taken only twenty-five minutes. Yumatov had walked down the steps, enjoying engulfing humidity and repressing an urge to scream out and punch his fist in his air. Yes! He was back. They had killed and invested because they needed him and respected him. A black Chevrolet SUV had been parked with two men waiting for him, one in a blue shirt and loose denim jeans, the other more formally dressed, but without a jacket, and with the sleeves of his maroon shirt rolled halfway up to the elbow. Both were around thirty.

The smartly dressed one had pointed to a long-range Gulfstream 650 barely a hundred yards away. He opened the door of the SUV, and they had climbed into the back seat. He asked Yumatov for the canvas pouch given to him in the helicopter and handed him a similar one. Inside were two more passports, again Russian and German, more money, a driver's license, a residency document for Dresden, and credit cards. His name now was Albert Paul Onstad. The man gave him a briefcase containing a Glock 22 with five magazines. Outside the vehicle, Yumatov shook hands, first with the smartly dressed man, then with the casually dressed one, whose handshake was firmer and his skin sandpaper rough. As he leaned forward, his collar slipped down and Yumatov saw a small tattoo at the base of his neck – the Kolovrat, an eight-spoked wheel, a symbol of the Slavic culture representing the path between good and evil. The Slavs were the largest ethnic group in Europe, inhabiting Russia, central and eastern Europe and some of central Asia. For many years, Yumatov was convinced that this ethnic identification would be the force that propelled Russia out of its abyss. The Kolovrat tattoo gave him a glimpse of evidence.

Yumatov had been free for barely an hour. He had not been told his destination. Nor had he asked. He had been given a tablet with Internet access which he looked through for any news story that could have prompted breaking him out. There was an opinion piece championing a new golden era of friendship between Russia and America, with a cartoon of an eagle and bear in embrace. He scanned a news piece on a summit in Bonn to launch the European army. A preliminary meeting was going on today in Warsaw. He found a small piece dated a month earlier about a new investment in Russia's massive Siberian natural gas project. He searched deeper and found that companies he knew to be linked to the Japanese Ariga corporation were among the investors.

After the Gulfstream 650 had taken off, the stewardess had explained that, as soon as it left US airspace, the aircraft would be switching its identity. An intrusive surveillance tracking system had recently been imposed on transatlantic flights. Previously, aircraft had only been in visual contact with air-traffic control when within radar coverage whose range was about 250 miles. In 2020, satellite surveillance became mandatory. Aircraft were permanently tracked throughout their journeys in a system known as longitudinal separation, like cars following each other on a highway at a safe distance. What Yumatov's flight crew was about to do was challenging but not impossible. A second Gulfstream 650, with the same year of manufacture, near-identical tail numbers and markings, was flying about a hundred miles behind at the same altitude of 39,000 feet. Each had been allocated a four-digit transponder code before take-off. For a nanosecond the pilots simultaneously turned their transponders on and off again. The result was that air-traffic controllers now saw Yumatov's aircraft from Baltimore as one that took off from Newark. The second aircraft would fly to Amsterdam's Schiphol, while Yumatov's would travel an extra thousand miles to Sofia, the Bulgarian capital or, more precisely, to the Vrazhdebna Military Air Base attached to Sofia International Airport.

TEN

The helicopter delivered Rake and Lucas to a rooftop helipad near Dupont Circle, from where a car took them to Lucas's apartment. Lucas fired up the coffee machine, opened his secure area and checked incoming details of Yumatov's escape. Forty minutes before the local farmer raised the alarm, Yumatov had flown out of Leesburg Executive Airport under the name of Olsen. At Baltimore he vanished. The one fatality among his rescuers had yet to be identified. He had a small tattoo of the Slavic Kolovrat symbol on his right arm. Total dead from Langston Farm was confirmed as seventeen. There were no wounded.

Lucas stared at the statistics. Langston Farm had begun as his operation. It had been his idea to wait Yumatov out.

'I took my eye off the ball,' he murmured.

'No good thinking like that.' Rake put his coffee next to him. 'There's a thousand people to blame, and like Carrie told me, it's no coincidence. If we want to find Yumatov, we need to find what's behind him and why, and why now.'

Lucas sipped the coffee. 'Thank you, Major,' he said formally, working the keyboard and bringing up new information referenced through the border firefight and death of Katia Codic. Aircraft movement along Russia's eastern coastline showed that a day before the crossing, an Mi-17 helicopter flew into the native settlement of Uelen, which had sediment and scree matching forensic findings on the inflatable power boat. The helicopter was on the ground for seventeen minutes before flying to Big Diomede.

'Could have been carrying the inflatable.' Lucas ran his finger along a map on the screen.

'How many military flights between Uelen and Big Diomede before that?' asked Rake.

Lucas punched in the search. Nothing came up.

Rake said, 'That's got to be the one.'

'We have more on Ariga Corporation.' Lucas keyed in more instructions, studied the file and said, 'They have fingers in pies all over the world, airports, ports, roads, hotels, casinos, and a historical interest in Uelen.'

'But nothing's there,' said Rake. 'Unless it's connected with the Bering Strait bridge.' An idea had been around for years to link America and Russia with a bridge or tunnel.

Lucas pulled up scans of old documents. 'Ariga has been all over it, arranging finance packages with Japanese, Chinese, Russians, whoever wanted to buy in.' The screen filled with a plan for a luxury golf course and hotel. 'This is early 1990s, a project to build a casino in Uelen. A high-speed rail track would run through the two Diomede islands and swing up through Uelen, bringing America straight into Russia and Asia. Like Vegas in the 1930s, a crazy idea in the middle of nowhere. But Vegas worked. This was the post-communist euphoria. Anything was achievable.'

Lucas moved to a grainy monochrome image. 'Eighth of September 1994. An old satellite image, before the days of drones.' There was a building with three rough-terrain vehicles outside. An armed guard stood by each of the vehicles, with two more at the door of the building. 'I'm checking who these guys are.'

'What's the building?' asked Rake.

'It's at the northern end of Uelen, about a mile from the settlement. An old Soviet Arctic research station built in the 1950s.' Lucas brought up a high-definition color image, showing the same building with vehicles outside and a small helicopter on the beach. 'Better images now. This is the eighteenth of May 2020.' He put a red circle around one of the plates. 'Twenty-five years later, and the same vehicle. As far as we can make out, the men guarding it in 1994 were from a section of the Russian mob, then called the Brothers Circle network, or Bratski Krug. The helicopter is private, yet this whole area is a military restricted zone, and we tracked it back to a company that has links to Gavril Nevrosky.'

'The guy in the photograph with Katia Codic and Ruslan Yumatov?'

'And Michio Kato, the Ariga heir.'

Rake stepped back to give himself distance from the screen with its statistics and changing images. 'So what makes this different from the Russian mob, a corrupt military and a casino project to launder black money?'

'The timing, the border shooting, Yumatov's break out. The threat of a weapon of unimaginable power.'

Rake let the harsh, bitter coffee bite into the back of his throat. 'You say we can't ask the Kremlin?'

'The President says it would show weakness.'

'And if we confront Nevrosky he would wrap himself tight in lawyers, Ariga even more.'

'That's sums it up, Major. You got any suggestions?'

'We go to Uelen,' Rake said. 'Just like we do in the Middle East. Just like they did with Yumatov. In and out before anyone knows what's happening.'

Lucas pushed back his chair and turned to face Rake. 'Madness or genius?'

'It puts us ahead. No one will expect it. If there is evidence, it will be there.'

'What evidence exactly?' asked Lucas skeptically.

'The Russian mindset is scrupulous on documentation. The local offices at Uelen would have records of the casino. We look at this Arctic research building and we start piecing things together.'

'And if you get nothing?'

'We won't.' Rake had been on many raids to remote places. None had failed to produce.

'How would we do it?' Lucas's switch from 'you' to 'we' told Rake he was moving from scrutinizing the problem to making something happen.

'We fabricate a search and rescue in the Bering Strait which will distract Russian attention.'

Lucas's fingers worked the keypad. 'The Coast Guard cutter *Alex Hayley* is in the Bering Strait.'

'There's a Russian Kamov Ka-29TB that we captured in Syria sitting at Elmendorf-Richardson,' said Rake. 'We can go in with that.' The Kamov was a transport helicopter for up to sixteen troops. It had two sets of rotor blades mounted one above the other, giving added stability

Surprise etched across Lucas's face. 'Why's it in Alaska?'

'The idea was to use it as a peace offering sometime. The Russians come across and pick it up, photo-ops and hand shaking. Hasn't happened yet. Moscow hasn't even acknowledged it's missing, and it still has its Russian military markings.'

Lucas nodded. 'We can use two Black Hawks and a Mark V on the water.' A Mark V was a high-speed patrol boat used to insert troops along rivers and coastlines. 'Timing?'

Rake outlined, 'From Wales, forty minutes to Uelen, fifteen minutes at the government offices, fifteen at the Arctic research station. Out within an hour max. We go in as a Russian special unit. No one will question.'

'If it goes wrong?'

'The Kremlin wants to keep the border shooting quiet. They would keep this quiet too.'

'I'll run it by the President,' said Lucas.

Rake was checking the weather. 'The fog's due to last another forty-eight hours, meaning we go now.'

ELEVEN

Warsaw, Poland

Stephanie Lucas's phone vibrated on the large circular conference-room table. Sergey Grizlov, a friend from her youth and now her Russian counterpart, needed to speak urgently.

'About what?' she messaged back.

An unfamiliar name appeared. 'Katia Codic.'

Thank God for bloody Sergey, thought Stephanie. Since six in the morning, she had been in a dreary meeting of regional foreign ministers ironing out details of how Europe would soon launch its own independent defense force, what the media called the European army. They had started early to get the agenda covered in a day so that everyone could return home. For Stephanie, it meant flying out of RAF Northolt, just west of London, at 23.00, getting to the British Embassy in Warsaw at 03.30, a couple of hours' sleep, and then to the ballroom of the Presidential Palace where she had learned in irritating detail about its eighteenth-century chandelier, which comprised five rings, eighty candles and 3,600 crystals. She sat amid counterparts from a rainbow of nations and craved sleep.

'Hello, stranger,' replied Stephanie. 'Talk in five.'

Stephanie's official title was Baroness Lucas of Clapham, a former Member of Parliament and once Ambassador to Moscow and Washington. To take the Foreign Secretary's job without the tedium of running for election, she had been elevated to the House of Lords, Britain's upper legislative chamber. She had met Grizlov in her twenties when she went to Moscow to get rich. Grizlov had helped her make her first million and they were briefly lovers. Stephanie's one short, tumultuous marriage had been to the American Congressman Harry Lucas, now a defense contractor close to the White House. Although divorced, as they rose in their careers, their paths continued to cross, as did hers and Grizlov's.

The Foreign Minister of North Macedonia was stressing how such a military force must not be dominated by Germany and France. He turned his gaze to Stephanie, saying how crucial it was that Britain joined and took a leading role. This was not about the European Union, but the defense of Europe. Stephanie tilted her head in acknowledgment and attempted to express a silent apology as she stood up from the table quietly and walked toward white closed double doors, her face etched with urgency to persuade the reluctant doorman to let her out. She navigated her way to a terrace looking over the courtyard with a statue that she knew to be of Prince Józef Poniatowski, one of those European generals who had fought for an array of different European rulers. She called Grizlov. 'Sergey, long time. How in hell's name are you?'

'All the better, Steph, now I'm talking to you.' Grizlov's tone was light but edged with urgency. 'Can we meet this evening?'

'No,' she said bluntly. 'Where are you?'

'Moscow?'

'Ah! That urgent. Can you say why?'

'Better face to face.'

'I'm in Warsaw, preparatory meeting for next week's Bonn defense summit. Not good for either of our careers to be all over social media having a discreet drink discussing Russia's planned invasion of Europe.'

'I've always said you have the wisdom of a street gangster.'

'Taught by you,' laughed Stephanie.

'When are you back?'

'Late tonight, and no, you can't drop by for a booty call. We're both too long in the tooth.'

'I doubt you are,' quipped Grizlov. 'Tomorrow?'

'Cabinet in the morning.' She tapped her phone diary, then chuckled. 'Technically, yes. It's my dad's eightieth. He's always wanted to meet you.' Stephanie's father raised her as a single dad after her mom had run off with a safer man. Clive Jackson had been a respected small-time crook who ran a neighborhood crime empire from his used-car yard in Clapham, south London.

'It's not that kind of meeting, Steph,' objected Grizlov. 'I need private one to one.'

'Then it's better. Dad's totally discreet. We talk in my house.

He'll be playing poker with his cronies. Anyone asks about your coming, we say it was a personal visit. If it goes viral, we show plane records and I've got bodyguards everywhere. You'll be a hundred per cent safe. But this rides with a condition.' All trace of humor left Stephanie's voice. 'I need to know what's so urgent.'

Behind Grizlov's silence, she heard a Russian radio news station, the volume turned down, and traffic hum. 'There's been a shoot-out on the border in the Bering Strait,' he said. 'A woman was trying to cross.'

'This is Katia Codic, and you want to know if we know her?'

'Do you?'

'Off the top of my head, Sergey, I don't, and I've heard nothing about an incident on your border with America.'

'It's a lot more than Katia Codic.'

Stephanie leant against the railings, not caring if rust or paint flakes broke off onto the jacket of her navy-blue suit. A US-Russian border flare-up on the eve of setting up the European defense force was not the finest of omens.

'You're right, Sergey. I'll check with the Prime Minister. Fly into RAF Northolt. A car will bring you to my house in Clapham.'

'Thank you.' Grizlov's tone was more gratitude than courtesy.

Stephanie closed the line and took off her jacket which was too small, biting into her armpits, the result of too many diplomatic canapés and not enough gym. Underneath she wore a white cotton blouse with a gray-black checkered scarf. A warm breeze blew over the terrace. She hooked the jacket over her shoulder and dialed her Prime Minister, Kevin Slater. The call went from the Downing Street switchboard to a special advisor who, knowing Stephanie's close relationship with the Prime Minister, pulled him out of a meeting.

'What is it, Steph?' asked Slater.

'Sergey Grizlov called, out of the blue.'

'About that bloody Bonn defense summit?' The Prime Minister had spent his early years in office untangling Britain as much from Europe as voters demanded, only to find the same voters were now insisting their government take a lead in the creation of a new European defense force. Dunkirk and the Battle of Britain were back in the headlines. Stephanie told Slater about the Bering Strait. 'Why in hell's name don't we know about it?' he replied angrily.

'Moscow and Washington want to keep a lid on it. That's why Sergey has come straight to me.'

'I don't like it, Steph,' said Slater. 'The Russians are being very tricky at the moment.'

Slater had arrived in Downing Street filled with ideology. It had taken time for reality to sink in, the realization that his days would be filled not with the firebrand activist oratory that had propelled him to office but with decisions and compromises that would often betray what he thought were his own beliefs.

Stephanie looked up. A hum of conversation rolled toward the terrace as the ballroom doors were flung open and European politicians headed out for a coffee break. Stephanie heard herself being hailed. 'Lady Lucas, we are so delighted the British decided to join us at the table.'

'For God's sake,' muttered Slater. 'Is that Angelo?' Christiano Angelo was the rotund Italian Foreign Minister, who constantly berated Stephanie for supporting Britain's leaving the European Union. She waved, indicating that she would be with him in a moment.

'It is,' she said. 'Coffee-break time. I offered Sergey tomorrow evening in London, but said I needed to clear it with you.'

'Do it, Steph,' said Slater. 'Keep me looped in.'

TWELVE

Bering Strait, Alaska

With its blades whispering through fog-laden air, the Kamov transport helicopter lifted off from the tiny settlement of Wales on the far western coast of Alaska. It carried Russian military markings painted on a pastel camouflage with a red star on its two tail fins. Through Rake's headset came a fabricated distress call designed to divert Russian attention. '*Mayday, Mayday, Mayday – Chinese trawler 05708, position 66 degrees 22'17.7' North, 167 degrees 31'06.8' West.*'

A measured American male voice replied. 'This is US Coast Guard cutter *Alex Hayley*. How many persons to be rescued, and injuries?' There was no emergency and no Chinese trawler. Radio traffic started up between American and Russian search-and-rescue teams. The operation into Uelen was underway.

Rake and Mikki sat on either side of the aircraft by each door. They had put together a small team, people they had worked with who were between deployments. Next to Mikki was Jaco Kannak, a sniper and tracker from the Alaska National Guard whose job would be to protect the aircraft on the ground. Dave Totalik, a fluent Russian speaker, would handle team close protection. Kay Arlook, also fluent in Russian, would be with Mikki gathering evidence, data, documents and forensics. Kay's brother Charlie, who was a special forces medic, had just agreed to go when his wife went into labor with their first child. Rake had called Carrie to fill in.

Seventy miles to the northeast, a Sikorsky UH-60 Black Hawk, with state-of-the-art stealth technology, took off from the tiny airstrip at Shishmaref, 105 miles due east of Uelen. Its task was to give cover and keep watch while Rake's team was on the ground. The Coast Guard cutter carried a Sikorsky MH-60T Jayhawk, a variant of the Blackhawk, which was also in the air.

It was 18.09 Alaska time on Wednesday, making it 15.09 Uelen time on Thursday. The International Date Line ran along the border. They would be there in twenty minutes. Carrie clipped down her medical pack. Jaco Kannak and Dave Totalik worked on their weapons. Totalik checked his three concealed pistols, one on his ankle, one in a hip holster covered by his tunic, one strapped to the small of his back. Kay Arlook booted her laptops, both military grade rugged, one a Panasonic Toughbook, one a Gridcase, together with an array of tablets, boosters and drives. Rake had watched Kay work in Syria, against the clock and under fire, yet unfazed and knowing when to cut out with what she had. Mikki Wekstatt leant back against the side of the fuselage and did nothing. Rake had never worked out how Mikki could always be relaxed yet ready.

The helicopter would come in over the stony beach, high enough not to be threatening, and land on a hard-surfaced metaled square 150 feet from the village's government offices and close to the lagoon on the other side. According to Lucas's intelligence, there would be staff in government offices who would cooperate with Rake's unit, thinking they were Russian. With Carrie, Rake now had three fluent Russian speakers. Getting the files on the casino development should take only minutes. They would then go to the Arctic research station which Lucas's intelligence showed was unguarded. The closest Russian troops were in Lavrentiya, fifty miles to the southwest. If trouble broke out, with flying time and Russian bureaucracy, it would take at least an hour for them to get there. By then Rake and the team would be gone.

The aircraft shuddered as the rotor blades speeded up. Carrie squeezed Rake's arm. She brushed loose strands of hair from her face, gave him a smile and tapped the inside of his right forearm where he had a small dark circular tattoo with a line coming out from the side, showing that his blood group was O-negative. She had persuaded him to get it when they decided to marry. The tattoo happened. The marriage didn't. Probably for the best.

Fog came and went. As the pilot brought the Kamov down, Rake glimpsed white-water waves, washing back and forth over the beach of small brown-gray pebbles. Single-story buildings with white, gray and red roofs lined the shoreline. There were three rows and then the flat water of the lagoon. Most buildings were compact and square. Some were longer, more sturdily constructed – the school, the government office, the sports hall. A battered brown wooden Russian Orthodox church with a tower stood out, its green roof capped with a gold dome and cross.

A raging southerly wind buffeted the aircraft. It might have been early summer, but this was the Bering Strait and the outside temperature was in the low forties, just six degrees Celsius. Rake gave a thumbs-up to the team. The aircraft juddered and skewed as it got caught in a gust. Summer winds were changeable in the Bering Strait, mostly southerly, like now, but they could switch in a moment, without letting up their ferocity. As they hovered over the roof of the government offices, the down-draft scattered loose pebbles. Children ran toward them, then scampered back, holding their heads against the sudden blast of cold air. The Kamov touched down, and its huge coaxial rotor blades slowed, drooping like swans' wings.

Rake slipped on goggles and opened the door. He was out first into the full force of the wind, followed by Jaco and Dave. The three set up a taped cordon around the aircraft with steel posts to prevent anyone, particularly kids, getting too close. This was Jaco's task. Once done, Carrie, Kay and Mikki jumped down. There was a smell of seaweed and dampness. Dogs barked. Children shouted. The helicopter was the biggest show in town, attracting attention. Rake led, pointing to the building they had just flown over. Mist churned around. One moment, he could barely make out Carrie. The next he could read determination etched into her face. He could see further, too, through to the beach which was when he realized that something was very wrong.

Lucas's intelligence had established that the government building would be open, with staff willing to give information to what they thought was a Russian military unit. Far from being open, the building was sealed off. He signaled to slow. The mist came back, meaning he couldn't double check what he thought he had seen. He kept up a fast walk, skirting the side of the building into the main street covered with black gravel. Briefly, a blinding squall blew away the mist, revealing a chain-linked fence around the building topped with razor wire that was higher than the roof. There was a gate in the fence opposite the double wooden doors at the entrance. It was padlocked. Red and yellow signs in Russian Cyrillic script each side said, 'Keep Out.' They did not say under whose authorization.

THIRTEEN

Rake could not afford hesitation. There were dozens watching, clustered on each side of the street in alcoves of buildings to shelter from the wind. By the time they reached the fence, Mikki held a pair of bolt cutters as if this were what they had expected. Rake, Dave and Kay set up a covering arc, no weapons on display. Carrie stood by Mikki, holding his gear. Mikki was about to tackle the padlock when the front door of the building opened.

'No need.' A tall figure with a long gray beard, dressed in jeans, a seal-skin hat, jacket and green ankle-length boots, jumped down the two steps and walked toward the fence. 'You're a day early. They said you were coming tomorrow.'

He reached through the gate, undid the padlock and opened it. The hinges were silent, well-oiled, new. He ushered them in as if to his home. 'I am Korav, chairman of the Uelen municipal council. Come.' He beckoned them toward the main door which he wedged open with a gray plastic doorstop.

Rake stayed quiet. He had no idea who was meant to be coming tomorrow. He followed Korav in with Mikki and Kay. Dave stayed outside, keeping watch with Carrie. Korav closed the door, dampening the roar of the wind enough to hear tribal music, an album Rake recognized from an Alaskan Eskimo dance show. Korav picked up a remote and snapped it off. 'I'm sorry, sir. You weren't expected until tomorrow,' he repeated. 'They fenced us off. I'm here alone.'

Who put up the fencing, thought Rake? Who was coming tomorrow? They would be armed and military because that was what Korav expected and what Rake's team was. So soon after the border firefight and about the same time that Yumatov was broken out, a team put up a razor-wire fence around the Uelen government buildings. Most likely they were still here. 'Our instructions are today,' said Rake.

The room stretched the length and width of the building. Light streamed in. There was gray laminate tile flooring, a white ten-foot-high ceiling, white walls with government posters about health, the Motherland, jobs and security, and narrow plastic molded work desks with computer terminals spaced out on alternate sides. Several carried colored Post-it notes, and photographs of families. A child's red jacket hung over a chair. Shoes had been left on the floor. There was personal work stuff seen in any open-plan office. To the right by the front wall was a sturdy old wooden table that looked out of place, draped with a dark green embroidered cloth that hung to the floor. On top were three stacks of bound files and a transparent plastic box of loose data drives.

'Everything we have is there,' said Korav. 'The resettlement from Ratmanova. Some came here. Others went down to Lorino, the other side of Lavrentiya. There are records of the crossings, the visits, the closing of the Gvozdez Islands border. The KGB files on those who wanted America to invade.' Korav let out a bellow of a laugh. 'I bet that's more than you bargained for.'

'And the Uelen development?' asked Kay, opening her laptop, picking up a thumb drive at random.

'All there. Just as instructed.' Korav waved his hand toward the boxes.

'Which ones?' Kay was testing a thumb drive whose contents unfolded on her screen. Korav looked over her shoulder and laughed again. 'I doubt you want that. The municipal district accounts.'

Korav pulled a folder from under a pile and flipped it to a laminated page showing architects' plans for the Uelen beach-front, high-rise hotels, neon signs, helipads and cafés. The Ariga logo was splashed across the top. 'The dream casino that never happened,' he said, 'The drives are numbered. If it's that project you want, I can get the person in who dealt with it. They're two minutes away.' He readied his fingers to make a call.

Rake put his hand over his phone and said, 'No calls. We're OB.' OB was the highest level of Russian intelligence classification.

'They never said that.' Korav's sea-hewn face creased into a caution matched with a slight smile. Rake moved away. Korav pocketed his phone, his gristly face hard with concentration, filling with uncertainty. Rake could almost hear him rearranging his thoughts, the same way Rake was doing.

'The archive?' pressed Kay. 'Where do you keep it?'

Korav tilted his head toward the wooden table. Mikki hooked back the green cloth to reveal stainless-steel hinges of what looked like a trapdoor. Korav crouched down, released a spring lock and pulled it open. There was a waft of damp, stale air. Korav turned on a light. Peering in, Rake saw a tunnel-like room stretching back into darkness, lined with metal shelves. Korav ran his fingers down his beard and stepped back.

Mikki played his flashlight down. 'Two minutes,' said Rake. The material Korav had gathered may have been sanitized. In the basement, there would be random files from which to gather forensic evidence. A fingerprint could stay on a clean plastic folder for ten years or more.

Kay checked a larger drive plugged in with a cable. She looked at Rake as if to say, do we have enough, the same question as Rake was asking himself. He had been on compound raids in Afghanistan with Kay when they had no idea what they were looking for and often came out with gold dust. Korav might have the answer, but it would risk their cover. Rake turned to him and saw a calmness, a man conserving energy, familiar with the unexpected. He wasn't looking around, wasn't twitching, his mind wasn't working on trying to fix something that couldn't be fixed. Rake recognized it because this is exactly how he would act in the same situation.

Korav was a Chukchi, and this was his land. In his mind, it would not belong to Russia or any government. It belonged to the native people. He and Rake were the same people, maybe not in language or clan, but as Bering Strait natives. They were not white people. So far with their masks, helmets and monosyllabic conversation, Korav may not have known. He might have detected their style, the way they moved and worked together, the patches of skin color on their hands and visible parts of their faces that told who they really were.

Korav took a match from a red crumpled box in his pocket, split it with his fingernail and used the sharpened end to pick between his stained, jagged front teeth. He kept his eyes on Rake. He dropped the match on the floor, rolled saliva onto his tongue and let it fall out of his mouth next to the broken match, making the point that Korav was his own man.

Rake took a risk. 'Did they fly a speedboat out from here?'

Korav snapped the other half of the split match and dropped it to the floor. 'You have the records.' He held both his craggy hands out in front of him, palm down, then turned them palm up, as if inspecting his skin.

Kay answered, because her Russian was better than Rake's. 'We need them.'

Korav stiffened, his charm from a few minutes ago gone. 'You tell me where my brother is, and I'll tell you about the boat.'

'What do you need to know?' asked Kay.

'He was told to go on the helicopter with the boat. He's not answering his phone. He hasn't come back.' Korav spat again, a projectile of saliva, this time hard, no finesse.

'I'll find out,' said Rake. 'You have my word.'

Mikki appeared from below. They were good to go. Mikki and Kay filled heavy-duty plastic bags. From outside the building, Dave's voice in his headset in Russian. 'SUV coming fast from the west.'

'Get in here,' said Rake.

The door flew open. Dave and Carrie ran in. Dave shut the door hard behind them. Rake stepped to Korav, right into his space. 'How many?'

'Who are you people?' Korav said.

'We're on your side.'

'Think you fucking own us.'

Mikki and Dave took up positions on either side of the door. Carrie took over from Mikki filling the bags. Rake stayed central with Korav.

Rake drew his pistol. 'How many?' he asked again.

FOURTEEN

There were two. One kicked in the door. The other ran through, weapon raised. They were in civilian dress, green jackets, denim jeans. One was slim with a pockmarked face, the other chubby, clumsy. They were both around forty. By the way they moved, Rake judged they were trained men, out of the military for some years and with fading levels of fitness, not of the caliber who freed Yumatov.

'Relax,' Korav shouted to them. 'They're from Eastern Command.'

The pockmarked one kept his weapon on Rake and Korav. The chubby one swung round to see Kay and Carrie with the bags. They had not spotted Mikki and Dave.

Rake made one of those split-second decisions which end up saving lives or getting people killed. No one would know until it was done, usually seconds after making the call. First up, the Eastern Command didn't sway these men. Rake's team remained the enemy. So far they had clocked Rake, Kay, Carrie and Korav. In the next seconds they would see Dave and Mikki. Rake chose to give them one chance. If they hesitated, they would die.

'Hey guys, lay down your weapons,' Rake spoke casually. They didn't. Rake ramped it up. 'Now. And I mean NOW!'

They tensed around their weapons and kept looking. Mikki sent a long-bladed knife in expertly controlled flight into the back of the neck of the slimmer man, who jolted forward with a yelp. He took an uncertain step, tangling his feet as blood reddened around his skull. He tripped and fell forward onto the hard floor. Dave had less success. His target, distracted by his colleague's plight, moved to his left. Dave's throw went wide, and the man's reaction was fast. He fired his automatic. Dave shot him. It wasn't precise and it wasn't quiet. The man was hit almost point-blank in the face, blood and bone fragments spraying over him while his own magazine emptied around the room.

Kay dropped a bag, sank to her knees, but stayed upright.

Carrie ran to her. Blood gathered beneath Kay's body armor. Her face creased against the pain. 'I can walk . . .'

'No,' insisted Carrie. 'I'll fix it first.'

Dave heaved the bags onto his shoulders. Mikki was at Carrie's side.

Rake said, 'We need to go.'

'If we go now, Kay dies,' said Carrie.

'One minute,' instructed Rake, knowing with Carrie there had to be a firm deadline.

Korav's gaze skirted the room. He chewed the end of a matchstick, neither helping nor getting in the way.

Carrie zipped open her medical rucksack. She gave Mikki a bandage which he opened. She removed Kay's blood-soaked tunic and the armored vest underneath. She tore open a bag of QuickClot, poured the granules onto the bandage and pushed it tight against the area of the wound. Kay winced, her eyes squeezed shut. Mikki held Kay steady, while Carrie tightened the bandage. They helped her to her feet.

Mikki and Dave looped their arms around Kay to create a seat. Carrie and Rake took the two bags.

The bodies lay skewed on the tiled floor. The slim one that Mikki killed had small bloodstains around his neck. The other lay in a pool of his own blood. With arteries severed, the adrenalin-driven heart still pumped weakly.

Korav tilted his head a fraction, met Rake's gaze, but said nothing. He didn't move. He stood, arms folded, to show he wasn't a threat, wasn't taking sides.

'Ninety seconds out,' Rake told Jaco, who was keeping watch by the aircraft. 'One wounded.'

He went first. The heavy mist had become light haze. A black Mitsubishi Pajero was parked diagonally on the street outside the fence. No one was in it. There was a splayed crack on the left side of the windscreen as if a stone had hit it. The padlock hung loose on the gate. The street was empty, not because of wind or cold, but empty like a place gets when civilians are afraid.

Moving randomly to avoid sniper fire, Rake checked as best he could, then signaled for the others to come. Mikki and Dave

took Kay, fast and smooth, toward the aircraft. Carrie followed.
Rake looked back into the building. Korav had gone. Rake ran
crab-like, covering his people from behind. Just as a fog cloud
enveloped him, he glimpsed Jaco, perfectly still, scanning through
the scope of his rifle. Had Rake positioned him fifty yards out,
he would have been able to cover the entrance of the government
building. But that would have left the helicopter exposed. *Don't
dwell on it.* Kay was hit bad. Rake tracked drops of her blood
falling in a curving line toward the Kamov. The blades turned
in a rhythmic thump-thump, their stealth design creating only a
slight downdraft. The pilot watched, and the co-pilot stood at the
open door of the main cabin, two guys pulled off a regular shift
from the base. Carrie handed up the first bag. Rake saw a shard
of light through the haze, immediately knowing what it was. He
had seen it too many times before, a weapon's muzzle flash
coming into contact with closely packed water droplets inside a
fog cloud.

He threw himself forward against Carrie's legs, wrapping his
arms around her to cushion her fall while pulling her back from
the aircraft. Flame erupted around the cockpit. A high-intensity
explosion from a rocket-propelled grenade tore open the metal
and sent fire back through to the cabin. Flames engulfed the
co-pilot. Metal shards tore through his torso, tumbling his body
to the ground. Shock waves pushed Rake and Carrie further back.
A wall of heat hit them, then vanished to a wall of brutally cold
wind.

Jaco, out of the arc of the blast, held steady, his eye on the
rifle sight. He fired five spaced shots, dropped out his magazine,
reloaded, shifted position to take cover behind a disused rusting
oil drum.

'Mikki?' Rake yelled.

'Good. Kay and Dave are good.'

The co-pilot was dead. The pilot could not have survived.
Mikki and Dave came into view, carrying Kay, her face covered
in grit from the ground. Carrie scrambled to her feet, pulling her
rucksack tighter onto her shoulder, and went to her.

'We need to move further away,' instructed Rake. There was
a risk of the fuel tank exploding.

At the edge of the landing area they reached an alley running between two brick buildings giving cover on two sides. One entrance faced the burning helicopter, another the main street and through to the beach. A girl's face pressed against the inside of a window. Adult hands pulled her away and out of sight. They laid Kay down. Her eyes rolled back. She was going into shock.

For the first time since they were on the ground, Rake spoke to Lucas. 'Are you getting this?'

Lucas said. 'We're bringing in the Black Hawk.'

They all had Lucas's voice in their earpieces. Morale lifted. Jaco swung round and pointed at the second bag left behind, perched on the edge of the burning helicopter.

'I'll go,' said Dave.

'No. You protect.' Rake sprinted forward, swerving left and right, expecting gunfire any moment. He approached the heat of the flames. A stench of burning synthetics from the melting seats caused him to catch his breath. There must have been a high-explosive anti-tank warhead on the RPG, designed to pierce armor and kill people inside. A spark flared from an electrical short. He jumped to his left to avoid stepping on the torn-apart body of the co-pilot. As he reached for the bag, he heard the throbbing hum of the Black Hawk overhead concealed by mist. Its crew would know the hazards of a war operation in a civilian area. They would work with its technology to find threats and take them out in the short time needed to extract Rake's team safely. That's what these guys did.

Rake said, 'Weapon was HEAT RPG.'

'Copy that,' said a voice of the Black Hawk crew. 'Landing lagoon side of your location.'

To the east of the wrecked Kamov were three store sheds clustered together. To the north was the extension to the government building where they were taking cover. To the south was flat open land that ran all the way to the lagoon, a large enough space for the helicopter to land with a hundred-yard run.

'Stay close to the lagoon edge,' instructed Rake. Their thermal imaging would break through fog to show the shore and the burning Kamov. The pilot needed to bring the aircraft down between the two. The hum became all-encompassing with the rolling noise of blades cutting through cold air. Pebbles and scree shifted with the downdraft which fueled the flames of the Kamov.

'Bring them out, Dave. NOW!' ordered Rake. He turned to Jaco, who was scanning to the east. The only place with a clear field of fire for an RPG was the ridge of high ground. That didn't mean there weren't snipers somewhere else. Rake told Jaco, 'Cover until they're in.'

The skids of the Black Hawk appeared through the bottom of the fog cloud.

FIFTEEN

Rake ran to the edge of the lagoon, positioned himself in front of the cockpit and gave a thumbs-up to the pilot. Head down, against the blast of cold air, he reached the side as the door slid open. He handed up the bag. Mikki and Dave lifted Kay high enough for three crew members to take her securely inside.

'She needs oxygen and blood.' Carrie reached out to be helped up to be with her patient.

'Oxygen and blood,' repeated Lucas. 'Tell Nome we're coming in now. Critical wounded.'

Dave went next with the second bag, Mikki behind him.

The Black Hawk's rotor blades pushed oxygen toward the burning Kamov, creating leaping flames of bright yellow. They needed to get out before the aircraft exploded.

'Jaco?' said Rake.

'You go. I'll cover.' Jaco was twenty yards behind him, walking backward toward the aircraft, eyes on the high ground. As Rake reached up, foot on the skid, a high-powered rifle round smashed into Jaco who convulsed. It wasn't clear from where. Jaco's legs buckled. Rake ran toward him and Dave jumped back to the ground. Mikki and one of the crew reached down to lift Jaco up. Dave went in with him. A second round smashed into the helicopter's skid. Rake again had his foot on the skid, and a third round smashed into the fuselage an inch to his right. Mikki had Rake's wrist, hauling him up, but Rake got wrenched away as a deafening roar and a blast of hot air pushed him hard to the ground. A rocket-propelled grenade fell short, exploding on the shore of the lagoon. Rake was on his back, heat from a nightmare inferno and cold lagoon water spraying down on him.

'Get out of there,' Lucas in his headset.

The Black Hawk began to lift off. Mikki and Dave reached for Rake. If he could get to the skid, they could haul him inside. Rake tried to get to his feet but stumbled. Or it may have been instinct. A line of heavy machine-gun fire cut up the metaled ground between him and the ascending helicopter.

'Take them out,' Lucas commanded.

The Black Hawk's laser threat technology pinpointed the sources of fire. A gunner, inches away from Mikki and Dave, fired three bursts at the top floor of a building in the middle of the settlement, a hundred yards to the west. From the other side of the aircraft a Hellfire missile sped toward the high ridge from where the rocket-propelled grenade had been launched.

The helicopter ascended. Through his headset, Rake could hear Mikki and Dave yelling protests. The pilot continued. Dave unclipped his pistols and dropped them with belts of ammunition. His Uzi followed. Mikki threw out a jacket and a woolen hat, civilian stuff because he was thinking ahead. If Rake were the pilot, he would have done the same. Kept going. Saved those on board. Rake ran across to collect the weapons. Another sniper's round tore through the belly of the Black Hawk. A second spewed up gravel behind Rake as he sped back to cover.

'Incoming,' came a voice from the Black Hawk.

A streak of fire headed toward the climbing aircraft, but too soon, too fast. It rushed over and in front.

'Sorry, Major,' Lucas said.

'Copy that, sir,' said Rake.

'Fuck you, Lucas,' said Mikki.

Jaco said, 'Tough shit, Rake. My round must have been meant for you.'

Rake leant against the brick wall, far enough inside the alley for when the Kamov blew. He squatted down, resting, letting himself feel the aches, allowing a moment to acknowledge that Jaco must be OK. That was good. The mission was half a success. They had two bags of documents and hard drives. His team was out. There was another feeling too, unexpected; like the old village chairman Korav had said, this was his land. It didn't belong to any government. Rake was with his people. He would find a way out. There was static in his headset, then Carrie said, 'Thank you, Rake. Kay has a chance of pulling through.'

'Who are they, Harry?' Rake asked.

'Get back to you,' Lucas replied. Then there was quiet. Someone had ordered radio silence.

Rake had two Glock 22s, his own with thirty rounds in three 10-round magazines, and Dave's with thirty rounds in two 15-round magazines; a micro Uzi with two 22-round magazines; a SIG Sauer P320 semi-automatic pistol with a single 10-round magazine and a suppressor; and a compact Ruger LC9 with a 9-round magazine which Dave would have kept in his ankle holster. He had two knives, an Ontario Mark 3 six-inch double-edged stainless-steel combat knife, and the slimmer seven-inch Fairbairn-Sykes given by the British soldier in Syria.

His cover would last a few minutes at best. He had to move. It was good he had weapons, but this wasn't a situation he could shoot his way out of. There was nowhere to walk to. He needed a boat. He needed everyone to stay frightened inside their homes, the streets and the beach empty. He needed his attackers to stay frightened too, civilians on a payroll, unlikely to break cover after seeing the Black Hawk at work. The men who had challenged him were ill-prepared, which is why they ended up dead. They hadn't known what was going on, had been called out unexpectedly, hadn't had time to check. But a sniper had set up within the settlement and an RPG on the high ground. Rake assumed the Black Hawk had killed both the sniper and the one with the RPG, which meant at least four dead. How many left? Six? Eight? Enough to put up the razor-wire fence and keep the place secure. Korav had said more were due tomorrow, and that his brother was missing after flying with the inflatable power-boat to Big Diomede. So, this must be a part-Russian government operation, a faction from the many turf fights within it. How much of it was the same as from Lucas's satellite images from 1994 and 2020?

The Kamov exploded, the noise loud and vibrating, trembling the ground, a flare of energy, a rush of heat down his alley, flames pumping higher and falling quickly.

Rake's next move would be toward the beach. He looked for a fog cloud that he could use to reach a point of cover on the beach before the cloud swept away and left him exposed. From there he would have to find more, moving from cover to cover. And he needed a boat; not just any boat, but one that would take him twelve nautical miles from the shoreline of Uelen into international waters.

With more men, the enemy would beat him. With helicopters, they would shoot him out of the water. With cooperation from the Uelen people, they could do a search sweep through the town and find him. His chances were not that good. They would want revenge. It was pointless waiting for nightfall because there wouldn't be any. Three in the morning was as light as three in the afternoon here. He removed his military camouflage jacket and put on the one Mikki had thrown to him. He took the headset from the helmet, slipped the radio into the right jacket pocket and the Bluetooth headphone into his ear. He put the helmet on the ground. He arranged his weapons around his pockets, with the Uzi strapped over his shoulder and concealed under the jacket which he left unzipped. He kept the two knives in sheaths on his belt, the Ontario against his right hip, the Fairbairn-Sykes against the small of his back.

He studied immediate weather patterns as he had done for as long as he could remember. The temperature was too warm to create freezing fog. Rake was looking for sea fog, where the air was warm and the water cold, when water vapor condensed around microscopic particles of salt. Uelen was perfect for flash fog which would form and vanish in seconds. Fog and mist were Rake's closest friends.

The southerly wind blew a long flat patch of fog, ghost-like, toward him. It came, enveloping, hiding, bouncing over scree and stones, wrapping itself around the old church, whisking away and back again, and he saw how he could move through it, how it would curl round to the center of the beach where he had spotted two old dinghies and a wooden shed. That would be his next cover. He waited for the fog to come to him.

SIXTEEN

Carrie forced her focus on the two wounded. There was nothing she could do about Rake. A single round had gone through Jaco's shoulder, tearing muscle and chipping bone. 'You may need physio, but you'll live,' she said, tightening the bandage.

Jaco smiled, mixing gratitude and sadness. There was little worse than leaving someone behind. She folded a second bandage into a sling for Jaco's damaged left arm.

'They want us straight to Elmendorf-Richardson,' said Mikki, who was sitting across from her. Because of the helicopter's noise, his voice came through the intercom in her headset.

'How long?' she asked.

'Four hours.'

That was too long. Kay lay on a stretcher with monitors on her blood pressure and heart rate. The most serious bleeding came from just under her left armpit. Carrie had stemmed it and given a transfusion. The Black Hawk's medical supplies were good, but Kay was a long way from being out of danger. She needed an emergency room in a fully equipped hospital. 'How long to Nome?' Carrie asked.

'Forty-five minutes.'

'We go to Nome.'

'Did you hear that?' said Mikki to whomever he was talking to. Carrie wasn't looped in. Mikki argued her case. 'If we go to Anchorage, the patient may die. If we go to Nome, she has a chance.' Mikki signaled Carrie, then said, 'I'm switching you across to her.'

It was Harry Lucas. 'Sorry, Carrie. It got rougher than we all thought.'

'You got a track record for that, haven't you, Harry?'

'Can you—'

'Go to Anchorage? No way,' Carrie broke in. 'Kay Arlook needs good treatment, fast.'

'It's the President's instruction.'

'Since when did the White House write the Hippocratic Oath?'

A smile rippled across Mikki's face and spread to Jaco and Dave, who could only hear Carrie's side of the conversation.

'Carrie, please. Hold back. Listen.'

As a doctor, Carrie had great control. As a person, she knew she let fly too often. She drew a long breath. 'I'm listening.'

'The hospital at the base is better equipped than Nome,' said Lucas. 'Kay will be well looked after there. The President has made the right call.'

The Black Hawk shuddered through an air pocket. They were flying low, skimming the gray-blue sea below, the sun high to the west.

'How many gunshot wounds do they treat at that secure air base? They do it all the time at Nome. Merrow doesn't want us to go to Nome because he wants to keep this quiet, even if it costs Kay her life. That's a political call, not a medical one.'

Harry Lucas shouldn't even think about crossing her. Not here. Not now. Not with Rake gone. Not when Carrie had a patient critically injured, whom she was going to keep alive. 'We may have lost Rake. We're not going to lose Kay. Not in one fucking sick afternoon.'

'I'm reading you,' said Lucas quietly.

Her voice softened to dampen uncontrollable rage surging through her. 'We do what we were going to do with Katia Codic,' she said. 'We go to Wales, air ambulance from there to Elmendorf-Richardson.' She was trembling, which was not good. She took another long breath.

'Jumping in here . . .' The pilot came across the intercom. 'We got hit back there. Oil pressure is dropping. Anchorage is out. We're ten minutes out from Wales. I've radioed in the Alaska Air Ambulance. It's equipped for two patients.'

Wales was the airstrip from where they had left.

'Thank you,' said Lucas. 'I'll notify the President.'

Carrie let go of her breath, thinking she had overreacted until the cockpit panel slid back and the pilot peered round. He was a kid, early twenties. He gave her a thumbs-up. Mikki returned the signal with both thumbs, mouthing to Carrie that the pilot had made it up.

'What are you doing about Rake?' Carrie asked Lucas.

A cloud sped past. Out of the right window she saw the two Diomede Islands, sunlight brushing across their high points in a shimmering haze. Little Diomede, Rake and Mikki's home, smooth and flat on top as if sliced with a sharp knife. Russia's Big Diomede, rough and craggy like an old man's face, military watch towers, birds circling. Given what had just gone down in Uelen, it was uncannily quiet, as if there were no border there at all, no conflict between governments, just two barren islands in a wild sea.

'We've lost contact with Rake, Carrie. We have no visuals on the ground. We're trying to get him out.'

'What are you going to do, fucking invade?'

It didn't matter that the whole thing had been Rake's crazy idea. Helpless frustration kicked Carrie in the pit of her stomach, a craving to smash something up. She had taught courses on survivor guilt, how it can chew up a person for years. She felt Mikki pushing back the left side of her headset. He cupped his hand around her ear. 'Bet a dollar, you and Rake have dinner tonight.'

Harry Lucas worked from a room within the North American Aerospace Defense Command at the Elmendorf-Richardson base outside of Anchorage, the joint US-Canadian organization tasked with protecting both countries' borders. He kept trying, but there was no word from Ozenna.

He understood Carrie's yelling at him, felt like doing it himself. Rake Ozenna was stranded in Uelen, and Lucas had no known way of getting him out. Carrie's Black Hawk was touching down in Wales. The Alaska Air Ambulance would be there within minutes to take critically injured Kay Arlook, and Jaco Kannak with his shoulder wound, to the base hospital.

Lucas began to compose a letter in his head to Ozenna's next of kin, except he didn't know who they were. His adoptive father, the boatman Henry Ahkaluk, on the island? Mikki Wekstatt, the detective, to whom Ozenna looked up as an older brother? Carrie Walker, the fiancée he never married? Ozenna was the best soldier Lucas had ever worked with, and too often it was the best who stayed behind. He couldn't risk another helicopter crew. The Mark V Special Operations Craft was three miles outside Russia's sovereign maritime boundary. There was no point in it crossing that border until they knew Ozenna's exact location.

Lucas fought off an attack of negativity, the same destructive part of his character that had lost him his seat in Congress and ruined his marriage. He had four phones at his workstation. Two general purpose, one for the White House, and one highly personal. Only a handful of people had the number. It lit with a call from his ex-wife Stephanie Lucas, now the British Foreign Secretary. Stephanie didn't respond well to self-doubt, and Lucas answered with a cheerful, strong, upbeat tone. 'Hi, Steph. What's up? Aren't you meant to be in Warsaw or somewhere for this European defense talk-fest?'

'Working on it, Harry.' Stephanie went straight in: 'What's happening in the Bering Strait?'

'Who's asking?' Lucas matched her tone for tone.

'I am.'

'What have you been told?'

'A border shooting. Grizlov wants to see me in London tomorrow. Throw me a bloody crumb, Harry.'

'You and who else?'

'The Prime Minister, of course. The Kremlin wants to keep a lid on it, or Sergey wouldn't have called, so we can keep it small. I don't need chapter and verse, but give me a bloody large crumb or tell me to fuck off.'

'Is Grizlov back in favor?'

'Yes. Lagutov seems to have brought him in from the cold.'

'For the Prime Minister's ears only?'

'OK.'

Lucas encapsulated the border firefight. 'It was meant to be about the Kremlin reaching out to the White House, and we need to know what she was carrying.'

'What did they tell you it was?'

'Technology on a new weapon. No details.'

'What went wrong?'

'Not certain. Looks like the military taking on the Kremlin. Sergey should know, and that must be why he insists on seeing you.'

'Is that it, Harry? If you want my help, don't leave out any surprises.'

Lucas's attention was distracted by a priority flagged alert that a Russian aircraft had taken off from Lavrentiya heading north. Uelen was fifty miles away, about twenty minutes. It must be after Ozenna. He could tell Stephanie about the Uelen raid. He could use her to leverage Grizlov to get Ozenna out. But that would leave the White House in the Kremlin's debt and Russia with an American prisoner. He told Stephanie that was it. There was nothing else. If Grizlov knew what Katia Codic was carrying, to pass it on.

The Russian troop-carrier helicopter was due in Uelen in less than fifteen minutes. Sending in the Mark V would be useless. The Russians would see it coming long before it reached shore. There was still no word from Ozenna.

SEVENTEEN

The MI-8 helicopter landed on the gravel road next to the beach, close to where Rake was hiding. He counted twenty troops jumping down. There may have been more. Cloud obscured some. He hoped they would deploy through the settlement, along the main street toward the government building and the burning wreck of the Kamov helicopter. Some did. Most fanned out along the beach toward him.

He had good but limited cover, behind two small fishing boats, one of blue and white wood, and the other gray metal. Their bows formed a V-shape pointing to the settlement. At the stern of the gray metal boat was a weather-battered shack, its door unlocked and hanging open. Inside hung fishing tackle, a couple of oilskins, boots, stuff for going out to sea and a smell of rotting fish and human urine.

He resisted any thought that the troops would pass right by him. These were professional soldiers, and this was not turning out to be a lucky mission. He had cover on three sides but was exposed to the sea which was fifty yards behind him. Alternating mist and fog clouds were great when they were with him, but they were unpredictable. The wind blew in his favor from the shore. He might be able to move with a cloud toward new cover within the settlement. But there was a risk it would scatter along the way, leaving him exposed. His advantage was that he was in civilian clothing, spoke some Russian and looked like a Chukchi. If challenged, he had a chance of passing as a local.

The Russians operated in pairs, which allowed them to cover the area more quickly. It signaled they did not expect trouble, or too much of it. They set up no cover positions for themselves. There was little sense of combat-readiness, as if they did not know that Rake was there. Maybe no one saw that one American did not make it out. Maybe they hadn't even been told the Americans had been here. This was a mop-up. They chatted as they moved through. Some smoked. In their minds, the enemy was gone, and they were playing catch-up.

He lay prostrate on the beach, watching through a gap between the bows of the two boats. He attached the suppressor to the SIG Sauer and chambered a round. If he had to use it, and the shot accompanied a gust of wind, the suppressor might do its job well enough. If it were quiet, it would not attract attention. Best would be a knife. He would go first with the Fairburn-Sykes – its blade was that vital inch longer.

Two soldiers, privates barely out of their teens, were close enough for him to hear the crunch of their boots on the stones. Their dark green uniforms were surprisingly well-pressed and laundered, their boots polished. The insignia on their sleeves showed the Russian flag and the red and yellow striped emblem of the Eastern Military District, so bright that it reminded Rake of Japan's images of its Rising Sun.

There was a chance they would check the boats and leave the shack alone. Slight, but it was there. He took advantage of a howl of wind, eased himself up by the hull of the metal boat and stepped into the shack. He closed the door. There was a small rusting bolt that locked from the inside. It used to be an outhouse toilet, maybe still was. There was a dirty plastic cream commode with nets, hooks and waterproof sheeting piled on top of it. From somewhere came a stronger stench of rotting fish. Arctic sea fish smelled bad because of the enzymes they produced to balance the effect of salty water. Enzymes rotting, together with bacteria from decaying flesh, produced the throat-stopping smell that forced Rake to put his hand to his mouth and check the urge to retch. The upside was that the stink could deter the young soldiers from looking too closely, and their lives and his would be saved. The wooden planks that made up the shack were skewed and disjointed. Light came in, and Rake could watch out. Filthy water dripped from the ceiling.

The soldiers knocked the two boats with their rifle butts, laughing like kids at the different sounds. The thud of metal on timbered wood. The clang of metal on metal. Rake caught odd conversation about an upcoming deployment to Syria. At least they would miss the Siberian winter. Not all Syrian girls were Islamic. A rifle butt landed against the shack, loosening a plank that slipped down. The one closest exclaimed about the stink. He shone a flashlight, playing the beam around inside. Rake pressed himself into the narrow space between the commode and the back wall. He felt something cut into his neck, some piece of metal. He levelled the suppressed SIG Sauer at the flashlight. The beam went to the ceiling, brushed over the closed bolt, ran up and down the fishing gear hanging on the wall.

'Let's go,' said the soldier.

'Do you know Petrov Kusnetsov?' asked the other.

'Of course.'

'He messaged me from Tartus. He's in love with a Syrian girl, wants to marry her and bring her to Vladivostok.'

'Idiot. Come. Let's go.'

Their boots turned on the shingle. The conversation continued, boot steps and voices getting more distant. Rake relaxed. A fishhook had embedded itself in an exposed part of his neck above his left shoulder. He pulled it out, licked blood from his fingers and heard another voice from a different direction.

'You two – have you checked inside that hut?'

The footsteps stopped. 'From the outside. With a flashlight, sir.'

'Go back. Check inside. Give it the all-clear.'

The Russians' footsteps quickened. The crunching became louder. If Rake had more time, he could try and disguise himself among the tackle and hope their check would be impatient and rushed. But he didn't. The knife would be not be fast enough. It would have to be the suppressed SIG Sauer, just as the door opened. Except . . . then what? The commanding officer was onto them. If they didn't report back within a minute or so, more troops would be here. What would be the point? He would be taken like a cornered rat, after ending the lives of two boys who talked about Syrian girls. More troops would be onto him than he could handle. Killing these two kids would be for nothing.

Which meant surrender. He needed to make himself known before they opened the door. Young and badly trained, they would be trigger-happy. He would do everyone a favor. The kid soldiers would get medals. Carrie would be pleased that he hadn't killed anyone. She had nagged him a lot about that part of his work. Maybe they would do a prisoner swap somewhere down the line. Or maybe Merrow would disown him and let him rot in a gulag.

The wind whipped up, shaking the shack. Rake sheathed the knife, unscrewed the suppressor, fitted it and put the weapon into his jacket pocket. It was as it was. Sometimes you just didn't make it through. He thought he heard louder wind. He peered outside and wasn't sure what he saw or what it meant. Not the wind. The engine of a quad bike, tearing up the beach stones with heavy-duty tires. The driver held his right hand in the air, waving it round and round, gaining the attention of the two soldiers who stopped and turned. They both levelled their weapons as the quad pulled up next to them. It was a powerful machine with single seats at the front and a bench at the back. The driver kept the engine running and got down with both hands in the air, so he could be searched.

He had his back to Rake. He pointed to the shack. 'My cousin Maxim. He's in there. He's not right in the mind.' He tapped his head, then circled the air with his forefinger, emphasizing that his cousin was crazy.

One of the soldiers patted him down and said, 'The old man is clean.'

'He gets frightened,' continued the driver. 'He feels safe here. That's why it smells so bad. He shits and pisses in there because he's afraid to go out.'

'We'll go get him,' said the one who frisked him.

'No. He'll scream and become madder. He needs a familiar face.' The driver pulled out a wallet to show his ID. 'This is who I am. Everyone knows me. Check with your commanding officer.'

The driver turned and, to Rake's astonishment, it was Korav, the Uelen chairman. The steeliness Rake had seen before now dominated. This was not a man to be messed with, not even by the Russian army. Korav was lying to them, and he knew the risk.

Rake had no time to work out why Korav would help him, if that's what this was, nor could he allow time for the soldiers to involve their commanding officer. He needed to take the lead. He slammed his arm against the flimsy wall of the shack, and let out a bellow, allowed it to run in an undulating tone of terror and madness. He smashed his arm against the wood again, spilling filthy equipment onto himself, cold slime and wet rags. He ramped up the bellow into a shriek to mirror the insanity of the human mind. He rattled the door, slid back the lock, kicked it open and hurled himself out, stumbling, losing his footing, recovering, continuing to howl like a broken man transformed into a deranged animal.

He assessed the situation around him. Korav was twelve feet away, directly ahead. One soldier was paralyzed with indecision. The other had slipped his trigger finger inside the guard of his AK-47. Rake feigned tripping again and stumbled. Korav caught him, putting himself between Rake and the soldier. He hoisted him up, wrapped Rake's right arm around his shoulder, showing enormous strength for a man of his age. Rake let out a demonic cry.

'What's going on?' the commander queried over the radio.

Korav walked Rake to the quad and tore off his hood so they could see he was native.

'A crazy guy,' answered the soldier with the weapon. 'Not an American. The chairman is here, helping.'

'In the hut?'

'Yes, sir.'

'The chairman is Korav?'

'Yes, sir.'

'Let them go. He was the one who called us in.'

Shaking, pushing his arms backwards and forwards, Rake climbed onto the quad. Korav shouted, 'Tell your commander I will settle Maxim, then be back to help.'

Korav roared away, the tires throwing up stones and a cloud of black smoke belching from the exhaust.

EIGHTEEN

Rake lay on the back seat, shivering, his thumb stuck in his mouth, keeping up the act, his right hand in his pocket around the butt of the SIG Sauer. There was a radio scanner on the dashboard. Korav drove west, keeping to the shoreline, going beyond the edge of the settlement where the shingle turned to a thinner gray scree, then to pebbles, a patch of sand, and back to shingle again.

Korav alternated between keeping his eyes on the changing terrain and glancing back toward Uelen disappearing behind them. Rake heard another Russian helicopter in the sky somewhere. The radio scanner picked up the chatter of the sweep through Uelen. For all Rake knew, Korav could be taking him into a situation that would make the Russian army seem like sanctuary. The landscape became damp scree and mud and then a metaled driveway that led to the old Arctic research building on Lucas's satellite imagery. Rusting rain marks ran down buckling steel walls. Korav pulled up.

'Come.' He climbed down. The large paint-peeling double doors were shut with a new combination padlock hanging from a metal bar. Korav opened it and slid one side of the door open. He drove the quad bike into a large dark empty space and cut the engine. The floor was cracked, chipped concrete with sea shrubs growing through. Along the high ceilings were brown rusting girders with broken strip lights and chains hanging down. A small, dirty yellow forklift stood at the far end. There were no windows, no electricity that worked. In the middle, on a red boat trailer, sat a green and black rigid inflatable raiding craft, the same model, as far as Rake could see, as the one that tried to cross from Big Diomede. At the back were two 300-horsepower Yamaha outboard motors, making it a very fast piece of equipment. Korav let out a low wolf whistle. A door opened at the back near the forklift truck. Four men walked in. They carried rifles over their shoulders in a way that made them look more like hunters than fighters.

'This used to be part of an Arctic research station,' said Korav. 'Where they said they would build their fucking hotel and casino.' He looked across to the men walking toward them. 'They'll get this down to the water for you. From there, you'll be on your own.'

The Russians had one attack helicopter in the sky. Another that could be here within a minute. There was no way Korav would go free once they knew he had arranged Rake's escape. Rake wrestled to understand his motive, work out how to get away from Korav if he turned bad, how to get through the Russian cordon if Korav did what he was saying.

A smile flitted across older man's face. 'Do you understand? Is your Russian good enough? I don't have our language. Do you?' Korav was talking about the native Bering Strait dialects. 'No,' said Rake. 'The American school system taught us English, not our native language.'

'Nor ours.'

'I understand enough Russian.'

One of the men hooked up fuel lines in the inflatable. Another man kept watch through the front doors. Another monitored the radio scanner of the quad.

Korav said, 'Every time the Cossacks tried to come here, we thrashed them. They never beat us. The Russian empire called the Chukchi "aliens not fully conquered." You understand me, Eskimo soldier, because you are one of us.'

'I do,' said Rake.

'The Soviets beat us. They broke up our communities, moved us around like dogs. They violated our graves.' Anger flared in his deep brown eyes, the same way Rake had seen with Henry Ahkaluk sometimes when discussing issues of culture and heritage. Burial rituals were a core part of the culture. Cemeteries were sacred grounds. In some communities, bodies lay in open coffins so the souls could find their way to the other world.

'You're not just helping me because of that,' Rake said.

'I need you to find my brother. His name is Vanya.' Korav slapped the edge of the boat. 'They delivered two of these back in the nineties. Ninety-three or -four. Part of the casino project. They picked one up three days ago and ordered my brother to go with them.' From his phone, he showed Rake a photograph of a man in his sixties, with a deep bronze face laced with red veins, and black-gray curly hair, thick and unkempt. There was no reason to doubt he was Korav's brother. 'We loaded the boat onto the helicopter. Two days later, a different set of people flew in and fenced off the government offices.'

'Who?'

'White people. I thought they were government.' He looked up to the ceiling and cast his hand around. 'From 1990 through to 2019, this place was sealed off. We couldn't come here. That's nearly thirty years.'

'By government?'

'I thought it was. But I thought you were government. This is Russia, anyone can be government. The men you killed fenced off my office. They worked for those who used to run this place.'

'Not these troops?'

'I don't think so. They are regular army.' Korav focused again on the inflatable. 'I am Mickael Korav. My brother is Vanya Korav. He is the best boatman, and he is not military. Plenty of boatmen could have done the job. They wanted him because if it went wrong no one would care. He's just a Chukchi.'

Rake thought back. Katia Codic had been at the wheel of the inflatable. There had been no sign of anyone else.

'I help you because I trust you to find Vanya. The number is in there.' Korav handed Rake a phone and gave him a print-out of the photograph on a waterproof laminated card.

Rake was about to zip both into his top jacket pocket when Korav handed him a full-length black wetsuit. Rake stripped off to his underwear and stepped into it. Korav produced heavy-duty waterproof bags for Rake's weapons. Rake strapped the seven-inch knife around his waist. He kept out the Uzi and a Glock 22, and sealed the other Glock in one bag with its ammunition and the SIG Sauer and Ruger ankle holster pistol in the other. He hooked both to clasps on the wetsuit. He sealed the phone and photograph in an outside upper pocket. The wetsuit was cold and clammy. It would warm up. It was too big for him, but better to wear than not.

'Is there a cellar here, a basement?' asked Rake.

Korav stamped his foot on the concrete floor. 'Under here. Yes. I saw it as a kid. Not since.'

'Access?'

'They sealed it off. It was back there, by that forklift. What were they doing here for thirty years, promising to make us all rich with their fucking casino?'

'Give me another bag,' said Rake.

Korav handed one over. Rake's eyes scoured the abandoned building, as three men lifted the boat trailer and pushed it toward the door. He picked up broken concrete chips from the floor, scraps of old paper, scree and pebbles kicked in from the beach over the years. He used his knife to peel paint off the forklift and rust from metal girders. He found the different shaded concrete that covered the entrance to the cellar and scraped off more. Forensic examination would show what had been going on here. Karov looked at him with the same flat expression he had worn throughout the killings in his office. He handed Rake a black life vest. Rake slipped it over his shoulders and tied the cord around his waist.

'When you go, we will create a distraction on the cliffs to the east,' said Korav. 'That will draw their attention and we will ask for their helicopter. It will give you a few minutes.'

The man watching through the door raised his hand. A low-lying pure white bank of fog was rolling in from the sea. Rake checked east toward the settlement. A grayer, denser cloud was gathering there. This far north, at this time of summer, the tilting of the Earth's axis barely allowed the sun below the horizon, but temperatures dropped, cooling the ground and creating evening fog. It was happening now, giving Rake a chance to get out to sea where the fog was even thicker.

Rake couldn't stay completely hidden. The Russian helicopter would have direct visuals and thermal imaging, some of which the fog would obscure, some not. He calculated that he could bring the power boat up to fifty miles an hour, possibly more, depending on the wind strength and how it whipped up the water. The twelve nautical miles to get to international waters would take fifteen minutes, a lifetime in an exposed combat situation. Even after that, there was no guarantee the Russians would not pursue. This was not like the Diomede islands where the border ran between two sovereign territories. If they really wanted to get him, Rake would be equally at risk in international waters.

'Start the diversion,' said Korav. The Chukchi monitoring
the scanner passed on the instruction. Rake heard radio chatter,
skewed by static.

The men opened the door. With two at the back pushing
and two pulling from the front they moved the trailer down across
the uneven scree to the water, splashing in until it floated free.
They shifted the trailer away. Rake thanked Korav, promised to
find out about his brother. The old Chukchi embraced him. The
two engines roared to life, creating a swirl of white water that
mixed with breaking waves. Rake climbed in. Cold water splashed
up on his face, seeped through into the wetsuit. He opened the
throttle and eased the vessel forward, feeling it dip back on
the weight and power of the engine.

NINETEEN

S harp, cold sea spray hit Rake hard in the face. He tilted the vessel against a wave created by the rush of Bering Strait current. The inflatable flattened, and he increased the throttle again. The heavy engines pushed the stern into the water, lifting the bow, which got caught in a wind gust and skewed to the left, threatening to tip him over. Rake eased the wheel to correct it. The inflatable came down with a loud smack and more water slapped in his face. The fog was white and thick, Rake's visibility a few feet. He had no GPS, no lights, no goggles. He kept direction by lining up with the wind, reading the current. A glow of sun lit up fog to the west. Yes. He was heading out toward America. He stood midway in the craft, feet locked to the deck. He kept the wheel loose in his hands, letting the boat feel its way. He wore the Uzi on a strap around his chest. The other weapons, in waterproof bags, were secured to his wetsuit.

To the east, Rake picked out the throb of a helicopter, obscured by howling wind and the crash of the inflatable on the sea. As it became louder, he was convinced this was not the MI-8 troop carrier, but an MI-28 gunship with weaponry that would tear him out of the water in seconds. Without warning, the fog was gone. From barely seeing the bow, visibility stretched for miles. There was no more cover of any kind, no land either. Gray sea, rippling with white water, unfolded in front of him under a deep blue sky, peppered with light clouds. He saw the speck of the aircraft coming toward him, two minutes out at most. He could go back to hide himself in the fog. But thermal imaging would find him, and it would buy him minutes at best.

Rake was less than halfway to the twelve-mile line where Russian territory would end. If the orders were to stop him at all costs, his only chance was to outrun them. With the fog gone, the sea became choppier. Gauging the swell, he gave the engines more gas, easing up the speed, through fifty, through sixty, where he hit a rolling wave and levelled out, drawing back to forty-five and keeping it there. The MI-28 would be flying at around two hundred miles an hour. There was no way he could get to the line before it reached him.

Both hands hooked around the top of the wheel, Rake absorbed the rhythmic rise, fall and thud of the boat. The helicopter was closer, its sound superseding all else around him, fast and deliberately low. The rotor blades' downdraft and side wash buffeted him, merging with the wind, putting Rake inside a storm with the strength of a category one hurricane, swirling gales of up to a hundred miles an hour.

The inflatable handled well. But he had to slow right down. There was no ballast against waves that tossed it as if caught in a tsunami. Gusts and spray screamed ferociously, forcing Rake to gasp for breath. He could barely see for water around his eyes. He needed the strength of both hands on the wheel. If he guessed one nanosecond wrong, the craft would flip. He coaxed the throttle, sensing surges, a fraction to the left, a fraction to the right, speed up, slow down, correcting his own weight, as the inflatable tilted one way with a pitch, then got drawn back into the vortex that the helicopter created. It was like a rodeo with a wild horse, and it couldn't last. Any moment, a wave would capsize him. When it did, Rake would be in the water and he would have lost.

Suddenly, the helicopter ascended enough for the downdraft to calm. The inflatable was barely moving. The gauge read eleven miles an hour. The helicopter door opened. Two men in wetsuits, snorkels and flippers sat ready to jump. The aircraft flew ahead, right into Rake's path. The pilot let off a line of machine-gun fire into the water.

Rake let go the wheel, wiped water from his face and raised his arms in surrender. The two frogmen dropped into the sea so skillfully that they surfaced each side of the inflatable, clasping onto the looped rope along the green hull. A rope unfurled from the helicopter. A soldier, holding with gloved hands, boots hooked around the rope, rappelled down, stopping a few feet above. A fourth stayed in the aircraft covering Rake. The helicopter hovered at about 150 feet with minimal downdraft. The wind was manageable.

The plan must have been to bring him and the inflatable back to Uelen. They wanted him alive, which gave him a risk and an advantage. He indicated to the pilot that he would take the rope of the rappelling soldier, as if to help him down. The pilot acknowledged. As the rope swung close, Rake opened the throttle, kicking the power boat's bow in the air as its speed climbed, leaving a whirlpool wake and tipping himself back with the force of its acceleration. The two frogmen held fast as they were pulled through the water. The helicopter kept pace. The machine gun opened up again, but again as a warning. If they'd wanted to, they could have shot him out of the water. But they didn't. They had their orders.

Rake increased his speed. A smack of water obscured the dashboard. There was drag from the two frogmen, and the boat lurched to the left. He tried to right it, but it wouldn't move. The speed slowed and he saw that a frogman had pierced the hull with a knife. The helicopter's weapon fired again, this time close enough to cut into the bow. Both the SIG Sauer and the knife were ready to go. But Rake couldn't win. They had given him enough chances and now knew that if it went on longer, they only needed to radio back to get the green light to kill him.

'*Grebanyy sumasshedshiy*,' screamed the frogman who had cut the hull. *Fucking madman*. The inflatable was skewing badly. Rake hung onto the wheel to stay upright. There was a blast of wind and a surge of water into the boat. Rake stepped up the throttle, kept it afloat with speed. He thought he heard the machine gun again. But it sounded different. He realized the two Russian frogmen were no longer there. He was taking on water but was back in control. The Russian helicopter ascended, with the soldier swaying on the rope. There was wind and sea slapping against the hull, but it was quieter. The gunfire had come from the American side. Rake saw the black shapes of the frogman, lying on their backs waiting to be picked up and, to the east, less than a mile out, the shape of a US coastal patrol boat that had breached the border to pick him up.

TWENTY

The sprawling Elmendorf-Richardson military base just north of Anchorage covers a hundred square miles. Rake and Lucas worked in a bright, sparse room attached to an aircraft hangar where two F35B fighter planes were undergoing maintenance. It was adequate, isolated and quiet, apart from the routine roar of take-offs and landings from a nearby runway.

Rake wore a freshly laundered uniform from the stores. His hair was damp after a long hot shower which washed off the salt water, sweat, beach grit and blood, and eased his muscles, although he could not identify any part of his body that was not aching. It was less than four hours since he had been picked up by the Mark V special ops craft while the Russian helicopter abruptly turned tail and headed back from the border.

Carrie had seen Kay Arlook into intensive care where she was still critical. She had treated Jaco Kannak's shoulder wound and declared him fit, and he'd headed to join Dave Totalik at Camp Denali on the base, home to the Alaska National Guard. Mikki Wekstatt was in the forensic lab of the military police, examining the files he had plucked at random from the archives of the Uelen government offices, and the fragments of chipped concrete and flaked paint that Rake had brought back from the Arctic research building.

Lucas had draped a heavy-duty green tarpaulin over a table-tennis table, on which he arranged documents and computer drives in chronological order. The older documents were browned, dog-eared and faded and the newer ones were fresher and more stylish, with higher digital resolution in the photographs. The early computer data was stored on large floppy disks which Lucas would only be able to access through a lab in Washington, DC. But there was enough to piece together a story.

The material went back to the late 1980s, when Soviet reform began and multinationals were sniffing around for opportunities. China was backward then. Japan was expanding, and Ariga was one of several companies with an interest in developing the Russian Far East. In 1991, Ariga put together an investors' pack on the casino and hotel development in Uelen. It would take advantage of a high-speed rail link across the Bering Strait, running between the Alaskan settlement of Wales and the now-abandoned Russian settlement of Naukan, from which the Soviets had forcibly removed people in 1958. Uelen was less than twenty miles north of Naukan, and easily accessible: It would be a magnet for the Japanese who had no casinos in their home country. The crossing's halfway point would be the two Diomede islands. The rail lines would take the United States directly into the Asian markets of China, Japan and South Korea. The brochures cited history: A crossing had been suggested in the nineteenth century under Tsar Nicholas II. Joseph Strauss, project engineer on San Francisco's Golden Gate bridge, had written a thesis on a Bering Strait bridge in the 1930s. In 2011, Vladimir Putin backed the idea.

'A Japanese company raises money for a construction project that never gets built,' said Rake. 'Yet, the plans keep getting redrawn. New money keeps coming.'

Lucas said, 'I got caught up in a firefight in Afghanistan in the early days, 2002. There was a mining contract and one warlord planned to take it from another. We went in to knock heads, explain to them about democracy, how the contract belonged to the legitimate government that would be elected by the people. All that shit, when we thought democracy had a chance of working. The old warlord belonged to the old Taliban. The new one was run by a group in Pakistan that was in the pay of a Chinese company, which turned out to be in partnership with a Japanese company with dozens of irons blazing in fires between them.'

'And the parallel here?' Rake stepped back from the table, coffee cup in hand, and took a sip. It was over-brewed and stone cold but, apart from sandwiches, nuts and water, it was all that was on offer. He sipped it again, looking at the spread of files, papers and drives.

'Investors know it will come good in the end because it's not about a hotel and a casino. It's about buying power.' Lucas leafed through papers. Some fell on the floor. They were both tired, mentally drained. Rake was about to call for a break when Mikki appeared at the door and did it for him. 'Harry, Rake. You need to leave all that stuff where it is and step out of the hangar.'

Four men from a hazardous material unit stood behind him in dark green military camouflage, their hands gloved, each holding a mask. The team commander instructed, 'Step over here where we can check you.'

Rake and Lucas walked out of the hangar. Arms stretched up like at airport security, they were scanned with a military-issue portable Geiger counter and dosimeter.

'Good, sir,' said the one who checked Rake.

'Good here too,' said the one with Lucas.

'Check the material on the table.'

Two men put on masks and went in.

Mikki said, 'Preliminary forensics on the bag of grit, scree and stuff shows up traces of weapons-grade uranium.'

Lucas glanced at Rake. The question asked a few minutes back might have become irrelevant, or it might be getting the start of an answer.

The HAZMAT commander said, 'We're pretty sure this is U-235. We're sending it to Oak Ridge for a closer look. Each processing centrifuge carries its own signatures. Oak Ridge holds records of the exact materials from dismantled Soviet sites, so they should be able to determine where it comes from.' U-235 was the ninety per cent plus enriched uranium used to build nuclear weapons. Oak Ridge National Laboratory in Tennessee led the international program to prevent nuclear proliferation.

A warplane screamed to a landing on the nearby runway. As the noise subsided, the two HAZMAT men came from the workplace with files sealed in a transparent bag marked with three bright purple triangles forming a 'propeller' on a yellow backdrop, warning of nuclear materials.

Mikki said, 'That's the stuff from the basement archive in Uelen.'

'Welcome, welcome,' Gavril Nevrosky's eyes, beaming and filled with enthusiasm, danced on the screen in front of Yumatov. 'Like the magician he is, the great Ruslan Yumatov has risen from the dead and is speeding toward my doorstep.'

Over the years, in conversations like this, Yumatov had hunted for clues that Nevrosky would cheat him or could not deliver what he promised. He had found none. His escape proved that Nevrosky was well-organized, efficient and ruthless. He had a quality of being generous, straight and brilliant, which was why he had succeeded in gathering power while keeping his profile low.

'Thank you, Gavril,' answered Yumatov. 'You are indeed a master at what you do.' A throat irritation prompted him to cough. He was unfamiliar with conversation, unused even to speaking.

'The pleasure is mine, and besides, I need you. Gavril Nevrosky is no altruist. I have an instinct for the torn currents of the European soul. Its time has come to be reconstructed in the image of the great Colonel Yumatov.'

Yumatov was unsure exactly what Nevrosky meant. After more than two years away, he had no idea what networks and operations would still be intact.

'Is Astrid looking after you?' diverted Nevrosky, his childlike smile mixing mischief with innocence.

'Astrid?'

'Your beautiful stewardess who gave you the phone.'

'Thank you, Gavril. Yes. After where I have been, it is all delightful.'

'And your departure?'

'Smooth. Thank you.'

'There is nothing on the news which is good. The Americans want secrecy. They have questioned the pilot who flew you from Leesburg. He told them he saw nothing because he knows where his next paycheck is coming from. Mr Angus Olsen has disappeared into the Baltimore swamp, never to be seen again.' Nevrosky let out a rasping laugh.

Yumatov pushed himself up in his seat. His muscles told him it was time for his exercise routine. The escape, the organization, the different people, the talking, all made him realize how out of the world he had been. The calm of his imprisonment had been shattered. The control he had within its confinement was gone. His mind flooded with the fantasies he had been nurturing. He wanted them all, real and now.

'How are Anna and the children?' He tried to keep his voice level and unemotional.

'Your beautiful wife, Anna, is fine. Max and Natasha are fine. They have a lovely house in London. Good schools. She lectures at a university. You are a blessed man, Ruslan.'

'Do they know?'

Nevrosky became serious. 'They know nothing, so you and they stay safe. Once you are settled, you will have a beautiful family reunion.'

'Thank you.' Yumatov's cadence was hesitant. He did not like being in the hands of someone else, however generous they might have been, particularly when the situation was so deeply personal.

Nevrosky said, 'Soon, I will give Astrid an update. When we meet, we can go over details. I have Wagner with me. He is looking forward to seeing you again.'

'Rudolf Wagner?' Excitement swept through Yumatov. Wagner was one of the most talented nuclear physicists working for the Soviet Union. He must be in his late seventies now.

'Yes, Ruslan. We have Dr Wagner. He told me how you and he have worked together since the 1990s. We'll all meet soon.' With that, Nevrosky tantalizingly cut the call. The German was not a man who did not deliver on his word; Yumatov's escape was evidence of that. But he had deliberately withheld Wagner's involvement to show his dominance over Yumatov. With Wagner, Nevrosky must have a lethal plan in which Yumatov was to play a part for which it was worth breaking him out. Yumatov found himself engulfed in a mix of exhilaration and disquiet. Was he still up to it? Did he want it? Was it the right thing to do?

'Champagne, sir?' offered Astrid.

Yumatov shook his head and asked for sparkling water and unsalted nuts.

TWENTY-ONE

Clapham, London

Stephanie Lucas pulled back the slatted white blinds of her ground-floor living room and watched a nondescript, slightly shabby Volvo sedan pull up on the quiet south London street outside her house. Sergey Grizlov had kept his word about being discreet.

Stephanie had bought the run-down, corner house in the mid-nineties, flush from making her fortune in Russia when Grizlov had been her business partner and lover. It was an era of youth and fast-moving high ambition. Surprised at her own sudden wealth, Stephanie had been set on changing the world. Single and driven, she became a young and popular Member of Parliament and fell head over heels for Harry Lucas, recently elected to the American House of Representatives and with the added glamor of being a decorated Iraq and Afghanistan veteran. The marriage was passionate but long-distance, and an impossible dream. Its failure taught her the challenge of overstretch. High-achieving professions and a transatlantic relationship were steps too far. The separation hit them both, Harry harder because it unleashed war scars in his mind that until then he had success-fully covered up. She wobbled a bit, then climbed out faster than he did. Now, Harry was doing well. So was Sergey Grizlov. She might be crap at long-term relationships, she told herself, but she was skilled at attracting talented men.

Straddling the corner of two leafy Clapham streets, her old Victorian pile was far too big for her. Back then, she had envis-aged a husband, children and a dog. She had knocked down internal walls, done up the kitchen and the bathrooms, and kept meaning to sell or rent again, but hadn't got around to it. Now her father lived in the annex and would scare off any decent regular rent-paying tenant. A smell of cigarette smoke, mixed with whisky, beer and cigars, drifted up from the kitchen, where

Clive Jackson, turning eighty and sharp as a whippet, was playing poker around the table with six old friends.

Stephanie stayed most nights at her official residence in Carlton Gardens, just off Pall Mall. If she wanted quiet and fresh air, she headed for Chevening House, the Foreign Secretary's stately residence in Kent. She kept the Clapham house because she knew that any day she could lose her job, and this was home.

Grizlov came into her small front garden, with the neat rose bushes pruned by her father. She opened the door to greet him. The sun was warm, and the air had an early summer scent. Grizlov moved like the young man she had met more than thirty years ago, deliberate, filled with purpose, flawlessly dressed in a dark pinstripe suit and waistcoat, and polished black brogues. A glint of sunlight reflected from his silver cufflinks. She had expected as much and dressed down to complement him, as she had done when they were lovers, in a loose colorful kaftan in reds and blues, worn brown leather sandals, brown hair loose on her shoulders.

'Never seen you in such a modest car,' she quipped, throwing out her arms in welcome.

'What else can a humble foreign minister afford?'

Stephanie stepped inside, holding the door open for him. Grizlov wiped his immaculate shoes on the inside doormat and said, 'I remember this house.'

'I'd just bought it.'

'It was furnished with a fridge full of wine and vodka, and a huge brand-new mattress on the living-room floor.'

'Where we spent the night.'

'Just before you dumped me.'

Stephanie chuckled. 'I thought it was you who dumped me, for some lissome blonde from Vladivostok.'

They both smiled. Grizlov examined Stephanie's random decoration, a green bamboo holder for walking sticks, as if this were a country farmhouse, a long, stained mirror above, and next to it an antique barometer that had been in her father's car showroom and had never worked. There were framed silk Chinese embroideries in reds and greens, and a lithograph of Soviet art, with workers building a dam beneath a hammer and sickle. Stephanie led Grizlov into the large, high-ceilinged living room.

'And you still have this?' Grizlov pointed to a wooden chess set on a low coffee table.

'For some crazy reason, I love it.' Stephanie picked up a black rook. 'Here is the younger Sergey, his talent hewn from Clapham wood.' The pieces were carved to resemble negotiators from a long-forgotten trade conference, so tedious that Stephanie had used her classroom art skills to make it. Grizlov was the black rook and she made herself a white bishop.

Grizlov looked around as if her living room were a museum. He pointed with a smile to two framed posters of fast cars in Hollywood chase scenes.

'Those are Dad's,' said Stephanie. 'He's living in the annex.'

Grizlov waved his hand in front of his face, referring to the smell of cigarette smoke. 'I think I can detect that. And hear it.'

'His poker school, like I warned you. Did you ever meet him?'

'You wouldn't let me. You must have been ashamed of me.'

Stephane found herself smiling again. 'So, what's so urgent? Can I get you some coffee, or anything else?'

'No need.' Grizlov shook his head, nimbly switching his tone from personal to work, which she had always seen as a mark of their good relationship. 'And I won't keep you, Steph.'

She patted the back of the sofa for them to sit down. Grizlov shook his head again. 'Planes, cars, planes. If you don't mind, I'll use my legs for a bit of weight bearing.'

He leant an elbow on her limestone mantelpiece and recounted the border firefight much as she had heard from Harry Lucas. 'We didn't want to talk to Washington officially until we had a better idea of what was going on.'

Stephanie was about to ask why Grizlov thought she knew any more, when she heard footsteps on the stairs from the basement kitchen. The door opened and her father appeared, hand placed firmly on the jamb. Clive Jackson had presence. His eyes were as sharply blue as she could ever remember. When his hair thinned and grayed, he took to shaving his head, giving him the look of a street-corner bruiser, an image enhanced by a sinewy body with no surplus weight, a strong jaw on a long face and a scar that ran more than an inch from the edge of his left eye.

'Hi, Dad,' she said breezily. 'You remember Sergey.'

'Always wanted to meet him. Never did.' Jackson stepped

forward, hand outstretched. Grizlov took it firmly, placing his left hand on top in a politician's clasp of friendliness.

'Mr Jackson, it's so very good to meet you at last.'

Jackson examined Grizlov approvingly and tilted his head toward Stephanie. 'I kept telling her to marry you, and she wouldn't listen.'

'Never too late, Dad,' quipped Stephanie. 'But we're in the middle of—'

'See what I have to put up with.' Jackson waved his hand affectionately. 'I know. You have affairs of state. But an old man has a right to meet the guy who should have been his son-in-law.'

'It would have been a pleasure and an honor,' added Grizlov.

'She should have been Stephanie Grizlov, not this Lucas name she got by marrying a drunk American. Had the sense to leave him. But God knows why you cling to his name!'

'We've had this conversation a million times.' Stephanie let out an affectionate sigh. 'People know me as Lucas. Supposing Elvis Presley had changed his name.'

'Don't you love 'er?' Jackson said to Grizlov. 'Always knew she'd go far.'

'Thanks, Dad, but we're in the middle of—'

'Of course, of course – you said.' Jackson's expression hardened, made a point of examining Grizlov, like as a child she had seen so many times in his car showroom with a customer as he was about to close a deal. 'The thing is, Steph – and I ask as I'd have asked you if you were marrying him – do you *trust* him?'

Stephanie let out an embarrassed laugh and decided to answer head on. 'Sergey wouldn't be in this house if I didn't.'

'Good.' Jackson gave Stephanie a thumbs-up as if to nail the point. He turned to Grizlov. 'Your turn, son. Do *you* trust your President?'

Grizlov shifted his weight, smiled awkwardly as if taken off-guard, which would be what her father intended. He took a few seconds to answer. 'I do, Mr Jackson. I serve at President Lagutov's pleasure, as the Americans say, so he could fire me at any time.'

A shout came from the kitchen 'You in or out this hand, Clive?'

'I'm out. I'm with my daughter.' Jackson took a couple of

steps to perch on the arm of the sofa. 'I'll give you both a nugget, then I'll be gone.' He pointed behind him. 'Half a mile down that way, when Clapham was rougher than it is now, Steph was raised in my used-car yard. We lived above the shop, me and her. Her mum went off with another. To make ends meet, I bribed the police, so I could cut corners with the law. I taught my lovely Steph how to con, sell, forge papers, fix odometers, lie with a pretty face; all the dark arts of my trade. She was better than me, so I banned her from taking over the business and packed her off to university. Had a sense she would be better used lying for her country than lying about old cars. Point is, Sergey, I owned my parish, became a powerful man here, and a trusted one. Because I learned how to trust and who to trust.'

Jackson then pointed toward the kitchen. 'Those six geezers there round my poker table, I'd trust with my life. Not one word of your being here will be spread by them. So, here's the thing. A customer like you, Sergey, comes to my showroom. I size you up as a flashy guy, a need to show money and class, might look down on me, but not bent, not in a big way, not in way that's dangerous. I'd do business with you. Now, your Lagutov is different.'

Jackson was not yet done. Grizlov tensed.

'If he walked into my showroom, I'd think differently. He puts on this air of not caring. He doesn't dress right, he's scruffy when he's meant to be the boss. He talks too much about his old job, a university professor, making out he prefers it. So, he's in front of me wanting to buy or sell a car, and I'm thinking: you're not what you're making yourself out to be, and I need to know who you are if I'm to do business with you. That's it. I've said my bit, and I won't ask again whether you trust Mr Lagutov because it ain't a fair question, not here, not today on my birthday, in my daughter's house. Don't change my mind, though, about wishing you and Steph had got married.'

Jackson stood up, gave them a wide smile, raised his hand in a wave, left and closed the stairwell door behind him.

TWENTY-TWO

Stephanie shrugged. 'Well, you wanted to meet my dad.'

'What a character!' Grizlov attempted a laugh.

They were quiet, readjusting after what might seem an old man's rant, except both knew it wasn't. 'Why don't we speak as if we're two of his geezers around the poker table?' Stephanie suggested,

'Sure,' said Grizlov. 'Since we spoke, the Americans also went into Uelen, a Bering Strait coastline settlement.'

'I didn't know.' She tried to hide her surprise. 'When?'

'The past few hours. While I was on my way here.'

Stephanie had spoken to Harry and he had said nothing. 'Why?'

'I don't know. It has to be connected with Katia Codic. Lagutov was uncharacteristically edgy when we just spoke. He wants me to find out discreetly before he goes public which, with Uelen, he'll have to.'

'You're genuinely asking, aren't you? You're not fishing?' Stephanie thought she knew Grizlov well enough to see that his usual certainties were diminished.

'Yes, Steph, I am genuinely asking.' Grizlov's lips tightened.

'Is this why you've suddenly been shunted into the loop, for Lagutov to use you as a fall guy?'

'Could be. He called me to the Kremlin. All those billions spent on intelligence gathering and I end up at your dad's birthday party in Clapham.'

Stephanie smiled. 'On Katia Codic, as far as I know, the Americans were expecting a courier sent by the Kremlin. As she was crossing, your side shot her. So, everyone is confused.'

Grizlov pulled down the right cuff of his jacket then cupped his hand around his chin. 'The Kremlin didn't send her. Whomever the Americans were dealing with, it wasn't Viktor Lagutov.'

'OK,' she said cautiously. 'Sounds like that's one for you guys to sort between yourselves. Who does she work for?' She deliberately used the present tense so as not to confirm to Grizlov that Katia Codic was dead.

'She was recruited by the FSB in 2006, left in 2010. We're trying to establish what she has been doing since.'

'The Kremlin doesn't know?'

'I don't, and Lagutov says he doesn't. Or for whom she was working.'

'But you know what information she was carrying, or you wouldn't have taken such drastic measures to stop her.'

'My job is to work my contacts in Europe. I don't know what secrets she had.'

'That makes two of us. Broad brush, you must know more than me.'

Grizlov fell silent, smoothing his sleeve again, fiddling with his cufflink, eyes flitting to the door above the stairwell, across to the window. 'Lagutov said it jeopardized our Europe policy.'

'Being what?'

Before Grizlov answered, Stephanie's phone buzzed, the line currently kept free for Harry Lucas. She fumbled awkwardly deep for it, inside her kaftan pocket.

'Is Grizlov with you?' said Lucas.

'Yes.' She heard the harsh whine of an aircraft engine.

'I'm on the way to Andrews,' said Lucas. 'If he hasn't said anything ground-breaking, just say *No*.'

'No.'

'Preliminary forensics are just in from Uelen. Does he know it's me calling?'

'No.'

'I am going to tell you one of the results. When I have, I need your view on whether Grizlov would already know this and whether you should pass it on to him.'

'OK.' Stephanie was silently screaming for Harry to just spit it out.

Grizlov pointed toward the door. *Did she want him to leave?* Stephanie patted the air with her free hand. *Stay.*

'Tell him it's me and watch his reaction.'

Stephanie looked up from the phone and said, 'It's Harry.'

'Send my regards.' Grizlov was aware of Harry Lucas's connections and his profession. He kept his eyes on Stephanie, then calmly let them float around the room, allowing her space. There was nothing in his manner that reflected something bigger was at play.

'Uelen shows traces of uranium 235,' said Lucas.

Stephanie sucked in the inside of her cheek to conceal the shock of what she'd heard. 'How, exactly?'

'In rubble scree, soil, rusting steel, and chipped concrete in a building formerly used for Arctic research which was sealed off by the military from 1990 to 2020.'

'OK, I got that.' She tried to sound breezy.

'Do you read anything in Grizlov?' asked Lucas.

'No.'

'Has he mentioned Ruslan Yumatov?'

'No.'

'Do you trust him?'

What a question! The second time in the past five minutes. Her father's advice, running through her mind, seemed as good as any. Grizlov was looking through Stephanie's carved pieces, picking one up, inspecting it, putting it down, moving to the next. Stephanie read impatience more than nervousness.

'In big things like this, yes,' she answered.

'Then tell him and keep the line open.'

Stephanie laid the phone on the mantelpiece, put it on speaker and said, 'Harry asked if I trusted you, and I said I did in the big things.'

Grizlov stood up and smoothed an imaginary crease in his sleeve. He glanced behind him to the door down to the kitchen again, as if checking they were alone. He read the solemnity in her face, returned to his perch on the mantelpiece and waited for Stephanie to say more.

'They found traces of weapons-grade uranium 235 on material recovered from Uelen,' she said.

Grizlov shifted his gaze toward the window, a reaction Stephanie had seen many times when assessing new information. Under his breath, he went through names, some of which Stephanie picked up as Soviet nuclear weapons sites. 'There was nothing around Uelen that I remember,' he said. 'What material exactly?'

'Stuff gathered from around an old Arctic research building.'

'Hello, Harry.' Grizlov's brow creased. 'Is that why you went in?'

Lucas said, 'We knew something wasn't right. We had no idea it would be this.'

Grizlov kept casting his eyes around the room, taking in stuff Stephanie had on the walls, photographs on side tables, his expression etched with concern. 'Have you sourced the U-235?'

'Oak Ridge is examining it.'

Grizlov let out a sigh. 'It may be less drastic than it sounds. There are uranium traces all over the former Soviet Union.'

'And you don't know about Uelen?'

'I don't.'

'Then you need to find out, Sergey, either from Lagutov, or whoever sent us Katia Codic.'

'Is she alive?'

'Between the three of us? Yes. Katia Codic is alive and she is talking. We need to sort this out, Sergey, before it's too late.'

Lucas ended the call with real exasperation and anger in his voice. No one would know the wisdom of him lying about Katia Codic until it was over.

Grizlov's expression had not changed; his eyes were unsettled. He fidgeted with cufflink.

'Anything, Sergey?' prompted Stephanie.

'Lagutov spoke about the risk to our Europe policy.'

'The only thing that's risking your Europe policy right now is that bloody—' She broke off, amazed at her own blindness. Her tone softened. 'That European bloody army conference.'

'Cannot be.' Grizlov shook his head. 'It's been around for years.'

'I don't expect you to tell me everything, but, like my dad said, I trust you.' Stephanie took his hand, held it affectionately but hard. 'Whatever bad is going on, Sergey, whatever trick Lagutov is playing . . .' She trailed off as Grizlov's face shadowed.

TWENTY-THREE

The military Gulfstream 111 with flat-bed seats was designed for six passengers, and usually carried generals, admirals and politicians. Rake, Carrie and Mikki slept the way their kind of people did – whenever, as deeply, and for as long as they could. Carrie and Rake's seats were side by side and Carrie's arm draped across Rake's chest.

Lucas was awake, studying a new piece of information. He had asked his digital team to create a portrait from the figure waving goodbye to Yumatov and Katia Codic at the London town house. He had also engineered a heavy-handed warning to the reluctant chief executive of Chatham Mayfair, the private intelligence-gathering company that owned the town house.

The identity was now 100 per cent confirmed. He was Richard John Brenning, aged sixty-seven, formerly with the UK Space Agency, where he had worked on an integrated missile-defense system called Sky Sabre. He had then moved to the private sector and been appointed to the House of Lords. It was not clear why. As Lord Brenning of Knettishall – a village in Norfolk on England's east coast – he sat as a cross-bench peer, meaning he was not controlled by any political party.

Lucas called Stephanie and asked if she knew Brenning.

'Vaguely,' she answered.

'Why would he be in the House of Lords?'

'Don't know, Harry, off the top of my head. But I'll find out.'

'Have you met him?'

'Probably, bumped into him, at least. He doesn't have a huge profile. Not a big hitter. Speaks on defense, but I have no idea if he's for or against the European defense force.'

'Can you watch him?' Lucas meant deploy a surveillance team.

Stephanie let out a long, low whistle through her teeth. 'We could, but not with shoe leather. Slater and Merrow both want us to stick to back channels. If we start tailing a member of the

House of Lords, there's risk of a leak. But you can do it, digitally. We'll give you pointers, and I keep my hands clean.'

'Thank you.' That could work. Britain had some of the world's most intrusive surveillance legislation, which included intercepting communication, tracking websites and hacking into the bank accounts of private citizens.

'Merrow has asked for our security assessments on the Bonn summit, above and beyond the usual,' said Stephanie. 'He and Slater took one look at the U-235 and thought *dirty bomb*.'

'They may be getting ahead of themselves.' Lucas grappled to find a connection. 'We found the U-235 by chance.'

'No, Harry,' countered Stephanie. 'You and Ozenna had your whiskers twitching that something was lurking in Uelen. You found the U-235 because the Russians shot up a power boat that came from there. They are right to be extra careful. There'll be more than thirty European heads of government gathered under one roof, at the old Palais Schaumburg.' Stephanie paused and Lucas heard a softness in her tone. 'Remember that place I showed you back in ninety-nine, when the German government was moving from Bonn back to Berlin? That's where we'll be.'

Lucas did remember Bonn, before they began seriously dating, before 9/11, before Iraq, before divorce. 'I see the symbolism,' he agreed. 'It was the seat of the West German federal government, a victor of the Cold War. But when was the summit set up?'

'A month ago.'

'An attack like this would have taken years of planning. And how do Yumatov and whomever he is working with propose to breach the layers of security? I don't buy it, Steph. We're sending the Secretary of State, so the Secret Service will be all over it.'

'Yumatov tried in Norway.'

'And failed. At least then there was motive. Here, Russia sees an independent European defense force as an opportunity. It pushes the US away from Europe and weakens NATO.'

'Except, we don't know if this is Russia,' countered Stephanie. 'We don't know what the hell it is.' She stopped there, drawing back from argument. They might have been divorced for years, but they still had a tendency to push the wrong buttons and flare up with each other. 'Just passing it on, Harry,' she said quietly.

Lucas kept the phone on his lap and tilted back his seat. In the first months of separation from Stephanie he had found sleep impossible. Neither drink nor medication worked. He eventually conquered it by taking apparently unconnected elements of a problem and finding the dots that joined them. Usually sleep took him before he succeeded and then he found himself waking with a useful idea. He closed his eyes to the rhythmic hum of the aircraft engines and the higher pitch of Mikki Wekstatt's snoring. He was woken, not by a solution but by yet another dot to be joined.

The duty officer from Oak Ridge called. 'We've sourced the U-235, sir,' he said. 'It was enriched at the Ulba Metallurgical Plant in Ust Kamenogorsk in what is now Kazakhstan. The last consignment our records show from there was in 1989, to fuel the nuclear propulsion system of the Alfa-class attack submarine, based way across in Severodvinsk, near Archangel. I've asked for more details.'

'So not for nuclear weapons?' asked Lucas.

'It's dual use, sir, the same levels of enrichment. Ulba was one of the centers of Soviet defense research. The biggest brains of the Cold War had been assigned there.'

The call had also woken Rake. He walked across and Lucas summarized his conversation with Stephanie about Brenning, and what he himself knew about the origins of the U-235.

'Ulba Metallurgical Plant,' said Rake. 'That's Project Sapphire.'

Rake was quicker than Lucas. Project Sapphire was on the curriculum of every nuclear proliferation war college course. As the Soviet Union crumpled, a warehouse in the closed military city of Ust Kamenogorsk was found to be holding canisters of U-235. The CIA had flown them out in three Lockheed C-5 Galaxy cargo planes, directly to the Oak Ridge facility in Tennessee, which would explain why it had been so swiftly sourced.

Rake fetched them both coffee from a self-help canteen at the back of the aircraft. 'Those U-235 canisters sat in a warehouse for two years with no oversight,' he said.

Lucas scrolled through his tablet. 'From December 1991, the handover of power from the Soviet Union to Kazakhstan, until October 1993, when the Kazakhs came to us for help. During that time, rogue states from North Korea to Venezuela approached the Kazakhs to buy. Planes were landing from the Middle East, stuffed full of dollars. Libya's Qaddafi offered five million for a single weapon. The Kazakhs say they resisted and refused. They asked for help from Moscow, which was then chaotic and dysfunctional under Boris Yeltsin. Nothing happened. Only then did they come to us. We got a full inventory in October 1993, six hundred kilograms which we flew out in November 1994, everything accounted for. We don't know what might have gone missing before that.'

'Or how it ended up in Uelen,' added Rake.

The aircraft shook with light turbulence which woke Carrie. She waited for it to settle, ran her fingers through her hair, stood up, came back to join them. There was another shudder of the plane. Carrie stayed on her feet, using Rake's shoulder for balance. Lucas filled her in.

Carrie asked, 'Any luck with finding Yumatov?'

'A possible flight from Baltimore to Schiphol, Amsterdam,' answered Lucas. 'It hasn't checked out yet.'

She took Rake's cardboard coffee cup, took a sip. 'Christ, you like it strong.' She screwed up her face to make the point.

Rake said, 'Yumatov would have been – what, sixteen or seventeen? What are the chances of any theft of nuclear material back then having anything to do with him?'

Lucas nodded. 'Like I told Steph, we could be trying to join dots, when all we've got are coincidences.'

'Coincidence is God's way of remaining anonymous.' Carrie took another sip of Rake's coffee. 'Albert Einstein. Not that I know a lot about him, except that everything is relative. Einstein does space, light and time. I do the human body, the artery, the kidney, the femur. You guys do what you do, and we all try to join dots because the dots are there, all of them moving in ways relative to each other.'

Lucas glanced curiously at Rake, whose focus was on Carrie, holding his coffee, with her eyes squeezed shut, and her hand tight on his shoulder in case of more turbulence. Her eyes sprang open onto Lucas. She handed the cup to Rake and set her hands a foot apart. 'The furthest dot on my left is this nuclear factory in Kazakhstan.' She flipped out her left forefinger. 'On the right is this summit in Bonn.' She drew her right forefinger in a wave-like curve through the air to her left one. 'The one constant that runs through this is Ruslan Yumatov. We don't know how, but we think he's in there somewhere.'

Lucas gave her an interested, puzzled look.

'We don't know where Yumatov is,' Carrie went on. 'I treated him when he was dying. The one strand that runs through his life is his wife and children, who are in London. I know first-hand how much he adores her. I also know the evil that drives him. Anna Yumatov would know that too. She would know if he had been anywhere near this Ulba place, if there were any dots to be joined.' Carrie finished the coffee and rested the cup on the arm of a chair.

'In my experience, monsters like Yumatov don't give a fuck about their families.' Rake picked up the coffee cup before it toppled with more turbulence.

'In my experience,' countered Carrie, 'it's family that drives them, or failure of family and relationships. If Anna still loves him, she'll want to know where he is and to help him. If she loathes him, she'll be motivated to help us. Either way, her instinct will be to protect her children.'

'Will it?' questioned Lucas, plans spinning through his mind.

'Yes,' said Carrie, allowing a strain of impatience into her voice. 'Komodo dragons, sloth bears, pandas – even hamsters, dammit! – sometimes they eat their babies. But we humans, we protect our babies with our lives.'

The plane jolted again, and clouds sped past the windows, as the pilot announced they were beginning their descent into Andrews.

TWENTY-FOUR

Vrazhdebna Military Air Base, Sofia, Bulgaria

From the Gulfstream window, Yumatov saw dry grass, summer haze, and the gray metallic buildings of an old, Soviet-style air base. He had first been told they were flying to Dresden, then that there was a delay and a diversion. They had landed at an air base north of Sofia in Bulgaria. The stewardess, who introduced herself as Astrid, had apologized on behalf of Gavril Nevrosky. After three hours, she had offered Yumatov a hotel, although that would mean immigration and formalities and would not be as luxurious as the Gulfstream.

The screen in Yumatov's seat flickered and the cheerful, pock-marked face of Gavril Nevrosky appeared. 'I am so sorry, Ruslan, for this inconvenience. It will be a few more hours.'

Astrid topped up Ruslan Yumatov's sparkling mineral water.

'I have been used to solitary confinement and bad food,' said Yumatov. 'But should I be worried?'

'Absolutely not.' Nevrosky's moving hands blurred against the lens as they made his point. 'We are meeting at one of my places in Europe. I'm going through a messy divorce, squabbles about who owns what. We're now going to the farmhouse in the Elbe Sandstone Mountains between Dresden and Prague. Rudolf Wagner and I are on our way there now. Astrid will look after you. Just a few more hours.'

Yumatov thanked him, said how much he was looking forward to meeting. As the screen darkened, he slowly chewed on a mix of walnuts and cashew and thought about Rudolf Wagner, who must be pushing eighty now and was the most brilliant nuclear physicist of his generation. The Ulba Metallurgical Plant, where he had worked, was the Soviet center of excellence for nuclear weapons research. Yumatov had been just a kid, furious and adolescent. As one teenage girlfriend had reprimanded, Ruslan was so blind with fury he couldn't even see his own dreams.

He had been leading protests against Russian tricksters and American lawyers who had broken up his factory and stripped his father of his job. Before taking to the vodka, his father had pulled his son off the protest lines, telling him he could never win, and sent him to join the army. They had made the young Yumatov an officer cadet and, aged only seventeen, he found himself with a delegation visiting Ulba in the closed city of Ust Kamenogorsk, which was soon to become a city in the independent nation of Kazakhstan.

Yumatov identified with the anger among the Soviet staff there. Their sense of betrayal mirrored those at his father's factory. It was December 1991 and, within days, the nation to which they had given their whole lives would cease to exist. They had been working on making nuclear weapons more compact and powerful, on forging metals for delivery systems that were lighter and more durable. The corridors and conference rooms were lined with photographs of the heroes of Soviet weaponry. Yet those heroes were now reduced to worrying about their families, their salaries and their pensions.

The task of Yumatov's delegation was to conduct an inventory of a warehouse stocked with U-235 weapons-grade uranium, and then formally hand it over to the Kazakh government.

It was minus eighteen degrees Celsius with a bitingly high windchill. Dirty snow drifted against the walls of ugly square buildings. Thick pipes ran around the plant like highways, coated with grimy ice from which sharp glistening icicles hung like spears. Smoke belched from tall thin chimneys and, inside, as they were shown around, Yumatov saw clanging machinery, creaking conveyer belts, the buzzing of timers and the whir of dull black spinning centrifuges processing uranium to a grade pure enough to make nuclear warheads.

In Yumatov's delegation was an East German nuclear scientist, Dr Rudolf Wagner, who had worked for many years at Ulba. He had made a point of befriending Yumatov, insisting that just the two of them dine together.

'The Soviet Union leads the world in nuclear technology, and all that will be lost,' Wagner had said, speaking with his mouth full, his fork in his right hand, and waving his left in the air to make his point. 'The Americans will take our work and make it their own. Yeltsin will sell them everything and screw us over, just like your father was screwed over.'

Yumatov had been caught by surprise that Wagner knew about his father. 'We spotted your leadership, intelligence and passion,' Wagner explained. 'That day, you were barely sixteen, and you confronted those racketeers breaking up your father's factory. That is why you are here. We noticed not just your anger, but also the strength of your argument.'

Wagner had dark matted hair and a pink face whose shades changed depending on the level of his excitement. He was clean shaven, although badly. There was a clump of stubble under his left ear and around his chin, as if he had got distracted and then forgotten.

'All this talk of democracy only exposes the rottenness of any system,' he said. 'Yeltsin is a drunk and the West hails him as one of theirs. We think we can be like them, but we can't. The Caucasus will explode. Russia will become sick. Gangsters will move in.' Wagner leaned forward, and lowered his voice, jabbing his fork toward Yumatov. 'Who do you think advised and financed those who fucked over your family and your town? Western banks and lawyers, with their free-market bullshit. I am only a scientist, Ruslan, yet even I can see what is happening.'

Yumatov had noted the familiar use of his first name. They finished their food and ordered coffee. Neither man was drinking. Wagner scooped up his white linen napkin and dabbed his food-specked lips. 'Give me a moment.' He dropped the napkin back on the table and walked out of the dining room, rubbing his hands excitedly together. Yumatov waited. Their table was next to a tall window which overlooked a dark copse of trees, through which he could see the blackness of the Ulba River. Half of the dining room looked old, with chipped timbers embedded in the wall and the ragged stuffed head of an elk over a large fire-place. This was where technicians and other scientists from the delegation were dining, loudly. Yumatov's area was of solid, unimaginative Soviet design, all square wooden tables and off-white walls, a place for people to eat and then go back to work.

Wagner returned with a second man, not part of the delegation. He was in his mid-thirties, short, with close-cropped hair and wide shoulders. Although in civilian clothes, Yumatov guessed from his manner that he was in the military. He began to get to his feet, but Wagner waved him to stay where he was. 'This is naval Captain Alexander Vitruk,' he said. 'He has flown in from Vladivostok to see us.'

Vitruk went on to become commander of the Eastern Division and led the ill-fated Diomede operation. He had pulled out a chair and sat down. He did not ask who Yumatov was and said only, 'You have the inventory?'

'From the warehouse? Yes, sir.'

'How much?

'A total of two thousand two hundred kilograms of nuclear material, sir, including six hundred and seventy kilograms of U-235.'

'How is it packed?'

'Beryllium alloy casing, sealed in reinforced stainless-steel canisters, ready for transportation.'

Vitruk stared out of the window into the gloom of the winter night.

'Seventy?' he asked Wagner.

'Four, maybe five,' the German scientist answered. At that moment, Yumatov had no idea what they were talking about.

Vitruk, his gaze still outside, nodded to Wagner who said, 'My specialty is the small and powerful nuclear weapon delivered with the lightest possible metal. We are experimenting with a magnesium-based alloy, light like aluminum, strong like titanium.'

At exactly that point, Yumatov knew what he had to do, while also realizing this was what he wanted to do. Had he refused, he suspected he would have ended up dead, that night, his body thrown into the icy depths of the Ulba River. Wagner and Vitruk planned to siphon off seventy kilograms of U-235, which would make four or five nuclear weapons, and give them and whatever organization they were forming an independent nuclear deterrent.

Yumatov caught Vitruk's eye in the window reflection and asked firmly, 'What do you need from me, sir?'

'Send the inventory as two thousand one hundred and thirty kilograms, including six hundred kilograms of U-235.'

'Yes, sir.'

Vitruk left. Yumatov adjusted the log as instructed. The next day a military unit specializing in the transportation of nuclear material removed seventy kilograms of highly enriched uranium from the warehouse in containers, and loaded them onto a closely guarded railcar.

Wagner retired and settled in his home city of Dresden. Yumatov was later transferred to Russia's Eastern Military District, which fell under the command of Admiral Alexander Vitruk.

TWENTY-FIVE

RAF Northolt, Middlesex, UK

'Major Raymond Ozenna? My name is Bridget England, special advisor to the Foreign Secretary.'

It was Rake's first time in Britain, and he was first down the steps of the US Airforce C-37 A, which had taxied to stop outside a square white terminal building at RAF Northolt, west of London. England began with a half-salute, palm facing outward, then changed her mind and pressed her right hand against her left shoulder as a designated post-COVID formal greeting. 'Sorry. Got mixed up. When I'm not in my day job, I'm a captain 21-SAS Reserve. When I meet a soldier, I go military.'

Rake acknowledged with a full American salute, hard and fast to the forehead, fingers outstretched and palm facing down, face expressionless, but with a glimpse of play in his eyes, squinting against the soft sunlight. 'Thank you, Captain,' he said. 'They call my unit the Eskimo Scouts. We don't deploy to the UK.'

England smiled. Her attention shifted to Lucas, who came down the steps talking on the phone, followed by Mikki. Carrie was already in London, having flown commercial from Dulles, and was planning to meet Anna Yumatov.

Rake and Mikki had gathered weapons and gear at Andrews. Mikki was amazed at what Lucas had made available. 'It's like if you order cherry pie, you get cherry pie,' he had exclaimed as they unpacked, inspected and loaded assault rifles, pistols, a range of ammunition grenades, launchers, hydration packs, food and the rest.

The aircraft would stay at RAF Northolt to fly them to wherever they needed to go. A black Mercedes minibus, engine running, stood under the wing. 'You brought the good weather with you.' England pulled open the van door. 'Slight change of plan. The PM had wanted to see you here. But he's been caught at Chequers. A row within his party over the joint European defense force. It'll be a forty-minute run.'

Once on the road, England stayed quiet in front, working her phone and tablet. Lucas took the jump seat at the very back, with Rake and Mikki in the middle. Rake saw that the landscape was neat and old in a way that the United States could never be. The roads were narrower, even the highways, and the cars smaller. The traffic lights stood on solid black posts and didn't hang from high wires at intersections. He took it all in, realizing he had barely got rid of the taste of salt water and blood from the Uelen raid.

When they turned off onto a country road thick with summer greenery, England went into tour-guide mode. 'This is Victory Drive. It leads to Chequers, which has been the Prime Minister's official residence since 1921. The house is of Gothic design, dating back to the sixteenth century. These beautiful beech trees on either side were a gift from Winston Churchill.'

She spoke as if this were a recitation repeated to foreign delegations, week after week. No one responded. The van drew up outside a heavy-set building of red-brick and gray stone. Rake recognized the Foreign Secretary, Baroness Lucas of Clapham, standing outside a dark wood front door.

'A heads-up, gentlemen,' England turned in her seat. 'The PM's having to deal with a backlash in his own party about Britain signing up for the European Defense Summit in Bonn. Keep that in mind as he makes his decisions. He will meet us in the Hawtrey Room and take us straight out to the terrace. The PM is an outdoors person. He thinks more clearly in the fresh air.' England got out and slid open the back door. Stephanie Lucas stepped forward, wearing a light red and white polka-dot dress and sandals. 'Good to see you, Harry.' She tapped her shoulder. Formal COVID greetings were still all over the place.

'You too, Steph.' Lucas returned the gesture. 'You know the team?'

'By reputation.' She acknowledged Rake and Mikki. 'It's good to meet you both.'

'Likewise, ma'am,' Rake said.

They followed Stephanie and Lucas through the door where they were greeted by a young woman in a Royal Air Force uniform, standing by an aircraft-style scanner. 'Weapons?' asked England.

'We're clear.' Rake put key, coins, phone and the rest into a tray and walked through. Mikki followed. They went with England into the Hawtrey Room – named after the first owner, she told them – with its fireplace, old furniture and chandelier. England then led them through and out onto the terrace to the Prime Minister. Kevin Slater was tall, well over seventy but with a sportsman's build, and was dressed in a maroon shirt, crumpled cream pants and black trainers.

The terrace was old and crumbling and ran the length of the building. Beyond it the lawn folded into a wild garden then into meadow with grazing cows. The air was heavy with the scents of lavender and freshly cut grass. There was a long wooden table with papers and photographs on it, secured from the wind with a couple of flasks of water, a pair of binoculars and two heavy stones. Two of the photographs were copies of those Lucas had uncovered of Yumatov in London and Dresden. Half a dozen staff stood by.

'Sorry to drag you gentlemen all this way.' Slater spoke in a casual regional accent from the north of England. 'My numbers aren't what they used to be. Rebellious colleagues say they'll oust me as party leader if I engage across the channel about a European army. So this time next week, I may be out of a job. But I'll be damned if Britain doesn't have a seat at the table of a new regional defense force.' He swung his intense gaze toward Lucas. 'Congressman Lucas – you're here because you need my cooperation, so you go first.'

Lucas ran through events, from the border shooting through Yumatov's violent escape to the discovery of the U-235 in Uelen and its sourcing to the Ulba Metallurgical Plant. 'Do we know where this Yumatov is?' asked Slater.

'We were fairly certain he flew from Baltimore to Schiphol,' said Lucas. 'But he hasn't been located from there.'

Familiar with setbacks, Slater accepted it and moved on. 'We need to get the last Soviet inventory from that nuclear facility, the one handed over to the Kazakhs.'

'The White House is keen we keep things tight,' said Lucas. 'Such questions will open them up.'

'Except the clock may be against us.' Slater signaled one of his staff. 'Jon, see if you can get President Merrow for us. In the cellar. Give us ten minutes.'

TWENTY-SIX

The Prime Minister plucked the photographs of Yumatov off the table. He handed Lucas the one taken in the Japanese restaurant in Dresden. 'This is Nevrosky?'

'Yes, sir,' said Lucas. 'The other is Michio Kato, heir to the Ariga empire. The Katos are a wealthy family whose political influence has grown alongside the rise of Japanese nationalism. Nevrosky is a Dresden businessman. Fingers in many pies in the old Soviet bloc.'

'Where is Nevrosky now?'

'Neither at his main residence nor in his office.'

'We need to get the Service onto it and work with the Germans. Discreetly.'

Bridget England glanced at Stephanie who said, 'Bridget has come up with something.'

'Then spit it out, Bridget,' instructed Slater.

'A number of companies based in Saxony and Bavaria have been using a London company, Future Forecasting, to help them gain local influence through elections. The targets have been football clubs, trade unions, charities, anything – it seems – that needs an election to its board. This company specializes in data harvesting and neuromarketing, in getting inside the minds of voters, and made its name here with Brexit. It has clients all over Europe, Catalonia, Estonia, Scotland. The common strand is that it targets areas that are vulnerable to extremism. The owner is Stephen Case, a hi-tech whizz kid, who boasts he will never work on an election he can't win.'

Slater's gaze stayed sharp on England while he summoned across a staffer. 'David, check we've never used this company, either the party or the government. If we have, make sure the press office has an explanation.' He turned back. 'Sorry. I call it bud-nipping: stopping shit before the sewage tank breaks. Bridget, please, go on.'

'Only to say, sir, that Stephen Case is now turning down

contracts in those same areas. We're still trying to find out why.'

'Is Nevrosky a client?'

'Not directly, sir. But there's a political pattern and we're still checking.'

'Good,' said Slater. 'Now, how does the Ariga corporation fit into all this?'

'Japan is more opaque, sir,' said Stephanie, glancing across for Lucas to pick up.

Lucas said, 'The Kato family is heavily entwined with Japanese politics and believes the country should never have lost the Pacific War. Unlike here and back home, organized crime is embedded in Japan's institutions. There is no strict prohibition to being a member of a crime syndicate. The police have files on tens of thousands of members. There is no red line dividing that from legal commercial and political activity. The Kato family founded Ariga, which is a pivotal force within the Yakuza network.'

Slater studied the photograph with a frown. 'I'll need more before confronting the Japanese government. We've lost so much leverage because of bloody Brexit.'

'Ariga was raising funds for the Uelen project over the same period that the U-235 was there,' said Lucas.

'I'll need a smoking gun.' Slater picked up the second photograph. 'Steph, you say we have a name for this blur of a man behind the window?'

'He is Lord Brenning of Knettishall,' said Bridget England. 'He was elevated as a cross-bench peer because of his knowledge of space defense. In government he worked with what is now Sky Sabre, our integrated missile-defense system. In the private sector, his last staff position was with a Cambridge-based company called Compact Space Technologies, which launches small private satellites.'

'Anybody know him?' Slater's gaze swiveled around everyone at the table.

'Met him,' said Stephanie. 'Heard him speak. Can't remember a word he said.'

The others shook their heads.

'Family?'

'Divorced, wife got the house in Kensington. Two daughters,

grown up and married. He lists his address as Armstrong Road in Acton, West London.'

A staffer signaled that the line to the White House was ready. Rake, Mikki and England stayed outside, while Slater led Lucas and Stephanie back through the Hawtrey Room and down a flight of stairs to a low-ceilinged room with a small conference table and a bank of screens at one end. Peter Merrow's on-screen face was turned away, talking to someone. He touched his ear, alerted that the British Prime Minister was now on the line. 'Kevin, thank you for helping out,' he said. 'I see you have Harry Lucas and the Foreign Secretary with you. And I understand we have lost Ruslan Yumatov.'

'We have, sir. Yes,' said Lucas.

'As Prime Minister Slater knows well, I hold the US-Russia front against China close to my heart. I do not intend to jeopardize it without good evidence, which we are lacking.'

From Merrow's measured tone, Stephanie judged this would not all be going their way. 'We have lived with the threat of a dirty bomb contaminating a city since before 9/11,' said Merrow. 'To run into U-235 traces in what was once a closed Soviet military district means nothing. The casino resort appears to be a routine money-laundering scam. Yumatov is most likely a spent force. Yes, it was a well-executed and bloody break-out, but more in tune with a drug cartel than the Russian state. The German, Gavril Nevrosky, appears to be a run-of-the-mill gangster, businessmen, politician. We have them here. You have them in Europe. The view from the Oval Office is that we should stay alert and keep investigating. I would put my money on there being a narco connection, nothing more.'

Slater's eyes were on Stephanie to respond, which she took as an instruction to push back, but not too much. 'Thank you, Mr President,' she began cautiously. 'The China-Russian interference in Europe is reaching critical levels, impacting the poorer parts of Europe where Nevrosky has most influence – Hungary, Greece, Bulgaria, Romania, to name a few. He has been undermining democratic institutions through transnational crime as cited in US presidential executive orders dating back to 2011.'

'Except this isn't 2011, Madam Secretary, and I'm not buying that argument,' said Merrow. 'This rise-of-the-right fear has been going on for some years now. The latest polls show it is declining. No democratic government is under threat.'

Slater contributed, 'What do you suggest, Peter?'

'Harry Lucas reports directly to me,' replied Merrow. 'He carries the full support of my administration.'

With Harry in London, Stephanie immediately saw how Merrow was giving them a way forward while keeping his own hands clean

'Then, we'll liaise closely,' concluded Slater. 'Thank you, Mr President.' The screen went dark. Slater led them out through the Hawtrey Room, back onto the terrace. The sun was dimmed by light gray clouds, making it cooler with a stronger breeze. Mikki was talking to Bridget England. Rake stood further away on the edge of the terrace, talking on his phone.

Slater said, 'Steph, work closely with Harry. For the next twenty-four hours we do what Peter Merrow asks and keep it tight. Is Sergey Grizlov still here?'

'In the Russian Embassy,' said Stephanie.

'Harry, talk to Lord Brenning and Stephen Case from this company Future Forecasting. We'll support from behind.' He paused while a gust blew across the terrace, then said, 'And the wife, Anna Yumatov—?'

'This is Carrie Walker,' Rake cut in. 'She's about to intercept her.'

TWENTY-SEVEN

C arrie stood in front of the window of an antique furniture shop at the intersection of Kensington Church Street and Peel Street in west London's Notting Hill. She listened to Anna Yumatov talking to her children, who were heading to school, from the steps of her rented town house.

Carrie had been met off her plane's airbridge at Heathrow, taken around the immigration lines and shown into a van that smelled of new seat leather. On the journey into London she was fitted with a near-invisible earpiece and equally discreet microphones and cameras. She was given a larger version of her pass to Washington General Hospital, which identified her as a trauma surgeon with her name bold and clear so it could be read at a distance. She was handed a tablet with bullet-point details on Anna Yumatov. Most Carrie already knew – forty-three years old, a professor at the London School of Economics, lecturing in central and eastern European modern history, a disciplined jogger, and so on. There was Anna's daily and weekly routine of sending Max, aged ten, and Natasha, aged seven, to school with a live-in nanny, identified as Hanna Kravets from eastern Ukraine, who would also pick them up while Anna was at work. The section was entitled Pattern of Life Analysis, yet another pigeonhole conjured up by the multi-billion-dollar security industry, thought Carrie.

Notting Hill was a wealthy neighborhood with expensive properties. Anna Yumatov rented a modest house on Peel Street, just south of the main thoroughfare and subway station. Morning sunlight peppered the narrow street as Anna stood outside the open dark blue door, wearing a maroon tracksuit with black trainers and a backpack. After seeing off the children, she was due to jog four miles east through Kensington Gardens and Hyde Park, past Buckingham Palace, then through Green Park and St James's Park, to her work at the university in Aldwych. She was holding tutorials during the day then delivering an early evening lecture – 'Consequences of the European Union's Expansion into Central and Eastern Europe'.

Carrie's van was parked on the corner of Peel Street and Kensington Church Street, opposite Kensington Wine Rooms. It was a Harry Lucas operation, although all but one she had met were British. There were four watchers on the street with Carrie.

'Get ready,' she was instructed. She turned away from the antique shop and crossed into Peel Street to see a typical morning family scene. The bickering Yumatov children reminded her of her sister Angie's children being rushed out of the house in Brooklyn.

'I don't need to be taken to school anymore,' complained Max, standing upright, his feet apart as if the narrow sidewalk were a parade ground. 'I'm not a child. I can walk by myself.'

'You're a child until you're eighteen,' countered his sister Natasha, hitching a yellow and black satchel onto her back.

'Lots of boys go by themselves when they're ten or eleven.'

Natasha turned to face her mother. 'Do they, Mama?'

Hanna the live-in nanny answered, 'Now, Max, you don't want to put me out of a job, do you?'

'No, we love you, Hanna,' said Natasha. 'So, Mama, tell Max to stop whining.'

'I'm not *whining*.' Max took a step away to make the point that he was setting off by himself. 'I'm fighting for dignity and independence. Our father would be proud of me.'

Both children wore smart school uniforms with dark blue blazers; gray shorts for Max, a skirt for Natasha. The file said that since going to school, they had begun talking to each other in English. They slipped back to Russian at home and when arguing.

'*Go past to get visuals,*' Carrie was instructed. From the opposite side of the street, she walked toward the family, feeling both fired up and calm. This wasn't her natural work, but tension, and the possibility of calamity were a familiar part of trauma surgery. She had been on the move since Uelen, had slept and eaten when she could. She might be tired, but she was operating at full capacity. It was how she worked best.

As Carrie walked briskly toward them, she recognized the style of watch Max held in his hand. It was a Soviet timepiece given out for long service. Her parents each had one. Theirs showed medics. She wondered if Max's showed factory workers.

'There's no rush, Max. Wait another year and you'll be big enough.' Anna ruffled her hand through his thick blond curly hair.

'See?' said Natasha. 'I'm right. We're still children, but I'll be grown up before you because girls are more mature than boys.'

Carrie walked toward them. Anna gave her a quick apologetic smile. 'Stop blocking the pavement, Max,' she said. 'Let this lady pass.' Max stepped onto the road between two parked cars. Hanna took his hand and guided him back to be with Natasha so she could shepherd the children west toward Campden Hill Road. 'My lecture finishes around seven,' Anna told her. 'But call if you have any problems.'

'*Now, Carrie,*' came the instruction. '*Before she goes inside.*'

Carrie made sure her pass hung in full sight around her neck and turned back. Anna was still on the steps, speckled in warm sunlight, half an eye on the children, half on her phone checking messages. A loud motor scooter broke the urban quiet, black smoke belching from its exhaust, and Anna glanced up. The cloud of filthy air was a prompt to head back in. She took a step toward the open front door as Carrie, a few feet away, said, 'Anna? Dr Yumatov? A moment, please.'

Anna slid her phone protectively into her tracksuit pocket and studied Carrie, who held up her hospital pass. She put her hand on the door, didn't move. Carrie said, 'My name is Dr Carrie Walker, I'm an American physician. It's about your husband, Colonel Ruslan Yumatov.'

Anna's body tightened. Her dark hair was pinned back, but not neatly, and strands hung down onto her neck. Her face looked stern, curious and strong. She was about to respond, when she read Carrie's name on the laminated ID card and put her right hand to her chin. 'Dr Carrie Walker,' she repeated. 'Of course. I know who you are.' She looked to her left and right up and down the street. 'Are you alone?'

'I am, yes,' Carrie lied.

'What is it?' Anna pursed her lips, examining Carrie. She switched to Russian. 'Ruslan is long dead.'

'Do you have a moment?'

'You knew him, didn't you?'

Carrie pointed to the open door. 'Can we talk inside? It's important.'

'Of course it is important, or you wouldn't be here.' Anna held herself stiffly and didn't move.

'*Show her,*' came the instruction through Carrie's earpiece.

Carrie unfolded a sheet of paper from her jacket pocket, printed with two photographs. One was of her treating Yumatov in an ambulance just inside Norway's border with Russia after Rake had saved his life. The other was of Yumatov lying on his bed, hands behind his head, in his prison cell at Langston Farm.

'Your husband is alive, Anna.' Carrie handed the paper to her. Anna looked, cast her eyes skywards as if to contain her disbelief, then back to meet Carrie's gaze. 'When was this?' She tapped the lower picture from the cell. Her hand trembled.

'Two, three days ago,' answered Carrie.

Anna turned and walked inside, leaving the door open for Carrie to follow.

TWENTY-EIGHT

The narrow hallway with light red terracotta tiles, a pale blue wall and white skirting boards, looked as if it were trying for a Mediterranean look. Except, far from being a Greek island, this was a house of small proportions in central London. The hallway widened into a kitchen where light streamed through windows and skylights. A varnished wooden staircase ran up to the first floor. Anna went left into a living room, elegantly designed in the same style, but with the scattered mess of young children, a train set on the floor, a pink doll on the couch, a drink with a red straw on a coffee table, a circular stain under the yellow tumbler.

Anna sank into a dark blue sofa with big cushions and hooked her right leg over her knee. She showed strength and composure. She had kept her feelings in check when learning that her husband was alive. She had showed no delight in the news, no fear, no anger. Carrie recognized her reaction, a familiar blocking mechanism. Anna was not asking how it was he was alive, or where he was. She had her work, and the children in the evenings, no room for personal feeling. It was about conserving strength and managing things.

Family photographs stood on a table by the wall. Carrie recognized Anna's father, the St Petersburg academic. There was Anna's graduation ceremony, surrounded by parents and siblings, then a recent one, feeding ducks with Max and Natasha in a London park. There was a school photo of the children and what looked like a school play with them both taking a curtain-call bow. There was none of Ruslan Yumatov.

'Open the drawer underneath,' said Anna. Inside was a pile of loose photographs. Carrie lifted them out. Anna shifted on the sofa as if Carrie were an old friend who had unexpectedly dropped by. 'I thought he might not be dead. Strange, isn't it? Ruslan has that kind of magnetism.' Anna sorted through the pile, pulling out a shot of a small military ceremony on the banks of a river.

'They sent me this, his memorial service in Khabarovsk, head-quarters of the Eastern Military District where Ruslan was based.' Her finger hovered over dignitaries. 'That's the President, Viktor Lagutov, the Foreign Minister, Sergey Grizlov, the commander of the Eastern District, Gennady somebody. I forget his name. They invited me, but I said no.' Her eyes welled. 'I had a feeling Ruslan's death was just one lie among the mountain of falsehoods in my country. Ruslan sent us to London, arranged everything. We were just a few weeks in London when the embassy contacted me. They told me he was dead. The next morning, I woke alone. I often did when Ruslan was away. But this was different because I knew he wasn't coming back, that he would never be in my bed again. I felt calm, peaceful, it was just me and the children and I didn't mind.' She plucked a white tissue from her tracksuit pocket, wiped her eyes, and gave an embarrassed smile. 'Sorry. I don't know why, after so long and with a stranger, my stupid brave face collapses.' She blew her nose, crumpled up the tissue and dropped it in a bin beside the settee. Carrie stayed silent. There was no instruction in her earpiece.

'He spoke about you, Carrie,' said Anna. 'That is why you are in my house. He respected you. He said you were a real Russian living in the wrong country. I saw you on television during the Diomedes crisis, giving that American presenter hell when she challenged you. Do you remember?'

'I do,' said Carrie softly. Russian troops were on Little Diomede and Yumatov had been second in command. Carrie had been caught there and ended up on American network television. Because of her Russian-Estonian heritage, she had been asked about her loyalty to the United States. It had not ended well for the anchor.

Other photographs of Yumatov lay on the sofa between them. There was a military mug shot, piercing eyes straight into the lens; the wedding, Yumatov in uniform with medals and Anna elegant and poised in a slim white dress. There was an evening at the Bolshoi Ballet, Yumatov in uniform again and a long purple evening gown for Anna. 'There he is with his father,' said Anna, pointing to a monochrome of Yumatov as a child, standing by a man in blue overalls pinned with Communist Party badges. 'The steel factory in Magnitogorsk, Ruslan's hometown. He was so proud and so angry at what happened all over Russia.' Anna kept looking and talking, as if she didn't want to ask about her husband in the present day but wanted Carrie to stay.

'*Need to move in, Carrie,*' came an instruction.

'Has he contacted you, Anna?' she asked.

Anna stiffened, her expression turning defensive. Panic laced her eyes. She gathered up the photographs, stood up, put them back in the drawer and said, 'Forgive me, Carrie. I was so astonished that I forgot to ask why you are here and what you want.' She stayed on her feet, beside a small mantelpiece with white silk flowers in the unused fireplace.

'*Go in hard,*' came the instruction.

Still sitting down, Carrie gave Anna another sheet of paper, showing the slaughter at Langston Farm. She studied Anna's face as she absorbed it, then said, 'Your husband has been broken out of detention.'

'Where is this?'

'I can't say, but you can see there the empty cell where he was being held, and the casualties.'

'And that's why you're here?' Anna handed the sheet back to Carrie.

'Yes.'

'But you're a doctor.'

'They asked me because I know Ruslan.' Carrie deliberately used the familiar first name.

'No, he hasn't contacted me.' Anna took a toy sailboat that had got onto the mantelpiece and put it next to the tumbler on the coffee table. 'As I said, I sensed something wasn't right, but I have tried to move on, to look after the children.'

'Did he share his plans with you?'

'You mean now? No. As I said, I thought he was dead.'

'Sorry, I mean in the past.'

'His stupid visions, yes.'

'Like what?'

'How to cure injustice, that sort of thing.' She swept her finger along the mantelpiece as if checking for dust. 'He called it Shock and Adjust, you know, from that American slogan Shock and Awe. Ruslan's idea was to create an atmosphere of chaos and fear. From that, people will accept an adjustment to their lives, receptive to creating a fairer and more equal society.'

'Have you any idea what he might be planning now?'

'I don't. He's gone from my life and I am not sure if I can learn to love him again, to know him again.' Anna's brittleness was fading. 'When he sent us here, he told me nothing. He did it for us, for our security, and I trusted him. I was struck by bewilderment, a thousand fragments of life scattered around me in a strange city. One night I had a nightmare. Ruslan was dying, covered in blood like in a horror movie. I was racked with guilt that I couldn't save him. Except it wasn't a nightmare because he did die, and I woke feeling calm and happy that he was gone.'

'*She's repeating herself, Carrie. It may be a front. Go in harder.*'

Carrie stood up, level with Anna. 'You husband is a monster.'

'I know,' Anna said. 'Not to me. Not to the children. But in his work, yes, I know all about that.' She made a point of looking at her watch and put on a false, polite smile. 'Talking of work, I need to go.'

Carrie didn't move. 'In Russia, when I was with Ruslan, he said how lucky he was to have found you. He spoke about how much he loved you.'

'Yes, he did. My culture is about devotion to family at the expense of all else. If that requires cruelty and killing, so be it.'

Anna's phone rang. The ring tone was a Russian Orthodox liturgical chant. She recognized the number and ignored it. She looked at Carrie, but the earpiece was faster. '*From the Russian embassy.*'

'Take it,' said Carrie.

'No.' Anna pulled the house keys from her pocket, reached across to collect the cup of juice and toy sailboat from the table, then changed her mind. 'Oh, leave it,' she said to herself. 'Hanna will be back soon.'

'*Need to seal it, Carrie.*'

Carrie stepped in front of Anna. 'Ruslan may be involved in something dreadful, and we need your help to stop it.'

Anna looped past Carrie to the hallway, unlatched the door and held it open for her. 'He's made no contact with me, and I don't want to see him.' Out on the front step, Anna shut the door and double locked it. 'That was my embassy. You arrive. They call. I don't want any of it.'

'You can't run from this, Anna.'

'I'm going to work.'

'*Name-check Gavril Nevrosky.*'

Anna was walking east. Carrie fell into step. 'Did Ruslan ever mention a German businessman, Gavril Nevrosky?'

Anna didn't answer. She spotted something at the intersection ahead, swiveled around and checked behind them. She pressed a name card into Carrie's hand. 'You want me to help you find Ruslan and persuade him to stop? Is that right?'

'Yes.'

'You want me to betray my husband?' She used the Russian word *predatel'stvo*, which implied a deeper sense of disloyalty.

'You will know exactly what you'll be betraying him for.' Carrie looked at the white name card, embossed with Anna's name, title and contact details.

'*Jesus!*' came an exclamation from her team leader. '*They've got people everywhere. Warn her, Carrie.*'

She knows, thought Carrie. Her eyes showed it. Anna was one hell of a tough woman.

'You're not safe, Anna.'

'They've done this before. I can run from you, but not from them.' She began jogging on the spot. 'I will help you. But you need to keep the children safe, unaware, and at home.' She sprinted off along the narrow sidewalk, swerving to avoid two elderly women, then speeding up again. Carrie spotted pedestrians toward the intersection, shifting positions, more aware than they should be of just another jogger. Anna kept going, turning south onto a bigger road.

'Well done, Carrie.' Lucas's voice this time.

'For what?'

'She's onside.'

'Don't bet on it.'

Anna Yumatov was too smart to give much away. Carrie was about to reply to Lucas when the instructor's voice came through. 'They got her. Corner Campden Street and Kensington Church Street, outside the Churchill Arms pub.'

TWENTY-NINE

I n more than two years in London, Anna Yumatov had never stepped into Kensington Palace Gardens, a wide, tree-lined road closed to public vehicles and home to several foreign embassies. The property Anna was entering, a nineteenth-century building of faded neo-Gothic opulence, was now the official residence of the Russian ambassador to the Court of St James.

The drive in the back of an embassy limousine, wedged between two diplomatic security guards stinking of tobacco, took less than five minutes. As soon as Anna had seen Carrie Walker, she expected contact from the embassy. This immediacy underlined the urgency.

Anna's mind swirled with thoughts that Ruslan was alive. The grandeur of the building, the guards on the gate, showed how important her husband was to Russia. She was frightened and excited. And she was happy. Ruslan was a great man, which was why she had married him. He had the most brilliant of minds, filled with ideas, and was fired with a sense of injustice and a hatred of cruelty to others, and with great tenderness toward her and the children. Even in their early discussion, in their twenties and thirties, he showed her social changes which she hadn't spotted, told stories from Chechnya, Georgia, Afghanistan and Iraq, pointed out patterns of human behavior that were not discussed in Anna's more protected circles. Ruslan was the first to show her how the West was pushing broken dreams, and that Russia needed to be ready.

She had introduced Ruslan to her father, Dr Dmitri Semin, a man so trusted that he advised governments, mainly Gorbachev and Putin because Yeltsin had been too drunk to listen. Her father declared his daughter should marry the young streetwise army officer who had finely tuned political antennae, a rare asset in any soldier. He could protect her.

Standing at the gate of the Russian ambassador's residence was Colonel Nikolai Usenko, the diplomat who had told her that

Ruslan was dead shortly after she arrived in London and who came from the same elite close protection unit – Zaslon – as Ruslan. Usenko was well over sixty but kept himself in shape and exuded both courtesy and discipline. He opened the limousine door. Anna stepped out, the security men melted away.

'When do you have to be at work?' he asked, as if this were a scheduled meeting.

'I have tutorials at two,' Anna answered. 'I have a change of clothes at the university.'

He scanned her tracksuit and trainers and took her through an entrance framed by a massive double-sided curving staircase and into a small room with a dark wood table, a chandelier and mustard yellow tapestried upright chairs. In the middle of the table were two enlarged photographs that looked as if they came from surveillance cameras. She recognized Ruslan in both, with a woman in her thirties. One picture was in a restaurant, the other on the street, leaving a house.

A door opened at the other end of the room. She immediately recognized the Russian Foreign Minister Sergey Grizlov. In his expensive clothes, he resembled his suave and cultured media image, meeting her gaze with a hollowness that Ruslan had loathed. Many times, Ruslan had cited the story about how Grizlov and a team of American lawyers had fleeced and destroyed his father's factory. Every grand vision Ruslan had held for his new world order boomeranged back to that.

'Dr Yumatov, thank you for coming at such short notice,' Grizlov said. Usenko pulled out a chair and indicated Anna should sit there. He poured her a glass of water from a flask and said, 'Tell the Foreign Minister about your visit from Dr Carrie Walker.'

Anna's mouth went dry. Inadvertently, she glanced at Usenko for guidance. She understood the power of the Russian state because Ruslan had exercised it. She pressed her hands on the table to steady herself, inhaling the smells of the room: mustiness, fresh paint, stale cigarettes.

She took time to answer. With Carrie she had retained her composure. Here, she was not sure if she could. Usenko and Grizlov were unfazed, men who understood the power of silence. She tried to make her tone measured, free of fear. 'She intercepted me as the children were going to school. She told me Ruslan was alive, that he had been broken out of a prison and was involved in something dangerous.'

Pages of her life floated through her mind. The father of her children, the man she loved, feared, admired, who commanded her loyalty, her soul mate who had sent them to London, safe from a danger he was creating. She loved him. She hated the risk he brought to her life. He needed to stay dead. She yearned to see him. Her life in London was not Russia, but it was a good life and better for the children. Now, without even seeing him, Ruslan was bullying his way back, real, alive, magnetic. A chill ran through Anna.

Grizlov stayed quiet by the window. Usenko pulled out a chair and sat beside her. 'You are here, Anna, because we are working with the British and Americans to find your husband.'

To kill him again, she thought.

'Do you know where he might be going, who he may be working with, what he may be planning?' asked Usenko.

'No.' She shook her head furiously. Her hair fell over her eyes. She pushed it back. 'Nothing. You told me he was dead. I told the children he was killed in a traffic accident.'

Usenko reached for the photographs. 'Do you know this woman?'

She was in both shots, looked ten years younger than Anna. Her features were Asiatic. She had a playful, intelligent face. 'No. I don't. Who is she?'

'Her name is Katia Codic. They were colleagues.' Usenko gave her a thin smile. 'It was not an affair. And these men in the restaurant?'

One was Asian, the other European and overweight. Ruslan sat stiffly, while Katia was laughing and gesturing. 'I don't,' repeated Anna.

Usenko glanced at Grizlov, who stepped away from the bay window and leaned forward with both hands on the dining table. 'Dr Yumatov, I apologize for literally dragging you in here, but we have an emergency. We need to protect Russia, and we need to protect you and your children.'

Protection meant different things in different cultures.

Grizlov's face showed concern. 'Your husband was being held illegally by the Americans. Some fifteen people died in breaking him out. As of now, we know very little. There is a chance the story will leak, with pictures and your husband's identification. You are here under your real name. The press will find you.'

'Carrie showed me the pictures,' she said flatly.

Usenko shot a glance at Grizlov who said, 'I understand you have afternoon tutorials and a lecture in the evening.'

'At six, yes.'

Usenko stood up, his hand on the back of Anna's chair, as if he were a waiter at a banquet, easing it out for her to get up. Grizlov walked around the other side of the table, his eyes on his phone. Anna ran her tongue around the inside her mouth. She didn't want to speak and show weakness.

'We're going to see the British,' said Usenko.

THIRTY

Saxony, Germany

Ruslan Yumatov's urge to call Anna would have to wait. He had no phone, and he would not ask for one from Astrid, the stewardess, or the driver. Unlike in his prison cell, he was not in charge. The circumstances were new. He had to be careful. He was unfamiliar with an environment of compulsory trust. After too many hours on the ground in Bulgaria, they had flown 900 miles northwest to Dresden in Saxony, and he was now riding in the back of a white Mercedes SUV that had met the plane. Astrid, the stewardess, traveled in the front seat and said she expected the journey to take a couple more hours. He did not yet know exactly where they were going.

'I am sure you understand.' Astrid turned in her seat and gave him a full-on stewardess smile. 'Mr Nevrosky needs to be elusive.'

Yumatov leant back and closed his eyes, enjoying the breeze and the sunlight on his face. Confinement had taught him patience. He was free and alive. He could roll the window up and down and look out at the undulating European countryside. Nevrosky must need Yumatov and he did not know why. His reference to Rudolf Wagner gave a partial clue, but not enough. An idea from so long ago in Ust Kamenogorsk could have germinated into anything. They drove for more than hour, leaving the autobahn to use small roads, rejoining it again, leaving it again, eventually beginning a gradual ascent into the mountains. Astrid turned back round with the same hostess smile. 'Another half an hour, Colonel. Mr Nevrosky is waiting.'

The road narrowed and wound up a hillside, gray with protruding rocks and green with lush undergrowth. They drove through a village of white stone cottages with livestock in large yards, and an old church with a broken wooden cross on its tower. Two men fixing a fence looked up, uninterested, and returned to their work. He saw no one else. They crossed a fast-running river, went through a series of sharp steep bends, and turned right, where the road became a well-maintained single-lane track with a high fence on each side. The location made sense – only one road in and out.

Two men stepped into their path. They had hard, combat-tested faces and dressed in civilian fatigues, dark green pants and practical all-weather jackets with heavy belts, each with a knife and black pouches although their weapons were not visible. One came to the window. Astrid spoke to him, not in German but in Czech. Then, still beaming, she said, 'We've reached Mr Nevrosky's estate. They need your papers. The ones from Baltimore.'

Yumatov handed her the false Onstad passport. She passed it through the window. There was an exchange of words. 'Sorry,' she said. 'They need your pistol. They say it is registered in Germany and was good for the flight. We are now in the Czech Republic and it needs to go back with the driver.' He frowned. She smiled. 'It is the same for everyone. We have others at the farmhouse.'

Yumatov handed over the box. They ordered everyone out, driver too. A mirror on wheels was slid under the car. They used the bonnet as a table to go through Yumatov's bag, even though it had been supplied by Nevrosky. He took off his shoes. They were checked with swabs and explosive trace detectors like at airports. The men patted him down, not caring about privacy, and did the same to the driver and to Astrid; fast, professional, gender neutral. They gave an all-clear.

The driver eased away. The fence stopped, and the road climbed steeply through a forest of fir and beech trees, then through barren ground with huge dark boulders. The air became chillier. They leveled out onto a plateau with a meadow of wild summer flowers. Up another slope, through a copse of trees, there was a black wrought-iron gate that swung open for them. Orchards sloped toward an old farmhouse, not a grand property but big enough, three stories with a steep red-tiled roof, yellow walls and big windows with red wooden shutters. Modern buildings were attached at the back. Beyond it, Yumatov glimpsed the rotor blade of a helicopter. The front remained as it may have been for centuries, a gravel driveway, a weather-worn bronze statue of a naked boy on a grass island.

Two large Dalmatian dogs ran toward them. Astrid got out and opened Yumatov's door. 'So, Colonel, we're here.' No longer the air-hostess smile, more one of relief and tiredness, a companion at journey's end.

An old man appeared on the front steps, wafer thin, as if a light gust of wind would blow him over. He had wispy gray hair and a limp. He walked quickly toward Yumatov, his stick scraping the gravel, rheumy eyes glistening, and exclaimed, 'Is it really you?'

This was Rudolf Wagner, the nuclear scientist from the Ulba Metallurgical Plant who had drawn the teenage Ruslan Yumatov into his circle. Yumatov dropped his bag and embraced Wagner, giving him the respect he deserved, feeling the frailty. 'Dr Wagner. So, so good to see you again.' He kissed him on the cheeks.

'And you, Officer Cadet Yumatov. Look at you. I am an old man and what a hero you have become. This is like Christ rising from the dead.'

'Ruslan.' Nevrosky shouted down from a small balcony outside a set of French windows above the main front door. 'Welcome. You made it. Wait there, I'm coming down.'

Wagner stayed close to Yumatov, speaking softly. 'It is so, so good you are here. Your meeting with Brenning. Brilliant.'

'Brenning?' It took a beat for Yumatov to remember Brenning, the dry, pompous Englishman he had met with Katia. Yumatov had put Brenning in touch with Wagner and heard nothing more.

'Gavril will explain,' said Wagner, as Nevrosky walked out hurriedly, arms outstretched. He embraced Yumatov in a bear hug, stood back, hands on both his shoulders. 'Ruslan Yumatov, you are a stubborn, incorrigible man.' Enthusiasm filled his rounded face. He rested his hand on the open back door of the SUV and pointed toward an orchard on grassland that stretched away from the house. Yumatov spotted a blue and yellow plastic slide for children in the shade of orchard trees on the lawn in front of the house. There was also a red metal swing and a paddling pool with arm floats and inflatable rings next to it on the grass.

'For Max and Natasha,' said Nevrosky. 'Now you are safely here, we can make plans to bring them from London.'

THIRTY-ONE

London

'Dr Yumatov, you have just been informed that your husband is alive. Is that correct?' Anna's questioner was an official from Britain's foreign ministry, introduced to her as Bridget England, dressed in a navy-blue business suit and speaking in short clipped sentences while others looked on.

'Yes,' Anna whispered almost inaudibly. She was taking in the grandeur of the room, the dozen people gathered around, the heavy white door opening and closing as people left and entered. Nikolai Usenko sat next to her at a large, oval-shaped wooden table, just as he had at the Russian Ambassador's residence. Except this table gave off a light smell of fresh polish and was splayed with reflections of sunlight. They had driven three miles to the official London home of the Foreign Secretary at One Carlton Gardens, close to Buckingham Palace, the Houses of Parliament and Anna's small office in the London School of Economics. She knew the distances and route because she jogged it most workdays.

Those in the room were formally dressed, and Anna felt out of place in her tracksuit and trainers. She recognized the Foreign Secretary, Lady Lucas, standing at the shallow bay window with Sergey Grizlov. Carrie Walker was there beside a large white marble mantelpiece, still wearing her hospital ID card around her neck. Carrie had lied. She had not been alone. As Bridget England started questioning, Anna recognized Rake Ozenna next to Carrie. Ozenna was a soldier who played on Ruslan's mind like a toothache because he had beaten him twice. Her husband used to trawl YouTube for Ozenna's lectures at military colleges to find a weakness, to work out how to defeat him next time. Ruslan could not bear to think that Ozenna was a smarter soldier than him. Anna had tried to convince him that Ozenna had no big ideas like Ruslan. He didn't think things through. He had no understanding of politics. Ozenna was a thug. His idea of resolution was to kill. Ruslan was a thinker and a leader. But her husband had never accepted it. He had even brought up Carrie Walker after meeting her during the Diomede crisis. How could such a cultured, intelligent woman have been with an animal like Ozenna?

Even though Ozenna's head was lowered and his eyes looked almost closed, she felt his gaze directly, unshifting, only on her. He would be here to capture Ruslan, she thought, and, by God, she hoped he failed, and Ruslan beat him. Next to Ozenna was another military-looking man, older, but equally weathered. On Carrie's other side stood a man in his fifties, whom Anna could tell was American. He was better dressed, in a light sports jacket, his gaze mostly on Lady Lucas and Grizlov.

'Your husband has tried to contact you?' asked England. 'Is that correct?'

'That is not correct.' A rush of adrenalin ran through Anna. She shot a glance at Usenko, with an expression of bewilderment. He nodded for her to comply. She pointed across the table toward Carrie. 'I only knew this morning from Dr Walker that he was alive. I have not heard from him.'

England slid a sheet of paper across the table with phone numbers, times and dates. 'Can you explain a call that came from Bulgaria to this London number here, which automatically switched it to your office phone at the London School of Economics?'

Usenko reached forward to bring the piece of paper to them. Anna sensed he was as surprised as she. Grizlov too; he looked accusingly at Lady Lucas. If they were working together, why hadn't the British shared?

'I don't have a photographic memory.' Anna felt stronger, protected by her compatriots. 'If you want straight answers from me, you need to ask straight questions. I have not heard from my husband.'

England pressed. 'And the call?'

Anna spotted the number of her office phone, studied it, spun the sheet of paper around and slid it back to England. 'I teach Central and Eastern European history. Bulgaria is in that region.

I talk to people there all the time.' She pointed across to Carrie. 'Dr Walker can confirm that I was at my house in Peel Street when the call was made at eight twelve this morning.'

England didn't even look up because she already knew.

'As for these numbers,' continued Anna, 'I don't recognize them.'

Usenko rested his hand on Anna's arm, looked across to Grizlov and said, 'If we are to work together, we need full disclosure.'

'Keep going, Bridget,' instructed Lady Lucas firmly.

'The call from Bulgaria is registered to a football club in Vidin province, in the northwest.'

Anna shrugged and said nothing.

'It was made to a political analysis company called Future Forecasting, based in Hammersmith, west London. From there it was automatically diverted to your office phone which went to voicemail, and no message was left.'

Anna had done consultancy for Future Forecasting, which England would know. Her stomach tightened. She tried to work out the connection with Ruslan but couldn't see one. 'I know this company,' she said firmly, picking up her water glass with both hands to steady any trembling. England read from her tablet. Usenko looked straight ahead, his hand no longer on Anna's arm. Grizlov scrolled his phone. Ozenna had not moved, his concentration still on Anna, who met Carrie's gaze, friendly, unthreatening, as if Carrie knew what it was like to be hammered on all sides. She decided to tell it exactly as it was. 'They used me as a consultant once or twice.'

'How so?' asked England.

'They had contracts in central and eastern Europe. I gave them nothing more than I say in my lectures.'

'What more exactly could you have given them that you didn't?'

'The specifics, the places, the people, the institutions that make up the fabric of that region, the kind of detail I might go over in a tutorial.'

'Such as?'

Anna inhaled deeply, keeping air in her lungs, exhaling slowly to control her impatience. The room was bathed in a natural summer light. There was a rhythmic ticking of the wall clock above the mantelpiece. In this lull, as Anna decided how to answer, she listened to the traffic hum from outside and birdsong coming from St James's Park to the south.

'Such as, say, the Srebrenica massacre in Bosnia in 1995.' She checked the room like a class. Detail caught their attention. 'Serbian militia killed eight thousand Bosnians. Do you know it?' she challenged England.

'Yes, of course.' Now England sounded defensive. 'The worst atrocity in Europe since the Holocaust, and part of a genocide.'

'Correct. Yet now, so many years later, a Serb politician will not get elected to office if he accepts that genocide took place. The Serbian mayors of Srebrenica do not visit the memorial site of white crosses and graves, even though it is only a short drive from their office. In a democracy, accepting past atrocities is a vote loser.' Anna held England's gaze. 'Future Forecasting is a political consultancy with contracts in the former Yugoslavia, so this is detail that would be useful to them. I did not discuss it with them. I kept it bland.' Anna drank from her water glass.

England said, 'Are these things you discussed with your husband?'

'What things? Genocides?'

'European politics.'

'Of course.' Anna switched her gaze to Usenko and then Grizlov. 'All of us in Russia, we grew up with it. And you, Miss England, given that you are here, you should be familiar with it too.'

The older American next to Carrie moved forward, in from the wall. 'Dr Yumatov, I'm Harry Lucas, working with your Foreign Minister and Lady Lucas. It's natural your husband would try and contact you, but do you have any idea why he would do it through Future Forecasting?'

'I don't.'

'And do you know Gavril Nevrosky?'

Now Usenko reacted, pushing back his chair an inch. He must know. Anna didn't. 'Carrie asked me that this morning,' she said. 'I don't know him.'

'Did your husband ever talk about a place called Uelen?'

Anna had never heard of it. She shook her head.

'Of Ust Kamenogorsk in Kazakhstan?'

'It was a military city. That's all I know.'

'About a Japanese company called Ariga?'

'No.'

Lucas moved further forward so he stood over her by the table, his left hand pulling at skin under his chin as if thinking hard. 'How would you describe the interference of organized crime in the governments of your region?'

Lucas would know the answer. Everyone in the room would. He would want her version. She gave it to him. 'It's there, worsening with political extremism whose money comes from these black-market operations.'

'Did you discuss this with your husband?' England was back. A crease of irritation crossed Lucas's face.

'Of course. Ask Foreign Minister Grizlov. Everything we do in Russia has a connection to this.'

'I mean extremism, the right?'

'Enough,' interjected Usenko. He jabbed his finger at England. 'This is not the way to work together.'

THIRTY-TWO

England's expression remained unchanged. Stephanie Lucas broke into a smile. 'No, this is all informal. I'm really interested in Dr Yumatov's view.'

Grizlov cut in. 'If you want to go on a fishing expedition to invent a link between Dr Yumatov and her husband which isn't there, it is best we end this informal meeting and communicate through diplomatic channels.'

'Let's row back, everyone,' said Harry Lucas. 'What the British are clumsily asking because they beat around the damn bush so much is whether Dr Yumatov could be a co-conspirator with her husband or sympathizes with what he has been trying to do.' He looked directly at Anna. 'If you can give us that answer, Dr Yumatov, my guess is we can move on.'

'Yes, of course I discussed extremism with my husband,' Anna said decisively. 'Any intelligent married couple would, because we must secure a future for our children.' Her gaze was sharp and hostile on Bridget England. 'Transnational crime funds right-wing European movements. Some governments are more vulnerable than others. Bulgaria is one, where this call came from. But – and read my lips on this, Miss England – I have discussed no details with my husband of the kind you are suggesting, and if I had it would be nearly three years ago and thus irrelevant.'

England was about to speak, but Anna raised her hand. 'No, you be quiet, because I am finishing.' Her gaze went to Harry Lucas, bounced off Rake Ozenna and then around to others in the room. 'This Nevrosky, this Japanese Ariga, this Uelen, this Ust Kamenogorsk, you are asking if I know how Ruslan might be connected to any of them. My answer is, I do not.' She stared at England, who met her gaze right back. Anna pointed at Harry Lucas. 'I suggest you follow this man's advice about asking questions straight instead of trying to score points.'

Silence hung over the room until England pushed back her chair and stood up. 'Good. Now, we'll get you to work.'

'Thank you, Dr Yumatov,' Stephanie said. 'I know how difficult this must be for you.'

Anna shot a glance at Usenko, who was on his feet, his hand again on the back of Anna's chair. She followed England into the foyer, Usenko at her side. 'I'm sorry, Anna,' he said. 'You have to come with us back to the embassy.'

Anna's heart began beating strongly. 'I have tutorials. I can't just not turn up.'

'We've told them.' Usenko's face darkened. This was how it was. Anna had no choice. 'We've diverted the calls from your phone there to the embassy.'

'The children?'

'Hanna will be there.'

Anna leaned forward, hands on knees, breathing deeply to slow her heart rate. She yearned to be back in her little house in Notting Hill, playing with Max and Natasha, even back in Moscow, in the life she needed to forget. Usenko had a look that Anna recognized from Ruslan, when he was concentrating, distant from her, everything more important than the family.

'Are we working with them or not?' she asked.

'Never trust them,' said Usenko. 'You are Russian. You answer to us, and only to us.'

As Bridget England came back into the dining room, Stephanie Lucas moved out from the bay window to a seat at the end of the table. Sergey Grizlov stayed where he was, his phone in his hand, screen in view, which – Rake thought – was either really smart or really stupid, given the way England had tried to cut up the Russians. In a lot of places her superior, cold approach could get a person killed.

Carrie said quietly to Rake, 'Anna's telling the truth.'

'Doesn't mean she's on our side.' Rake had detected in Anna the swirl of heart-head conflict that often led good, smart people to do bad things because of family.

'Harry,' said Stephanie. 'Your take?'

'We need her. She knows her husband. She knows the politics. No point in alienating her, Steph.'

'Or my government,' added Grizlov sternly.

Stephanie ignored the reprimand. 'Bridget?' she asked.

'She's hiding something, ma'am. We need to go harder.'

'Go harder? How?' pressed Stephanie.

'Use her visa. She violated her work permit by consulting for Future Forecasting.'

'That won't work either way,' interjected Carrie.

'With all due respect,' said England. 'This is politics and national security, not medicine.'

'I agree there,' said Carrie flatly. 'In medicine we do not use family and children as leverage.'

'It will focus her mind.'

'Threatening to take Max and Natasha out of school and send them back to Moscow will shut Anna down as surely as cutting out her tongue.' Carrie fixed her gaze on Stephanie, demanding she step in.

'Sergey?' asked Stephanie calmly.

'Your side is talking bullshit, Steph, and you know it. You need to change your approach, because this high-handedness typifies all that my people resent about the West – superiority, privilege and ignorance. Anna Yumatov is no exception. You will not terrify her into cooperation.'

'What do you suggest?' asked Harry Lucas.

'From the Kremlin.' Grizlov held up his phone, screen lit. 'We have a team in Uelen now. We will share what we find. We're leaning on the Khazaks about Ust Kamenogorsk, and we will share that. We're investigating Ariga, the casino project and the Bering Strait crossing. We will share everything. But if you throw curve balls, as you just have, we will withdraw. Right now, as a Russian citizen, Anna Yumatov is under our embassy's protection. If you want her, you need us.'

The quiet was long and uneasy.

'Jesus fucking Christ.' Carrie rolled her eyes. 'The Brits slipped up because they can't even smell their own shit. Now you're doing the same. If you hold Anna, she'll fight you too. Let her go to work, then go home, live a normal day. I can be with her. I'll sit in on the lecture, go back and hang with the kids.'

The tension eased. Grizlov put his phone in his inside jacket pocket.

THIRTY-THREE

Harry Lucas walked up to the curved stainless-steel reception counter in a modern west London office block and asked to see Stephen Case, the billionaire owner of Future Forecasting. As the receptionist phoned up, Lucas thought that if he were Case he would have set up artificial intelligence software that found every aspect of Lucas's life embedded in the web and would highlight the safe and dangerous elements. Facial recognition alone would tell Case that Lucas was a former chair of the US Congress House Intelligence Committee and now a private contractor close to the White House. The speed with which the receptionist printed him a temporary identity pass and slid it across with a tag to hang around his neck told him his reading was correct. She pressed a button to open the security turnstile.

Lucas had chosen to handle Future Forecasting alone. He wanted Rake with Carrie because the Russians would be watching. They were now heading with Anna Yumatov to the London School of Economics. He had assigned Mikki to work with Bridget England on tracking down Lord Brenning, the space scientist identified in the London photograph with Yumatov.

The search for Yumatov was closing in. There had been two Gulfstream 650s, one leaving Baltimore for Schiphol, Amsterdam, and the other taking off from Dulles at the same moment with a flight plan to Sofia, the capital of Bulgaria. The longitudinal separation system had allocated them back-to-back flight paths, not by coincidence. The transponder codes to the two aircraft had been switched, indicating detailed operational planning similar to that involved in breaking Yumatov out of Langston Farm. The Schiphol aircraft had a crew of three carrying a cargo of engine pistons and plastic sheeting. The Bulgaria one was a private passenger jet which must have been Yumatov's. The two pilots were in custody. Both were of European descent with American citizenship. They had said nothing, and expensive lawyers had arrived to ensure their continued silence.

Future Forecasting's penthouse elevator opened straight into the office of Stephen Case, who sat with his bare feet on his desk, taking a deep draw from a green jade vape pipe. As Lucas stepped in, he swung his legs down and stood up, slipping on a pair of leather sandals. He was a weird stick-insect of a man, thin and bendy as a praying mantis, with sharp brown eyes under a high forehead and early receding hairline. One wall was covered with promotional posters – *Healthcare Analytics Saves Live*, *Global Insight Is About You*, and so on. Floor-to-ceiling windows on three sides commanded views of central London, the Eye, the Shard, the Thames, and the sprawling complex of the United States embassy.

'You know who I am. I know who you are,' said Case. 'You know why you're here. I don't, but I hope it's because Future Forecasting's unblemished track record is needed across the pond in the U S of A.'

Lucas smiled inwardly. After conversations tangled in diplomatic nuance, Case was refreshing. He gave himself more time to assess and answered the question with a question. 'Why is that? You're doing very well here.'

Case fidgeted with his pipe, his body language erratic. He walked over to a black leather office suite and low white coffee table, strewn with magazines and unopened bottles of mineral water. He waved his hand. 'You want anything, Harry? Coffee, tea, any of that crap?'

'I don't.'

'Then what?'

'Gavril Nevrosky,' he began. 'Does that name mean anything to you?'

Case didn't react emotionally. He spun round and returned to his desk, fingers hovering over the keyboard. 'Nevrosky? Doesn't ring a bell. Spell it.' Case typed as Lucas spelt Nevrosky's name. 'Nothing coming up, but that doesn't mean he's not in our arc. Where does he operate?'

'Dresden, with a reach through central and eastern Europe and some in Russia.'

Case worked more of the keyboard, whistled through his teeth and swung the screen round so Lucas could see. 'By central and eastern Europe, you mean the old Soviet bloc; around eighteen, twenty countries. We have eighty-nine contracts there. God knows which are Gavril Nevrosky's, if any. These guys tie themselves up in so many shell companies they could make their own beach. If you need it, I can find it, as long as it doesn't contravene any of the nondisclosure bullshit cluttering up my disk space. But it'll cost.'

'I'll pay.'

'You haven't seen the invoice.'

'I'll pay,' Lucas repeated.

'And you look like a guy I would be stupid to screw with.' Case pressed a button. 'It'll take a few minutes.' He placed the vape pipe on the desk, carefully positioning it between a phone and a tablet. 'Anything else? We're a full-service company.'

'What does Future Forecasting do?' Lucas pointed to the posters on the wall. 'Apart from all this promotional stuff.'

'We win elections. Everything is legal. We harvest personal data, design algorithms to target emotion that boost extremism and conspiracy theories. Good business has been coming from the poorer areas of Europe because this is where disappointment is at its highest.'

'In what way?' Lucas wanted to hear it from Case.

'No magic money tree that they were promised. People are fed up being told how to think and what to believe. The previous generation held out hope for that democracy beacon and, before that, for good old communism. This generation believes all that is a load of horseshit and is looking for something different.' Case took a long drink of water, put the bottle next to the pipe and wiped his lips with the back of his hand.

'We coordinate millions of data points to discover triggers of bias, anger, hope, all that stuff. It's a pattern I learned during the Brexit campaign. We got people to think with their heart and not their heads and inject them with the drug of hope. We persuade them to believe in the impossible dream of a glorious past. The dream might destroy them, but they vote for it because it makes them feel good. We persuade them that life is so black they have nothing to lose. There's some shit in our brain that makes us do this. The hippocampus, the cerebellum, the prefrontal cortex, the amygdala – I have people downstairs who are experts in what bits of the brain do what and why. We call it neuromarketing.'

'In Europe, with these societies, how does it work?' pressed Lucas.

'If I tell you this, Harry, you best tell me what the hell you're doing.' Case tapped his screen. 'I got you on facial recognition, so I know exactly who you are, your war record, your marriage to our Foreign Secretary. It's all been coming up as we've been speaking. But what I don't know is what you want and why you're in my office now. You look a notch above an investigator trying to crack a mafia boss.'

'If I decide to hire you, then you'll know, and I'll only decide if you keep talking.'

Case broke into a playful smile. 'We gather mountains of data under the radar and work on smaller-scale elections, entities less in the public spotlight like sports clubs and local companies. In today's world everything has a vote. If we can get enough of one political mindset controlling these smaller organizations, that same mindset will control government. The President or Prime Minister becomes your puppet. What we do is smart because it isn't obvious.'

'And the impossible dream?' said Lucas. 'Give me an example.'

'A defeated enemy is the most common. Many feel their lives are irrelevant. They are looking for a conspiracy, something, someone to blame, something easily understandable, like immigration, Islamic encroachment, gay sex, corruption, loss of tradition. War's the big vote winner, because it wraps up feral emotions – anger, guilt, love, the whole meaning of life.' He paused, gazing through the window. 'Having said that, Harry, things might be changing. Those flings with fantasy may have had their day, which is why I'm turning down business. There's a shift against extremism and it's difficult to manipulate an election when common sense and moderation prevail again. Which is why I'm looking for work across the pond.' He looked down at his screen. 'Here we are, an initial search on Gavril Nevrosky.'

Case sat down, squinting at the screen, letting out low whistles, his fingers hovering like birds of prey over the keyboard and striking occasionally.

'Bulgaria,' Case said decisively. 'If these readings are correct, Nevrosky's people run the country. He's done a lot with the German right, stuff in Estonia too, Serbia, Albania. This guy is a real dude.' He looked up. 'Nothing conclusive. These are companies and things that bounce through each other. It's incredibly complex. If you need chapter and verse, it's going to take a day or two and cost a day or two more.'

Case's file told how he cut his teeth with political neuromarketing in the presidential election in Mexico in 2012 and secured his reputation with the Brexit referendum in 2016. Since then he hadn't looked back. It would take any American intelligence agencies days to get to where Case was now, even if Lucas could get it prioritized. Lucas needed to either close a deal with Case or leave. 'With your software, could you get inside Nevrosky's system?'

'Inside it, where?' He eyed Lucas suspiciously 'Future Forecasting is not a spy agency. We're a transparent political consultancy.'

'If you want to work in America, you can start working for me.'

Case's expression lit but creased with skepticism. 'Doing what exactly?'

'Can you get inside Nevrosky's networks and know his thinking, and the thinking of those who work for him?'

'Yes. We could. Downstairs, I have people who could do that. But you're asking me to possibly betray client interest.' Abruptly, Case stood up and stepped to a window looking east, his finger in the air tracing the curves of the River Thames. 'But no . . . Harry, you are a genius. Not betraying, because Nevrosky himself is not a client that I know of. If he is, he's hidden behind a web of companies. And he must be contravening all sorts of compliance shit or you wouldn't be after him.' He swiveled back to Lucas. 'Who's your client, Harry? Treasury, FBI, some New York mafia prosecutor? You've got agencies that do this – NSA, God knows what – that have way more firepower than my little operation.'

'Do you want the work?' asked Lucas firmly.

Case reached for a bottle of mineral water and unscrewed the cap. 'It's important, isn't it?'

'Yes.'

'Like . . .?'

'I can't say, but are you in or out?'

'I'm in.' Case took a long drink of water.

Lucas didn't pause. 'Dr Anna Yumatov, London School of Economics.'

'Is that a question?'

'Do you know her?'

'Yes, I do. We've used Anna. She's very smart. Sexy, too, if you're that way inclined. There's no one better on that part of Europe. She put data in context for us.'

'Such as?'

'Such as . . .' Case tapped a pen on his desk, thinking. 'Christ, it's complicated saying it rather than computing it, but *such as* – what's the conservative right in Poland got to do with the conservative right in Romania? Is there any connection to the conservative right in Britain? What are regional trends? What does the anti-gay lobby have to do with the anti-immigration lobby? Anna knows all that stuff, how politicians sow disappointment with hope to get people to where they want.'

'Do you use her a lot?'

'I met her once, here, a couple of years back.'

'How did she come to you?'

'A contact in Moscow said she was the best. We'd been using academics who repeat each other's echoes. Anna's different. I tried her out. She showed she knew her stuff, so I hired her for a session with the tech people downstairs.' He tapped the keyboard and glanced at the screen for a couple of seconds. 'She's not on retainer, but we pay her if we need a one-off.'

'Anything lately?'

'Yup. Six months ago.' Case took another drink of water and said, 'I had a close shave with a client in Croatia. I called Anna and she said Europe was swinging away from populism. It would swing back, but not for another decade or so. That's when I started looking in your direction, Harry. So, yes, I value Dr Anna Yumatov.'

THIRTY-FOUR

Anna Yumatov, breaking into an elegant, practiced smile, addressed her young audience. 'You will see I have changed the title of my lecture this evening,' she said. 'Looking at you all, my new theme seems to have attracted extra interest.'

Rake stood to the side of the university's Hong Kong Theatre underneath a large arched window of the old banking hall. Carrie had a chair to the left of the stage. A few scattered fliers announced that the lecture would examine the consequences of the European Union's expansion. But between leaving One Carlton Gardens and getting to the university, Anna had decided to switch topics There was no flier, but word had gotten around. The venue's capacity was 220. Every one of the maroon flip-down seats was taken, and students had filed in for standing space, three or four deep.

Anna, wearing a loose white blouse, navy-blue pants with a patterned orange silk scarf around her shoulders, paced up and down in front of the light-wood-paneled podium and the empty white screen behind.

'Today, instead, I will examine how far-right ideology has become legitimized in European politics,' she said. 'It is encompassed within the Future for Germany party, what we know as ZfD, and was propelled toward popularity during the 2015 immigration crisis and the 2020 coronavirus pandemic. The ZfD's sentiments went on to challenge the government of every European country, including here in Britain.'

Rake scanned the audience. With their book satchels and summer student clothing, they were mostly white, Russian and Slavic-looking. The Russian embassy could have slipped in any number of watchers, as could the British and Americans. There were only a handful of Asiatics, people looking more like Rake.

'Far right extremism is the biggest danger to European democracy today,' said Anna. 'It breeds in times of chaotic leadership, undefined values and material uncertainty.'

The Asians were listening as if in a lecture. The Europeans were personally engaged.

'The driving force within this style of politics is that the established systems are close to collapse. The ideology of the right is infiltrating European militaries, particularly special forces units whose training is based on fast reaction to sudden crises.'

Anna reached the far left of the stage, close to Rake, and briefly caught his eye. She was sending a message about who she was and what she knew. She switched her brisk stride to a slow, ambling walk and stayed silent until she reached the center, where she faced the audience, her hands clasped.

'Those affiliated to a nationalist cause within European militaries and security agencies run to the hundreds of thousands. They used to refer to the time they were to move against the system as Day X, drawn from a failed plan in 2017 to assassinate liberal politicians. Since then, the network has become larger and stronger. They now refer to the start of their operation as Hour Alpha. The Beginning, the moment of the strike.' Anna adjusted her scarf and gave a stern smile. 'Day X you'll find in Wikipedia. Hour Alpha you will not. Or maybe you will in a few seconds, because I see some of you looking at your phones which are technically banned in my lectures.'

A ripple of laughter ran through the audience. A door opened. Mikki peered in, looking for Rake. Against the clean-cut face of the student holding the door, Mikki's battered features gave him a savage look. Rake slipped out. 'Harry's waiting,' Mikki said. 'He's got Carrie covered. The Brits have a location for Lord Brenning.'

The London School of Economics was set back from the Aldwych, a wide thoroughfare curving west to east. Mikki led them round the Australian High Commission, talking as if he knew every building, the High Court, St Clement Danes Church, designed by the same guy who built St Paul's Cathedral. Cities had never been Rake's thing. He half tuned in, his mind on Anna Yumatov, forgetting that the traffic drove on the left, and stepping into the road so Mikki had to pull him back. What exactly was Anna trying to say? Who did she think would decode her message? They crossed a wider road, waiting this time for the green pedestrian signal, and headed down a street to the river. Rake spotted Lucas outside a building marked Arundel House, home to one of London's think-tanks. Lucas was talking to a couple of men, who peeled away as Rake and Mikki approached. Lucas led them to a minivan parked across the street. The engine was running. They got in the back, sealed off from the driver by a transparent screen. Lucas closed the door. Anna's lecture was playing at low volume through the speakers.

'We're following up on Hour Alpha,' said Lucas. 'Her numbers and analysis check out.'

'She gave them in the hundreds of thousands,' said Rake. 'When the European army is created, they could fall under one command.'

'Yes, if the European defense force is activated, which would be during a regional crisis.'

'And if the wrong person heads that command?'

Lucas ran his hand along the leather on the side of his seat. 'Sergey Grizlov's been summoned back to Moscow,' he said. 'The military attaché, Nikolai Usenko, is running things here, liaising with the Kremlin.'

'Summoned?' asked Mikki.

'That's what he told Stephanie. She wants us to squeeze Brenning, find out his relevancy, before Grizlov gets to the Kremlin. Brenning is divorced, miserable and living alone in a row house someplace in west London. They call them terraces here. Stephanie is getting people down there but wants us to go now.'

Rake had conducted plenty of off-the-books operations. This was turning into something far more. The Brits were asking them to do their dirty work because Lucas was a guy who could cut red tape and get jobs done. He must have read Rake's skepticism. 'The White House has greenlit it, Major. We get first pick at Brenning's intel.'

THIRTY-FIVE

Rake rang the scratched white plastic doorbell of Lord Brenning's terraced house. Brenning opened the door, showing some surprise, but not enough, Rake thought later, on seeing two unannounced strangers. An overhead light dimly lit the hall. Unopened mail lay on a chipped wooden table, and a shirt and jacket hung over a chair. There was a whiff of microwaved meals and unwashed dishes. Brenning looked unsuited to the scruffy little house, his slice of the broken pie after a badly handled divorce. He wore a neatly pressed dark woolen suit with a blue cotton shirt, cufflinks and a carefully knotted blue and red regimental tie. Mikki was keeping watch from a sedan across the street, Bridget England from another three cars along. The British wanted the result, not the responsibility.

'Lord Brenning,' began Lucas, 'we're from the United States, and we would be grateful for your expertise.'

'So, the Yanks have come to my humble door.' Brenning's hand rested on the doorjamb. 'Have you found the photograph?'

Lucas feigned ignorance. 'This is about your work with Chatham Mayfair, your expertise in satellite technology.'

Brenning picked up mail that had been dropped into the wire letterbox on the back of the door, glanced through it, and tossed it on the table behind him with the rest. He returned his hand to the doorjamb, a symbolic barrier against Lucas's and Rake's entry. 'This is a strange manner in which to ask for my expertise,' he said. 'It is not difficult to contact me through the House of Lords. For government business, you can go through the Foreign and Commonwealth Office. Baroness Lucas is a friend and colleague.'

Lucas stepped back, to lessen the apparent intrusion. 'You met a Russian military officer, Colonel Ruslan Yumatov, at Chatham Mayfair.'

Brenning gave a sad smile. 'So, you *have* seen the photograph. Why didn't you say, and we would all know what this is about? I was expecting the British, even one of my former colleagues to soften me up. But I get the bloody Yanks.' His eyes narrowed. Then he dropped his arm. 'What is it you need to know? Yes, I met this Colonel Yumatov. We were looking into Russian capabilities in small satellites – all the rage now, you know. I was working with a Cambridge company specializing in that business. Compact Space Technologies, if you need the name, although no doubt you already know. We wanted to know the competition. I had some business with Chatham Mayfair, and we arranged that I'd see this Russian colonel there and we would share.'

Rake stood beside Lucas, one foot on old paving stones, the other on ragged lawn. He could see down the hallway, a lamp on at the top of narrow stairs with a worn blue carpet, more light from a room on the left.

'Did Yumatov approach you, or you him?'

'You'll see the date on that photograph coincides with the Farnborough Airshow. He was over for that, looking at new weapons kits. He contacted me out of the blue.'

Brenning looked out, scanning the narrow street, then turned to Rake, his eyes blank, not engaging, more assessing. 'You want more, don't you? Yet you haven't even introduced yourselves.'

Lucas brought out his security ID for the White House which had him attached to the National Security Council. Brenning examined it and pointed at Rake. 'My associate,' said Lucas.

'Your unnamed associate. Your bodyguard, more like.'

Lucas's tone hardened. 'This is important, Lord Brenning, or we wouldn't be here.'

'Then come in.' Brenning stepped aside. 'It's a bit of a mess. If you want me to come with you somewhere, I'll need firmer authorization.'

He led them into the narrow hall, which was when Rake spotted a change in him, like a man dropping a mask, anticipating something bad. He had seen similar shifting expressions among Afghan villagers professing to show friendship, a dull falseness of greeting, an offer of food, and then the face coming alive, eyes sharpening, as visitors were led toward lethal danger.

'After you,' offered Brenning, indicating an archway to the left that led into a shabby front living room. Lucas went ahead.

'Harry,' Rake began to warn, his hand around his back, resting on the Glock 9 mm tucked into his belt. A knife was inside his right pants pocket.

A suppressed gunshot hit Lucas, who threw himself to the ground. Another shattered a vase on a table by the window. Rake fired. Instinct controlled his aim toward the single human presence among inanimate objects, hitting a gunman standing in front of a scrubbed wood kitchen table. The first shot struck his stomach, the second Rake put into his heart. There would not be only one, not with Russian mobsters, because that's who they must be, and they worked in packs of at least two. From behind the door, the other kicked Rake hard in the chest, smashing his right wrist and throwing the Glock to the floor.

Why not shoot him, like Lucas? Did they want Rake alive, Lucas dead? Had they come to capture Brenning? Had Brenning asked for Russian help? This wasn't the moment to think through motive, but it did help to decide his next move.

His enemy was armed, a pistol leveled at Rake's chest. He was in his late thirties with buzz-cut hair and a rough, lean combat face. A former military private hire, Rake reckoned, out of practice in close combat, distracted by his dying colleague. Rake blocked Lucas from his mind, down and bleeding, until the enemy was dead. Instead he brought his left arm round in a looping curve to divert his enemy's attention from the real threat. The Russian deflected the blow, giving Rake a moment to draw the knife and hurl himself sideways to the ground. His enemy raised his pistol, by which time Rake had sprung up to drive in the knife, automatically choosing the neck in case he was wearing body armor, which was unlikely given Rake's shots to the first target had gone straight in. Either way, Rake implemented a death strike, not a wound. He pulled out the knife to a jet of warm blood. It was bright red, arterial not venous, which meant the man had seconds to live. Rake collected his Glock and checked the rest of the room, ending with his weapon on Brenning who stood dazed and silent in the hall.

'Any more?' he snapped, just as Mikki kicked through the lock of the front door and came in.

'Only those,' Brenning blurted.

'Watch him,' Rake instructed Mikki, turning to Lucas, who was pushing himself up with his right hand. Blood streamed from his left arm, dark red, bleeding from a vein. He would live. Lucas sat against the wall and said, 'Get their faces. Check for ID. We need to know who they are.'

Rake forgave him for stating the obvious. He took a first-aid bandage from his side pocket, crouched and fixed it tight around the blood-soaked shirtsleeve, telling Lucas to hold it tight on the wound. He stood up, took out his phone and got a picture of the pale, drawn face of the man he had killed with his knife. He stepped over the corpse to the one in the kitchen, whom he had barely glimpsed. The body lay on its side, twisted against the legs of a kitchen chair. The man was slim, with short, sandy-gray hair, in a suit and bloodied blue shirt. Rake pushed the shoulder with his boot. The body fell back, empty eyes staring up, and Rake found himself looking at the face of the military attaché, Nikolai Usenko, who a few hours earlier had been with them in Carlton Gardens. Not Russian mobsters, Russian diplomats. Or maybe one diplomat and one hired gun. It didn't matter. During that meeting, the Russians must have known all about Brenning or they would not be at the house now. The British had been right to throw hostile curveballs at them. Rake kept his eyes on Usenko's corpse for a second too long. He was about to tell Lucas when Mikki shouted, 'Don't!'

Brenning was reaching into his jacket. 'It's all there,' he said. 'Take it for, God's sake. Just take it.'

Mikki kept his weapon on Brenning, whose light blue flickering eyes showed confusion, as if a game had unexpectedly become bloodied reality. Rake flipped back the edge of Brenning's jacket. From the inside pocket, he drew out a sealed cream envelope bearing a handwritten address, *To Whom It May Concern*. Rake tore it open and extracted a typewritten sheet of paper with Brenning's House of Lords address embossed in black at the top. Rake skimmed the opening sentences. *I want you to know why I acted in the way I did. My whole career has been given over to the defence of my country.*

'We need to go,' said Lucas, hauling himself to his feet, using the mantelpiece for support. He was right. There was no time to read a broken man's confession.

'I need to get my medication.' Brenning pointed toward the kitchen.

'What?' asked Rake.

Brenning tapped his chest and touched his throat. 'Heart. Asthma.'

'Stick with him,' Rake told Mikki.

Rake kept scanning Brenning's note. *Many years ago, I made a stupid mistake which has led to this corrupt and illegitimate government trying to arrest me. I am not young. They might have broken me easily and my story would be twisted. It is better I tell it myself. I am a patriot.*

Bridget England appeared at the open front door, distracting Rake. 'Casualties?' she snapped.

'Two dead,' said Rake. 'One is Nikolai Usenko.' He offered no defense, no explanation. In case it was too much for England to take in, he added, 'The Russian diplomat.'

England's face turned white, mind whirling. 'You need to get out, out of the country. We'll clear up.'

Rake held up the letter. 'We may have something here.' He pointed through the arch. 'Brenning's through there.'

England strode forward and said loudly, 'Mikki, what's the . . .'

Mikki turned, and in that moment that everyone should have predicted, with a speed that caught everyone by surprise, under the pretense of fetching medication, Brenning stepped over the corpse of Nikolai Usenko, sank to his knees, scooped up the weapon and as Mikki, too late, threw himself forward to stop him, another roar of gunfire echoed through the house as Brenning shot himself in the head.

THIRTY-SIX

Around the table at One Carlton Gardens were the Prime Minister, Kevin Slater, Stephanie, Rake, Mikki, and Harry Lucas with his bandaged arm in a sling. Peter Merrow was linked in from the White House with principals from State, Defense and Homeland Security.

Bridget England stood by the tall mantelpiece with Brenning's confession letter, which had turned out to be a suicide note. Everyone had a copy. Slater and Merrow agreed England should read it out loud. She reached the part Rake had already seen – '*My whole career has been given over to the defence of my country . . .*'

Kevin Slater said impatiently, 'Can we skip the excuses?'

'Ma'am?' England deferred to Stephanie.

'It's best we hear it all, Prime Minister, the detail and his state of mind. It's not long.'

Slater nodded for England to continue. '*When I saw blunder after blunder committed by government after government, I decided I had to act. The United Kingdom was fragmenting into separate nations, with its defence controlled by the United States. I devised a method whereby we would create a completely independent nuclear deterrent. I am, though, a scientist and engineer, not a politician. This process proved me to be an appalling judge of character. I sought help from the wrong people, who have hijacked my project. I will now outline what it is.*

'*Central to the plan was a Russian colonel, Ruslan Yumatov, now dead, who had access to weapons-grade uranium, which was transported to the remote settlement of Uelen on the far east coast of Russia.*'

'We called that right to go in,' said Merrow. 'Sorry, Miss England, go on.'

England cleared her throat. '*I was introduced to Colonel Yumatov by Dr Rudolf Wagner, an East German nuclear physicist who shared my concerns. My expertise is in satellite technology.*

Dr Wagner specializes in building compact nuclear weapons. The entire explosive process of a nuclear weapon occurs through a closely synchronized burst of energy within a billionth of a second. We worked together for more than twenty years to make sure we got it right, the triggers, communications, weight, material. I must stress we were not a handful of disillusioned scientists and military officers. Wagner, Yumatov, and to some extent myself, could draw on institutional resources from like-minded people.'

'Do we know who they are?' asked Slater. 'These like-minded people?'

'We're following up detail, sir,' said Stephanie.

England continued, *'We built powerful simulations to test every step of manufacturing, and then each phase of the attack initiation sequence. We knew, too, that effects could go way beyond what we saw in the read-outs from the simulator.'*

'What's he talking about?' questioned Slater. 'What attack initiation sequence?'

'We're coming to it, sir,' said England. *'Dr Wagner needed to construct a weapon light enough to be carried in a satellite. He did this by building a fusion weapon in the form of a small hydrogen bomb, in which U-235 fuses with tritium that releases a burst of gamma rays. For the lay people hearing this, a kilogram of U-235 is the size of a golf ball. We used five kilograms. I will not reveal further details because I don't know who will have access to this. My satellite weighs 210 kilograms and is about the size of a large family refrigerator. We conducted a private launch from Japan, registering it as a communications and imagery satellite, and it is currently in a 253-mile orbit, circling the Earth every ninety-six minutes.'*

The threat was far more terrifying than anyone in the room had imagined. This was not a rogue missile strike or a silent submarine torpedo. It was a satellite in space, orbiting the Earth, armed with a nuclear weapon.

'Our satellite is registered for communications and imagery with the United Nations Office for Outer Space Affairs. It was launched from the Uchinoura Space Center in Japan. The cost was $25 million, the satellite build cost about $300 million. Its bandwidth annual fee is $2.3 million. The bulk of this was funded by Japan's Ariga Corporation. The weapon was constructed in

the Russian settlement of Uelen. The satellite, which was my responsibility, was assembled in clear view at commercial plants and won plaudits for its design of lightweight materials and nuclear polonium-210 batteries which would last for years.'

'The factories?' asked Slater.

'Working on it, sir,' assured Stephanie.

Merrow's chin was cupped in his hands, eyes closed. 'So, there is a satellite currently in orbit carrying a hydrogen bomb,' he said. 'Am I hearing correctly?'

'Mr Prime Minister, Mr President,' said Lucas, 'Brenning is talking about conducting an electromagnetic pulse attack. It paralyses electrical circuits. It could cripple civilization.'

'Which is not a nuclear attack?' queried Slater.

'Not exactly, sir.' Lucas looked up at England. 'Now he gets technical, doesn't he?'

England silently scanned more of the letter. 'He does, sir. Yes.'

'Read it, Bridget,' said Stephanie. 'Then, Harry, you tell us what it means.'

England went on, *'We created what is known as a super electromagnetic pulse weapon. To give an idea, the detonation with tritium fuel we used achieves temperatures as hot as the sun, producing gamma rays that strip electrons from the upper atmosphere. These electrons are rotating at the speed of light around the Earth's magnetic field lines. This generates the pulse that propagates downward through the atmosphere.'* England paused, looking around to see if she should continue. Lucas signaled that she should.

'The Super-EMP weapon causes damage by upsetting the equilibrium of titanic natural forces in the Earth's magnetosphere and atmosphere. It weaponizes them for destructive purposes, releasing far more energy than the bomb itself, akin to a man-made geomagnetic superstorm. Once these forces hit the ground, they weaponize all they destroy. Think of the match that lights the forest fire. A burning tree ignites a bush whose heat explodes a vehicle and so on. In our simulations, readings far exceeded 200,000 volts per meter. Every electronic system will be hit.'

'All right, Bridget,' said Slater. 'Time for some translation.'

'Harry,' instructed Merrow.

'Yeah,' muttered Lucas, arranging his thoughts. 'It's the

weaponization of mother nature and our society, sir. Think of a
tsunami, the ferocious impact of the tidal wave hitting land,
smashing buildings, pulling down power lines, picking up cars
and boats like matchboxes. Then comes the chaotic, swirling
destruction followed by the slower-moving but equally lethal long
surge of water at the end. In electromagnetic pulse, first comes
the shockwave, second the lightning strike, and third the pulse of
extreme gamma rays, what we call the magnetohydrodynamic
signal. EMP attacks electronic systems. Everything is hit instantaneously, and from that comes the weaponization of the systems
by which we live. High-voltage power lines will drop hot to the
ground and start fires. The demagnetization of metal will collapse
structures. Hospitals will cease to function. Train lines, water
systems, pacemakers, phones, planes, communications.'

'But surely these installations are protected?' said Merrow.

'Yes, sir. But most hardening allows—'

'What is hardening?' Slater interjected.

'It's physically protecting an electronic component, usually
with metallic shielding like steel or copper.'

'Don't we do that automatically?'

'Not everywhere.'

'Why the hell not?'

Stephanie answered, 'Cost, sir. Utility companies find it
expensive. They have a highly effective lobby in North America
and Europe downplaying the danger of electromagnetic pulse,
whether natural or man-made.'

'This is some of the most secret defense information,' added
Lucas. 'Military installations and critical infrastructure are hardened, but standard protection is 50,000 volts per meter. Brenning's
simulations resulted in readings of four times that and more.'

'So, we're not protected?' said Slater.

'Mr President, Mr Prime Minister,' Rake spoke for the first
time, 'I was involved in an electromagnetic pulse war game at
the Army War College. We had power stations and substations
adequately hardened. But we discovered that even then there was
breakdown because there was always a weak point in the system.
If I could give one scenario . . .?'

Rake paused until Merrow said, 'Go ahead, Major.'

'The only data we have is from the early 1960s, when we and

the Soviets conducted EMP tests. In ours, above the Pacific, electrical systems shut down eight hundred miles away in Hawaii. In theirs, fires started in power plants, which shut down electrical cables running three feet under the ground. A similar attack on the United States today is estimated to damage more than three hundred and fifty large transformers in the grids. Up to forty per cent of the population would be without power for between four and ten years.'

'Do you have more precise scenarios, Major?' asked Slater.

'Yes, sir,' said Rake. 'The EMP strikes. A driver loses control of his vehicle because its electronics fail, and he smashes into another. Both drivers are injured and bleeding badly. Their phones do not work to call an ambulance. A passerby's phone does because the manufacturer has hardened it. Maybe it is more expensive. An ambulance answers the call, but hits traffic because an inter-section's lights are down, and it cannot get through. The two men die. The chain reaction that begins has little to do with the EMP-protected power station. We gamed the Houston Ship Channel, the biggest petrochemical cluster in the US. The EMP found a weak point, igniting fires which cause leaks around the tanks. It is not long before there's a chain of explosions which flatten everything within two to three square miles and propel poisonous gas clouds into the air. And that's just Houston, sir. Fire engines cannot put out fires. Ambulances cannot transport the injured. Planes crash into densely populated areas. We gamed gas pumps, blood transfusions, ATM machines. A helicopter's electronics might be hardened, but the lights on a high crane at a city construction site are not. So, the pilot flies into it. Strip away the detail, sir, and what you get is firestorm after firestorm. Everything burning. Everything on fire.'

Slater had his worry beads out and was moving tiny bits of black Yorkshire rock along the thread with his brow creased and his gaze down.

'Is this fifty thousand or two hundred thousand volts per meter?' asked Merrow.

'That was fifty, sir,' said Rake. 'We didn't game two hundred thousand.'

Quiet fell on the room. Merrow talked to people offscreen. Slater looked up with a grimace toward Stephanie. Rake watched

Lucas write equations; it looked as though he was calculating the arc of the attack. England, standing at the mantelpiece, caught Rake's eye and gave him a cheerless smile.

Lucas broke the silence. 'In that orbit, around two hundred and fifty miles above the Earth's surface, the zone of impact would be about a thousand-mile radius from the satellite position. Above Kansas City, the entire United States would be affected, apart from Hawaii and Alaska. Above Brussels, say, it would cover the whole of Western Europe.'

'My people are telling me Brenning is spot-on with his description,' Merrow said.

'Do we need to hear any more from the letter?' asked Stephanie.

'Finish anyway, please, Bridget,' said Slater.

England obeyed. '*I am close to the end. Tell my two daughters, Emily and Nici, how I died. Please don't tell them I am a traitor, or anything like that. Tell Maggie, my wife. We have no love for each other, but she is my legal partner. She won't be surprised—*'

'Enough,' Merrow interrupted. 'I don't want to hear about that monster's family life. We need to find this satellite and shoot it down.'

'Mr President,' interjected England. 'Lord Brenning adds a postscript we should hear.'

'Go ahead, Bridget,' said Slater.

'He writes, *The outer casing of the satellite is equipped with sensors. Should there be an attempt to shoot it down, they will activate the weapon.*'

'We need to defeat this thing,' said Merrow. 'And I just lost the favorite option.'

'This must have been the information Katia Codic was bringing across,' said Lucas, 'Someone in Russia wanted to warn us.'

THIRTY-SEVEN

The President of the Russian Federation faced Sergey Grizlov in the same modest office from which Grizlov had been deployed such a short time ago. Viktor Lagutov, behind his desk and flanked by Russian flags, took off his spectacles, and laid them next to his computer keyboard. Grizlov had been ordered back to Moscow shortly after the meeting at One Carlton Gardens broke up. As he was shown in, he noticed a security presence not there earlier. In the office itself, they were alone.

'We have difficult decisions to make, Sergey.' Lagutov's expression was rigid, a man boxed in. 'Gavril Nevrosky has not been entirely straight with me, nor me with you. It is time for full disclosure.'

Grizlov had known the President for enough years to read that there were no easy solutions, and none would be pleasant.

'Our team in Uelen has discovered that, for almost thirty years, rogue military officers ran a facility beneath an old Arctic research station there,' said Lagutov. 'It was used to make an experimental nuclear warhead with U-235 stolen from the Ulba Metallurgical Plant in Ust Kamenogorsk. Gavril Nevrosky funded this together with the Ariga Corporation, a Japanese company, under the cover of investment in the Bering Strait Crossing, which planned for a hotel and casino complex in Uelen. They built a warhead small enough to go into a satellite that has been launched.' Lagutov sat down, put on his spectacles, kept his gaze steadily on Grizlov.

'It's up there now, Sergey,' he said, pointing his finger in the air. 'I asked the FSB to look into Nevrosky when he was offering a $300 billion investment in our Arctic energy project on the Yamal peninsula in Siberia. I wanted Nevrosky to come in because the Chinese have a thirty per cent stake and he would give it a European balance. Katia Codic headed up that investigation.'

Grizlov had known about the offer, but not that it came from

Nevrosky. His attempts to get more scrutiny were ignored. Lagutov had kept him out.

'Do you know if Katia is alive?'

'I believe she is dead, sir, or alive and not talking,' said Grizlov. 'I understand the Americans do not have any of her information.'

'But you are not certain?'

'I am not.'

'Katia was a computer and mathematical genius. She had turned down offers from Silicon Valley and China and stayed on her low FSB salary because she thought she was a patriot.' Lagutov's attention drifted elsewhere, elbows on his desk, hands fiddling with spectacles, eyes cast toward the ceiling. 'She ended up being a traitor. She had gone into Nevrosky's network and – among many other aspects detrimental to Russia – she had found out about the satellite. And she had discovered a rolling cryptographic code used to communicate with it. Do you know how that works, Sergey?'

'Not exactly, sir,' Grizlov answered cautiously.

'Nor did I, but I do now. The first level of the code is made up of 1,024 five-character blocks of digits and letters, like 1768A, F2F1D, and so on. They change every few minutes. The second level is the access code to a time-authenticated stamp. That is a mix of digits, letters and other characters, like currency signs, star signs, impossible to guess. Katia was carrying all this on a thumb drive zipped into her jacket pocket. I agree with you. I don't think the Americans have it or Merrow would have told me by now.' Lagutov indicated he now wanted his Foreign Minister's input.

Grizlov chose an anodyne question, one that would not incriminate him. 'Do we know why she chose the Bering Strait?'

'The Bering Strait was Katia's idea. She believed Nevrosky's tentacles were everywhere in Russia and Europe. A few minutes by speedboat would be far safer than a European airport and street. She reached out to Gennady Krupin, the commander of the Eastern Military District, who facilitated the crossing. He is now under arrest. He arranged it with the Americans, making out he had the authority of the Kremlin, which he did not.'

Grizlov pulled out a guest chair and sat down in front of Lagutov's desk. He wasn't so sure. Lagutov had a knack of authorizing and letting something run until he knew which side would prevail.

Lagutov said, 'Katia discovered that Nevrosky planned to explode the warhead in the satellite, blasting an electromagnetic pulse that would cripple all electronics in its arc.'

'Where?'

'Europe. Western Europe to be precise.'

Grizlov was aware of the threat of electromagnetic pulse. An electromagnetic Carrington Storm in 1859 was the first to show its impact, cutting telegraph transmission in Europe and North America. The Soviet Union's experimentation with it in the 1960s had been required reading, although lightly taught in the late eighties because everyone had thought those days were over. 'If Katia Codic had a drive, we have a copy. So, can we not stop him?'

'Exactly,' answered Lagutov quietly. 'We could. My question is, should we?'

Grizlov kept his gaze firmly on the diffident President, who was not meeting his eye. He chanced using his first name. 'Yes, Viktor. Of course, we should.'

'Which is exactly why you would make a lousy President, Sergey. Here is a weapon that is greater than anything the Americans have. If we share it with them and the weapon is dismantled, they will tear us apart like they tried to in 1989, with NATO, with Ukraine, like they tried with China after the pandemic. Yet if Gavril Nevrosky succeeds, Europe will be weakened – indeed crippled for a time – in our favor.'

Grizlov stood up, leaning over Lagutov's desk. 'The Americans are reaching out for partnership.'

'I know. They keep doing it.' Lagutov rubbed his eyes, blinked and looked up. 'But we can never live as brothers with America. It has taken this to make me understand that. Peter Merrow and I can forge a new relationship which the next president might over-turn. We must become self-reliant, Sergey. The weaker we make Europe, the more we can achieve that. The Chinese understood that long ago.'

'Does this mean that the attack . . .'

'Yes,' said Lagutov.

'Have you seen casualty projections?'

'I have.'

'Europe will be engulfed in firestorms. Russia's economic lifeline will be destroyed. Thousands, maybe hundreds of thousand will die.'

'I hear you, Sergey, believe me.' Lagutov's voice was stronger, assertive again. 'But if we interfere, Russia will suffer for more generations. How many Chechnyas, how many uprisings, how many Ukraines and Georgias? We cannot go back to that. Nevrosky is not targeting Russia. He is targeting Europe. His black-market hyenas will eat the spoils. Nevrosky is as much of the West's making as he is of ours. If America thinks there will be blood and carnage, it is up to them to stop it.'

Grizlov's time to respond was limited to a few seconds. He sensed Lagutov watching and evaluating, eyes steady, barely blinking, turning his spectacles back and forth on his desk. The flags that flanked him reminded Grizlov that neither had yet betrayed who they were. It was not about morality, or even values. It was, as Lagutov said, about Russia, its past and its future. He reminded himself of the new security guards outside the door. One hint of disloyalty and Grizlov might not live to see the end of the day. Then, he would be useless.

'Thank you for putting your trust in me, sir,' he said. 'How can I help?'

THIRTY-EIGHT

Elbe Sandstone Mountains, Czech Republic

Ruslan Yumatov followed Nevrosky through the farmhouse kitchen door into the backyard and out into the sunshine, with the two Dalmatian dogs scampering around his feet. Nevrosky stopped mid-pace as Astrid appeared from the driveway, wearing walking boots and carrying a stick. She whistled for the dogs to come to her, and they ran off. Nevrosky gave her a fulsome wave, turned to Yumatov and asked, 'What do you think?'

'They are beautiful and well trained. Where did you get them?'

'The dogs, they are scraps from my separation settlement. She has the children, a beautiful house in Cologne, numerous bank accounts and a new lover. I have two Dalmatians. But I meant Astrid – what do you think of her?'

'She's lovely,' humored Yumatov. 'Professional. Intelligent.'

'Indeed she is.' Nevrosky began walking again. 'You have Anna, Ruslan. Yours is a real marriage. I have never managed that. Love. Friendship. Astrid is loyal and she believes in what we believe in. At this stage of my life, I ask for no more.' He opened the door of a single-storied red-brick building directly across from the kitchen, about seventy feet long with a high sloping roof of solar panels. Yumatov felt a wall of air conditioning with a smell of new electronic equipment.

'Here is our little nerve center.' Nevrosky proudly pointed to a bank of screens near the door. 'Our surveillance covers every centimeter – laser microphones, infrared, ground sensors, everything. No one gets through without us knowing. The men who searched you are mainly Czech, recently retired from the 601st Special Forces Group. The Czechs are easier to run, more amenable to our type of business than Germans or Russians.'

At the far end, Wagner sat at a large oblong workspace, part stainless steel and part embedded with screens. The furniture was sparse. Yumatov tried to identify what reinforcement was in the structure of the building and saw nothing. The set-up and situation unsettled him.

Nevrosky's security would not last minutes against a government force. Yumatov had led enough attacks against remote and supposedly impenetrable properties which had collapsed in minutes. Private contract security men did not fight like government soldiers.

He would ask, but later. His priority was to establish exactly why he had been broken out of his American detention with such ferocity and skill and, if necessary, find a means of escape.

Wagner lit up his workspace. Liver spots covered his hands. His fingers were arthritic, his wrists like matchsticks. Loose skin hung from his thin bones and wrinkled around his eyes.

'Let me show you, Ruslan,' he spoke with the enthusiasm of a child. 'Thirty years ago, at that dinner in Ulba, I would never have imagined that this is what we would have achieved.' Wagner was trembling. 'We have the satellite containing a nuclear weapon. Five kilograms of U-235 injected with tritium and deuterium gas at its core, with an initial trigger of polonium-210 activated by a simple electronic signal. The electromagnetic pulse will cover western Europe.' Wagner's watery eyes burnt with energy. He drew red circles around European cities.

'Electromagnetic pulse cripples electronic infrastructure,' said Yumatov. 'What is its strength?'

'This is a thermonuclear device, Ruslan, making it not just an electromagnetic pulse but a super EMP. Simulations read two hundred thousand volts per meter at the target point, stretching out for five hundred kilometers and diminishing to one hundred thousand at the edge of the radius.'

Wagner decreased the map and brought up an image of the satellite itself in relation to Earth. It was currently over the Pacific Ocean. 'We use standard networks to control the orbit, as if it were an imagery satellite. The trigger runs through a separate system, protected by encryption that constantly updates itself, a self-teaching algorithm of artificial intelligence. There are signal transmitters embedded in solar panels on the roof of this building.'

'And on my other properties,' added Nevrosky.

Wagner opened a drawer and lifted out an oblong steel box, unlocked it through a combination to reveal a black satellite telephone in a waterproof transparent case. 'We have these. Enter the access code. Press "send" to trigger.'

Wagner brushed his hand through his thinning white hair. 'You are not my son, Ruslan, but I am as proud as any father of what you have achieved.' He turned his screen into a night-time aerial image of London.

'I chose London for a simulation,' he said. 'This is the eastern Thames crossing at Dartford, and here is Heathrow Airport in the west, a distance of just over thirty miles.' The screen dissolved into a yellow flash. The London image went black and then emerged as if seen through a night-vision lens.

'That was the strike of the gamma rays.' Wagner created a thin red matrix. 'This is the national grid. The main power stations are here, here and here.' He used a green cursor arrow to point to areas around London. 'None can withstand the pulse, not at two hundred thousand volts per meter.' Wagner's arthritic fingers clumsily worked the keyboard. The green cursor swept through firestorms, fleeing citizens, blacked-out hospitals, vehicle collisions, fallen power lines that sparked more fires. He went closer to a ward at St Thomas's Hospital, across from the Houses of Parliament, showing how blood transfusions, chemotherapy and surgery instantaneously ceased. No backup generators worked because their electronics failed.

'And this is not just London?' Yumatov had seen similar Russian projections.

'Exactly,' said Nevrosky. 'This is exactly your concept, Ruslan. A shock so complete that it forces people to change how they think.'

Ideas that Yumatov had kept alive in his mind for so many years were now laid in front of him in detailed reality. He had not known the science. That was Wagner's team. He was not looking for profit. That was Nevrosky's area. Yumatov sought fairness, so small people would not be trampled on as his family had been, as his hometown had been; so that talented Slavic people, like Carrie Walker, stayed in Russia and Europe and were not deceived into thinking that America gave better freedom; so that soldiers as skilled as Rake Ozenna, a native of land stolen by America, would not fight blindly for that criminal government; so that privileged thieves like Sergey Grizlov would be publicly punished for crimes against the people. They all needed to accept the truth that Yumatov would show. For an undisciplined moment, he was gripped by a thrumming elation.

Wagner had delivered a near-perfect weapon. Long before Yumatov had written anything down, he had discussed his concept of *Shock and Adjust* with Anna. She had tested it as if it were an academic paper, taken him level by level through the theory to an end result. She helped him understand the political difference between the blunt destructive strike of a nuclear explosion and an attack like this. The American shock and awe tactic created a backlash against an enemy and demands for revenge. People gathered around existing leaders. Yumatov's *Shock and Adjust* theory would propel blame toward the existing government because so much would break down. 'You are certain governments are unprepared?' he asked.

'Yes,' said Nevrosky decisively. 'Look what happened with the pandemic – no preparation until people were gasping for air and dying.'

'We have been working thirty years on this,' said Wagner. 'Yes, we are certain.'

One question kept playing in Yumatov's mind. Why did they need him here? Sure, if he had been working with them, but he had been gone for so long. With the high risk and cost of getting him out of America, there had to be something else. 'You don't need me for this,' he said. 'So why am I here, and why now?'

There was an abrupt change of atmosphere. Nevrosky shot a glance at Wagner who shut down his screens. Nevrosky's ebullience vanished. His expression became business-like; not physically threatening, but the bouncy, smiling façade was stripped away.

Another screen lit, this time on the wall. Nevrosky's hand was on Yumatov's right shoulder, guiding him. 'Can you stand just here, please?' Yumatov stood in front of the flickering screen. It settled to show Russia's President Lagutov, behind his desk, flanked by flags of national colors and the double-headed eagle.

Yumatov had little respect for the Russian President, as did thousands of like-minded Russians in the military and government. For too many years he had kept Russia treading water, following the Putin doctrine when Putin failed to go far enough.

'How are you, Colonel?' Lagutov's gaze was partly there, but also kept flipping down to his desk where he turned a phone around like a prayer wheel.

'I am well, sir,' replied Yumatov.

'I have thought hard about the future of our country, Colonel, as I know you have. You have been impatient with me, as I would have been at your age and with your vision. You have acted decisively and paid the price. Had you returned to Russia after your Norway operation I would have had you executed.' His hand left the phone and he gave a short smile. 'You were lucky, and we are now where we are. We both love our country.'

'Yes, sir.'

Nevrosky trembled with excitement next to him. In the arc of his vision he saw Wagner, transfixed, tightly clasped hands resting on his workstation. Yumatov kept his eyes unwaveringly on the President.

'I understand that Gavril Nevrosky has briefed you?'

'Yes, sir.'

'Good. Then I shall be quick. The weapon will be detonated thirty minutes after the signing of the treaty for the European defense force that will take place in the Palais Schaumburg in Bonn. The head of this force will be the Bulgarian defense minister, General Adam Sarac. He is one of us. Your current location is outside the arc of attack. You will not be affected. Soon afterwards, you will fly to Moscow. The world will be in political chaos. It will be too big a job for Viktor Lagutov. I will step aside and position you as my successor. Your reputation, as a soldier and Russian patriot, is second to none. You have a compelling story of suffering, bravery and sacrifice on behalf of the Motherland. With Europe paralyzed, people will seek leadership and answers. Your fame from the Diomedes crisis, your close relationship with the Kremlin, your skill at communication, will give them that. You will symbolize the stability of Russia against the chaos of Europe.' Lagutov fell silent. His hands again turned his phone.

'Thank you, sir.' Yumatov outwardly showed not one crease of reaction. Inside, his emotions swirled, part planning, part disbelieving. Everything – where he was, how Wagner had briefed him, the bodies strewn across his detention house in America – now explained why Nevrosky had done what he did.

'Our embassy in London is arranging for your wife and children to be flown back to Moscow. Russia will love her new first family.'

'Thank you, sir,' Yumatov said again. Images of his father's despair and his own son's pride flashed through his thoughts. The screen went blank.

THIRTY-NINE

Notting Hill, London

Lights turned off so she could not be seen from outside, Carrie looked through the front room window as two black sedans pulled up outside Anna Yumatov's London house. Police had cordoned off both ends of Peel Street, which ran four hundred yards west to east, parallel with Notting Hill Gate. Upstairs, Anna was packing, with squabbling children and nanny Hanna. The smell of fish pie came from the kitchen, though the oven was turned down, no certainty that supper would ever be served.

Stephanie had called Carrie toward the end of Anna's lecture, telling her to go with Anna to the house. They had been delayed by students with questions and a few wanting selfies with Anna. The security men who extracted them were not military, not police, more like the ones seen around rock bands, sent by Stephanie, and they were good. Carrie had worked and bar-hopped with the British Foreign Secretary a few times over the past ten years or so. For all her official titles, Stephanie was a hands-on person, sometimes dangerously so, willing to break rules and people to get things done.

Once outside the building, the security guys protectively flanked Carrie and Anna as they reached a black unmarked minibus illegally parked on Aldwych. Inside, Carrie had been given a phone. 'Stay with Anna. We'll collect you,' Stephanie had instructed.

Now Stephanie called again, tersely running through analysis of Anna's lecture then, almost in the same sentence, relaying in her matter-of-fact British manner the shooting in Brenning's house and his suicide. Carrie found herself caring, asking if Rake was all right, which he was, a couple of bruises and he had plenty of those, and Lucas's flesh wound. Stephanie finished by saying that the diplomat Nikola Usenko was dead and had been there.

'We're taking her in, Carrie. I don't want the police. You need to persuade her.'

Carrie dropped back the white blind she was holding. Across the street, people looked out through their windows. There were flashes of phone cameras, doors opening, police checking IDs, which the British hated. An unexplained interruption in a quiet London street was being displayed on social media platforms all over the world. Carrie went upstairs. Hanna had the children under control. Anna was in her bedroom, where Carrie spotted a photograph of her and Yumatov, a selfie in springtime woodland with yellow and purple flowers. Anna scooped it up and dropped it into a large gray carry-on case she was hastily packing.

'They're here,' said Carrie.

'Where are we going?'

'To the Foreign Secretary's residence, Carlton Gardens, where we were before.' Carrie put on an upbeat tone, as she would with a patient who might or might not make it.

'Will Colonel Usenko be there?'

'Not straight away.'

'I need to talk to him, before I do this.' Anna folded a dress and laid it in the case. 'I am a Russian citizen, the children too. The Russian embassy is closer.' She reached for a pair of jeans to do the same, slowing her pace. Her eyes were red, traced with suppressed anxiety.

Carrie played scenarios of how much to tell and how much to hold back. If she lied to Anna now, and was found out, trust could be weakened over something more crucial to come.

'Usenko's dead.' Carrie delivered a statement of fact, no color, no nuance.

Anna continued folding the jeans, running her hand down the ironed creases. 'How?'

'I don't know, Anna, but that's why the rush.'

Anna put the jeans in the case.

Carrie added, 'Foreign Minister Grizlov has gone back to Moscow. We need your help.'

Anna opened a drawer, lifted out underwear and laid it on top of the jeans. She pulled out the framed selfie photograph. 'That is why I gave the lecture. I thought it would be enough, that they would leave me alone.'

On the street, the two sedans were parked next to the minibus that had brought them here. Carrie could see the eastern end of the street, a blue light flashing from a police vehicle. 'These are your choices, Anna,' she said. 'You leave with Hanna and the kids under British protection. If you don't, the police will take you anyway. I don't know about here, but in the US, when that happens, you end up in a cell somewhere, and Max and Natasha go someplace else.'

'I can go to my embassy.'

'You won't reach it. Even if you did, you would never leave, and you know better than I what could happen there.'

'I never judged Ruslan.' Anna handed Carrie the photograph, her face covered in dread. 'I loved him. I understand him. Men like Ruslan need vision, or they wither.'

Ruslan Yumatov murdered an elderly woman in front of me, thought Carrie, pushing her anger deep inside. She placed the photograph back in the case. There was a rap on the open door. Max stood there, in his formal school uniform with a freshly laundered gray shirt and red patterned tie. 'Hanna says we're ready, and that I can take my granddad's watch.'

He showed it to Carrie. 'Do you like it?' Carrie had seen it that morning. Max held it up by the metal wrist strap, showing bold white markings on a black face with a tiny red hammer and sickle at the top underneath the twelve.

'That's a lovely timepiece,' said Carrie. 'My mom and dad have watches just like that.'

Both Max and Natasha stared at her expectantly. 'Are you Russian?' asked Natasha.

'What do your watches look like?' asked Max.

Carrie switched to Russian. 'Like that, except the numbers are black and the background is white. Maybe a bit smaller.'

'Mine was given to my grandfather,' Max stated proudly. 'He was foreman of the Iron and Steel Works at Magnitogorsk in Chelyabinsk Oblast in the southern Urals. Magnitogorsk lies one thousand and fifty-six miles east of Moscow.'

Natasha let out a sigh. 'Our dad gave it to him. He gave me my grandmother's brooch.'

'Where's your dad's watch from?' asked Max.

'The Hara Submarine Base in Estonia,' said Carrie. 'He was

a doctor there, and my mother was a nurse. They worked hard for the Soviet Union.'

'Of course, you can take granddad's watch,' said Anna. 'Now, wait downstairs with Hanna. We'll be with you soon.' Carrie listened to the children's feet patter downstairs, Hanna following with the bags.

'Are you going to help us?' asked Carrie.

'They'll kill him.' Anna slipped a bag of toiletries into a side pocket

'Unless you persuade him to give himself up.'

'For years we've been laying out the facts of what has happened to us, and for years no one has listened.' She zipped up the case and lifted it off the bed. 'I don't know if I can persuade him, Carrie. I don't know if I should.'

FORTY

Stephanie watched the Yumatov family and nanny head upstairs to a small suite of rooms at One Carlton Gardens where staff had prepared toy sets, children's books, jigsaw puzzles and supper.

Anxiety pulsed through her. There was silence from the Kremlin. Sergey Grizlov was not responding to her message. Attempts to reach Viktor Lagutov's private office were being stalled, contemptuously, according to Bridget England, who was tasked with getting through. Usenko had been acting on orders, as was Sergey. Far from being a friend, the Kremlin was an active enemy. She could see nothing good in what was unfolding.

She checked herself in the mirror that reflected the shiny black-and-white chessboard-style flooring in the entrance hall. Rake Ozenna's killing of Nikolai Usenko and another Russian, who turned out to be an embassy driver, had shifted goalposts into an unknown. Then, Brenning's letter had propelled them to another level completely. As with so many things, electromagnetic pulse was something everyone knew, but did little about. Now it might be too late.

She flicked white fluff off her navy-blue jacket and smoothed down the shoulders. She needed a change of clothes and a session with the hairdresser, for sure, if she had to go on television to explain Britain's way out of this mess. She let down her hair and pinned it back up again, making sure she caught the loose strands falling over her face. She reminded herself to button her lip from railing against Harry and Americans in general for their culture of guns, guns and more bloody guns. Except, if Rake Ozenna hadn't fired back, Brenning would now be with the Russians together with his letter, and Harry might be dead. Bloody untidy, the whole thing. Untidy – the word her father used when things were going to shit.

Stephanie stepped into the dining room to see the Prime Minister sitting stony-faced at the end of the dining-room table, playing impatiently with his Yorkshire stone worry beads. 'Ah, Steph,' he said, looking up. 'We have some minor good news. Go on, Harry.'

Lucas sat beside Slater, three phones and a tablet in front of him. 'We've located Yumatov,' he said. 'He's in the Czech Republic, at a property owned by one of Nevrosky's companies just north of a village called Tisa, in the Elbe Sandstone Mountains, sixty-five miles north of Prague and thirty-three miles south of Dresden, where Yumatov's plane landed. We think Nevrosky is there. Our advantage is that there is only one road in and out. It becomes a track and then a mountain footpath. Our disadvantage is that the property is well guarded by men, mostly drawn from Czech special forces, some from Germany and Russia.'

'We will discuss options with President Merrow, who will be joining us shortly,' said Slater. 'Meanwhile, Harry, update us on this company, Future Forecasting.'

Lucas splayed his fingers across his tablet to bring up details. 'The owner, Stephen Case, had contracts with dozens of Nevrosky-linked companies without realizing it.'

'Or so he says,' interjected Slater.

'At this stage, sir, my calculation is that we either trust him or don't use him at all. Case is now collating those contracts to give us a pattern of Nevrosky's reach. He is also trying to get inside Nevrosky's software. If Nevrosky has the trigger to the satellite, we may be able to neutralize it.'

'How long a shot is that?' asked Stephanie.

'Case's company has signed eighty-nine contracts in Central and Eastern Europe. One will have a weak entry point. Once in, Case believes his people could access the network. He doesn't yet know about the weapon.'

'Steph, take me through the politics,' Slater said. 'This weapon does not kill directly. It is not a strike on a person or even a building or a city . . .'

'Anna Yumatov's lecture was a warning, sir. She spoke publicly about Hour Alpha, now picked up on right-wing social media chatter, which was her intention. She also gave figures on how the European defense force could be infiltrated. The man designated to head it is a General Adam Sarac, outgoing Bulgarian defense minister, associated with the United Popular party. He is a strong advocate of Bulgaria leaving NATO in favor of the European Army, and Bulgaria is heavily influenced by Nevrosky.'

'By God, I read this wrong,' said Slater with a sigh. 'I insisted Britain sign up, and now I'll have to U-turn and it'll cost me my job.'

'I think we all got it wrong,' supported Stephanie.

'Britain cannot be a signatory. We have to withdraw from the Bonn summit.'

'Then we need to announce it now.'

The door opened, and Bridget England stepped in. 'The White House, sir.' A screen slid down above the mantelpiece. There was a low hum as blinds covered windows. Peter Merrow, wearing the same jacket and tie as a few hours earlier, his head tilted to the left as a technician's hand fixed an earpiece, then facing the lens, tiredness in his eyes.

'I've spoken with Lagutov,' he said. 'Not good. He says they've found nothing in Uelen. Our raid was an act of war, and there will be consequences. We're also picking up unusual military vehicle movements on Russia's European borders.' Merrow's face vanished, to be replaced by satellite and drone imagery. He kept speaking. 'This is on the Estonia border. Here at Kaliningrad which borders Poland and Lithuania. Here openly in Russian-controlled eastern Ukraine.'

'These are supply trucks.' Rake stepped close to see more detail. 'A mix of civilian and military.'

At Rake's side, Stephanie tapped a line of trucks on the screen. 'What are they carrying?'

'Water, medicines, fuel, basic supplies,' said Merrow.

'Necessities that European governments shattered by electromagnetic pulse cannot provide,' said Stephanie. 'Nevrosky's networks will be preparing supply lines like this all over Europe.'

'Hardened against a super electromagnetic pulse strike,' added Rake.

Stephanie turned to Slater. 'As you said, sir, this weapon is not designed directly to kill people or to turn cities into rubble. Its immediate purpose is to erode trust in government for failing to protect.'

'Harry,' said Merrow, 'what options have you identified at your end?'

'Nothing guaranteed to work, sir,' answered Lucas. 'The weapon can be triggered from a phone, like a roadside bomb. Whoever holds the trigger needs to be persuaded to surrender or be neutralized.'

'And we can't destroy it?' questioned Slater.

'Not if we believe Brenning's letter about the anti-attack sensors.'

Rake addressed Merrow directly. 'There is one option, sir, that has a chance.'

'Go ahead, Major?'

'We fly to Ramstein, our base in southern Germany. I put together a team of people heading to or from Middle East deployments. We fly on to Dresden, pick up vehicles and head toward the property in the Czech Republic. This is a Schengen border. No checks. No one need know we're coming.'

'Then what?' said Merrow.

'If Yumatov has the trigger, only one lever will stop him. We will have with us Anna Yumatov, his wife, and his son Max.'

Merrow leaned away, this time to his left, then came back. 'Do we really need a child in this fight?'

'Yes, sir,' said Rake. 'Yumatov is obsessed with his legacy, and sons bear the legacy of their fathers.'

'Does Anna Yumatov know about Nevrosky?" asked Slater.

'We don't think so.' Stephanie looked to Carrie to say more.

'What she knows is her husband's mind,' said Carrie.

'You've spent time with Colonel Yumatov, Dr Walker,' said Merrow.

'Yes, sir. He's clever, driven and lethal. If he has the means, he will trigger this weapon.'

'Can his wife talk him out of it?'

'I don't know.' Carrie kept her eyes on the screen. 'And she doesn't know if she wants to. She's unsure of her loyalty.'

Merrow didn't miss a beat. 'Major, what if the family doesn't work?'

'Most important, Mr President, is that we be there.'

FORTY-ONE

Ramstein US Air Force Base, Germany

Rake tightened one knife sheath around his right leg and secured the other to his belt in the small of his back. He cast his gaze around the five men who, like him, were preparing weapons and equipment in ways that suited them best. Three were Eskimo Scouts – Tommy Green, Eric Wolf and a medic, George Kameroff, on their way to the jagged and barren mountain ranges in Afghanistan. John Sanger and Dave Campbell were from 1st Special Forces Operational Detachment – Delta, better known as Delta Force, on their way back from Iraq. They all wore casual, practical civilian clothes: tough pants, blue or green shirts, light summer jackets with plenty of pockets, and heavy-duty boots, not out of place among trekkers and rock climbers in the Elbe Sandstone Mountains, whose 125-square-mile range straddled the border of Germany and the Czech Republic.

Carrie flew in separately with Anna and both children. She had argued to bring Natasha because the siblings should not be separated. Rake had agreed to Natasha coming, but without the nanny. Carrie's Gulfstream 111 taxied toward them, stopping next to Rake's US Air Force C-37A, parked just inside the hangar at Ramstein airbase, America's military hub for Europe. Rake's team worked inside the hangar with a constant roar of aircraft. His pilots filed a flight plan to Dresden, three hundred miles to the northeast.

So far, Stephen Case and his team at Future Forecasting had failed to get through impenetrable firewalls.

Rake and Mikki worked on putting packs of plastic-wrapped hundred-dollar bills into two separate bags to be used to bribe the security guards at Nevrosky's property. It might work. It might not. If one man took it, they would all have to, and in Rake's experience the amount received by each needed to be enough for them not to work again for at least two years, ideally for life. Lucas had offered $50,000 each. Rake got it doubled, and the final consignment turned out to be even more than that. It had been easier to get a straight million. One bag contained $700,000 for each of the men at the checkpoint, the other $300,000 for contingencies. No one showed surprise at seeing such a large amount of money strewn across a table. In the field, they had all handled dollar deals, luring enemies to be friends or getting from one place to another. The greenback was still king.

They zipped up bags as ground crew wheeled steps to the door of Carrie's plane. Rake's phone buzzed with a call from her. He looked up as Carrie appeared at the aircraft door. She spoke in a lowered voice. 'Can't tell if Anna is with us or not.' She came down, the rucksack slung over her left shoulder, making her gait lopsided. She scanned the massive hangar, quickened her pace, half-embraced Rake, brushed her lips over his cheek and whispered into his right ear. 'Big fucking psycho mess.' She pushed herself away, beckoning Anna. 'Anna, meet Rake Ozenna. He was the one who actually saved Ruslan's life.'

Anna's poise was cool and examining. The two children ran down the steps and huddled each side of their mother. Anna removed Natasha's thumb from her mouth and held her protectively against her leg. Max stood apart, hands by his side like a soldier, staring directly at Rake, holding the position for a few seconds, then breaking it to look around at the aircraft, vehicles, men getting ready for combat.

Anna said, 'I have been instructed to help you in any way I can. If I do not, we will be deported to Russia.'

'That is correct, ma'am,' said Rake. 'Do you and the children need the rest room or anything?' Rake asked Carrie to give the children whatever they needed. He walked Anna to the back of the hangar where there were maps, tablets and phones. 'You still hold that you know nothing about what your husband is planning?' he asked.

'Nothing,' said Anna curtly. 'If you wish to understand me, Major, you should know that my duty is to my children.'

'If your husband succeeds, many innocent people will die. You will be pivotal in persuading him to stop.' Rake gave her a tablet showing a map of the German-Czech border area.

Anna traced her finger along it. 'I don't know this place.' She pushed a loose strand of hair behind her left ear.

Rake couldn't read her, yet he needed to judge how she would act in those fractions of seconds when decisions were made. 'We fly to Dresden, about half an hour. From there we drive to the Czech border.' Rake enlarged the screen. 'Your husband is on a farm property north of this Czech village here. There is a guarded gate barrier a mile and a half from the house itself. The plan is for you, Carrie and me to go in to meet your husband.'

'Not the children?' Anna kept her gaze away from him, an angry glower spreading across her face.

'They stay back until we know it's safe. Once Ruslan is neutralized, then they come too. Your husband has no forewarning of our arrival. He will only know once you reach the property.'

Anna dropped the tablet on the table, her eyes hardening further. She turned and walked back toward where Carrie was playing a skipping game with Max and Natasha.

They drove from Dresden on a modern four-lane highway that ran through an uninteresting low-lying landscape, part forest, part agriculture. Mikki was at the wheel of a cream Mercedes Sprinter, decked with black leather seats, belts, cup holders, phone-charging sockets, television screens like in an aircraft. Rake rode next to Mikki. Anna and the children were behind, Anna facing Natasha, a gray, plastic table in between them, and Max with a seat to himself on the right, eyes transfixed out of the window. Carrie rode at the back, her medical rucksack on the seat next to her. Courtesy of the air base, its chassis and windows were armored, not to the level of a US presidential limousine, but enough to stop the first rounds of high-velocity automatic. The other two Mercedes G-class special utility vehicles were not. The three Eskimo scouts, Eric Wolf, Tommy Green and the medic George Kameroff, led. Dave Campbell and John Sanger, the Delta Force soldiers, took the rear.

Rake studied plans and imagery of Nevrosky's mountain farmhouse. There was a spread of living rooms on the ground floor with four bedrooms above, two bathrooms, and a loft under roof arches with a water tank. Outside buildings were attached, brick and timber, a garage for vehicles, a workshop, a smaller area for gardening equipment. A front lawn beyond the circular gravel driveway had children's playthings, a swing, a slide and a paddling pool with water rippling against the sides in a strong wind. Beyond that was an orchard.

There right now were Gavril Nevrosky, Ruslan Yumatov, Astrid Becker who had travelled with Yumatov from Baltimore, Rudolf Wagner, the nuclear physicist who had worked at the Ulba Metallurgical Plant in Kazakhstan, and five staff who lived either there or nearby. There were seven guards at the first entry point, but no details about the second or the overall size of the security force.

A black Jeep splashed with mud and a Volkswagen SUV were parked outside the house, both registered to separate German companies in which Nevrosky had shareholdings. The sedan that had brought Yumatov from Dresden was not there. Automatic number-plate recognition recorded it heading back to Germany shortly after it arrived. The farmhouse lay along a narrow one-lane road that rose gradually into the Elbe Mountains. This was the last house, and the road itself became a dirt track that turned into a footpath.

Lucas was deploying a British Protector drone with powerful surveillance systems but no weapons. Piloted out of RAF Waddington in Lincolnshire, the Protector had been diverted from a NATO intelligence-gathering operation over eastern Europe.

Anna was silent. Max was fascinated by the soldiers, studying and mimicking their every move. Carrie entertained the children. 'See, there, Natasha, on Max's side,' she said, leaning over the back of their seat. 'That blue sign with the yellow stars says we're almost in the Czech Republic. A prize for which of you counts the number of stars first.'

'Twelve,' said Max straight away.

'One prize. And what do the stars represent?'

'They're pretty, like Heaven.' Natasha pressed her nose against the window.

'They represent the dictatorship of the European Union,' said Max.

Carrie caught Anna's glance in the mirror, worried and uncompromising.

'Max and Natasha, close your eyes and open when I clap.'
Natasha squeezed her eyes shut, her face still against the window.
Max, head up, did not. Carrie clapped. 'Open! And there, and
see the sign and we are across the border in another country. No
passports. No checks.'

'Are we seeing my father?' asked Max.

'Yes,' said Carrie, her hand gently on his arm. 'Your mom's
going—'

'We call her Mama,' interrupted Max.

'It's all right, Max,' said Anna. 'Carrie's American.'

'She's Russian too. She has a watch like Papa's.'

'It *is* true, isn't it?' said Natasha, turning from the window
and looking pleadingly at Carrie.

'Yes. It's true. And your mama is going first because she
hasn't seen your dad in a long time.'

'He's Papa,' insisted Max.

'Then you children will come shortly after.' Natasha leaned
across to squeeze her mother's hand. Max remained detached
and rigid.

Three miles across the border they turned left through
the small town of Petrovice. Rake stopped just before the next
village of Tisa. This was where they would make the switch.
Rake, Carrie and Anna would go in an unarmored SUV, clean
of weapons. The children would be in the armored minibus with
George Kameroff, the medic, Mikki at the wheel, Tommy Green
next to him and Eric Wolf in the back. The farmhouse was a
couple of miles ahead, the first checkpoint in just under half a
mile. Sanger and Campbell, in the second SUV, would stay back
with the minibus.

FORTY-TWO

Ruslan Yumatov examined the schedule for the electro-magnetic pulse attack. Europe's heads of government were to arrive at the Palais Schaumburg in Bonn over a sixty-minute window between 17.30 and 18.30 that evening, to be greeted by the German Chancellor. All was running to plan, except the British had announced they were pulling out, citing technical legal issues. Even so, they were still sending Foreign Secretary Lucas as an observer instead of Prime Minister Slater as a signatory. The reception would last an hour. At 19.30 the Chancellor would give a twelve-minute speech announcing the international treaty that would lay out the structure of a European defense force. There would be thirty-one signatories, with Australia, China, India, Japan, the United States and now the United Kingdom and others invited as observers. Thirty minutes were allowed for the signing, then the Bulgarian defense minister, General Adam Sarac, would be named as the force commander. By 20.30 he would be in post and, technically, should a regional crisis break, Sarac would have control of troops and military hardware across Europe.

At that time, the satellite would be over the east coast of the United States, orbiting toward Europe. Half an hour later, it would be above Bonn and the thermonuclear explosion would be triggered. Electronic systems in western Europe would immediately fail.

Nevrosky, Wagner and Yumatov would fly by helicopter to the small Ústí nad Labem Airport fifteen miles to the south. A plane would take them to Chkalovsky Military Air Base north of Moscow. From there they would be driven to the Kremlin. Scheduled arrival was 02.00. President Viktor Lagutov would meet them for breakfast at 08.00. Europe's infrastructure and systems would be collapsing and anger against governments would be beginning. This would be made worse through an intricately planned social media onslaught exposing the lack of preparation on the part of European governments. False documents would be leaked on the refusal to harden electronic infrastructure. It would become apparent that governments knew about the threat of electromagnetic pulse but did nothing. Blame for the attack would deliberately confuse and challenge. There would also be accusations against every country that had a satellite in space, with an emphasis on Iran, Israel, India and North Korea. There would be counter-argument that this was a geomagnetic storm similar to what became known as the Carrington Event of 1 September 1859, when rudimentary electrical systems in North America and Europe failed. References would be made to the near-miss of a similar storm on 23 July 2012, and huge outages in London and Manhattan in recent years. There would be debates about sun cycles and solar spots, while in Europe communications and services would be ripped back to another age and firestorms would rage.

With blame diluted and muddled, people would ask why their governments had not protected them. Why was there no fresh water? Why did phones and cars not work? Why were loved ones dying? Civilian institutions would be unable to cope. The new European defense force, supported by powerful political momentum, would move in to deliver basic services. If there was unrest, the same force would restore order. Russia would pledge shoulder-to-shoulder assistance. Lagutov would appoint Ruslan Yumatov to a special cabinet role, tasked with saving Europe from catastrophe. Should he perform well, the Kremlin would be his for the taking.

'This is all your work, Gavril.' Yumatov made no secret of his admiration for the detail and planning.

'I have people, of course,' Nevrosky smiled. 'But I am a micromanager. I have to know it is right.'

'It is brilliant,' congratulated Yumatov.

'I will become wealthy. You will lead your country,' said Nevrosky. 'This is a strong plan, Ruslan. It will work.'

The door opened, and Astrid came in unannounced. Her hand shaking, she pressed a code into the surveillance keyboard to bring up a shot of the first guardhouse at the entrance to the property where Yumatov had been searched.

A black Mercedes SUV was at the barrier. The driver's head

was down, his face concealed by a baseball cap. There was a blonde woman in the front passenger seat and another woman in the back, her face also unrecognizable, obscured by the angle of the camera.

'The passport of the front passenger identifies her as Dr Carrie Walker.' Astrid hesitated before continuing. 'The woman in the back is Dr Anna Yumatov – your wife, Colonel.'

Yumatov expected Nevrosky to break into a huge smile, proud and happy to have delivered his family to him as promised. Instead the German looked surprised; and Astrid had rushed in confused and afraid. Seconds earlier, the atmosphere had been upbeat, Nevrosky in control of everything. Now, it was heavy, swirling with uncertainty, Astrid wanting answers from Yumatov, Yumatov wanting them from Nevrosky, and Wagner sitting silently, eyes down, tracing a thin crooked finger over a diagram. Yumatov realized he was watching an old man who knew his life's dream was about to be destroyed.

Yumatov moved to the surveillance screens. Yes, he recognized Carrie, the way she never could tuck all her blonde hair under her cap, the rucksack on her lap which would be her medical pack. Then, like a stone dropping through his stomach, he recognized the driver as Rake Ozenna. He couldn't see the face, but after the Diomede crisis he had studied Ozenna and learned his body language, watched his lectures, sought his weaknesses, tried to get inside his mind. He had even learned more about his people, the Eskimos, the Yupik, the Chukchi, and found nothing to help him. It was as if Ozenna protected himself with firewall after firewall, with no emotional feeling whatsoever, no sense of family, no children. His war-junkie relationship with Carrie Walker had failed because intelligent Carrie wanted more than this animal could offer. Ozenna was nothing but a subhuman killing machine. While Ozenna lived, Nevrosky's plan would fail. Therefore, to win, now, Yumatov had to kill him.

The vehicle at the checkpoint, with Anna in the back seat, showed this was an American government play and Nevrosky had lied to him. The Americans thought Anna would persuade him to change his mind. It was a smart move, except the future of Russia and Europe was a far, far greater cause than family. Anna would understand.

FORTY-THREE

'**A**nna and the children are meant to meet me in Moscow,' Yumatov told Nevrosky calmly.

'Talk to her, Ruslan.' Nevrosky was pleading more than suggesting. 'Find out why she is here.'

Yumatov watched Anna shift her position to look out the window. She looked serene and elegant, as she always had, not a day older than when he had last seen her leaving Moscow that evening with the children.

'Of course, I will, Gavril,' said Yumatov. 'But this satellite is you, Rudolf and Lagutov. My work comes after that in Moscow. So, I don't understand why Anna is here.'

'I don't know either.' Nevrosky's voice vacillated.

'But you were in touch with Anna. You said it was all arranged.'

'The Americans must have got to her through the British.' Nevrosky had been caught out. The Americans had identified the man who had skillfully hidden behind webs of companies for so many years. The paleness of his face, the shock in his eyes, the unexpected draining of energy – it was what Yumatov had seen many times in confidence-filled men who suddenly got shot. It would only be a matter of days, maybe hours or minutes, before Nevrosky's bank accounts and assets were seized. All this would be spiraling through the German's mind. America controlled the world's financial systems, and without money Nevrosky was nothing. For all his commercial and criminal brilliance, Nevrosky was a civilian not a soldier, and civilians, lacking military discipline, had a habit of pulling out when things got difficult. He could handle lying low in a secluded mansion. He could not handle prison.

'We need to adjust,' said Yumatov. 'We go now, to Moscow.'

'We can't.' Nevrosky's voice was even weaker, his gaze wandering toward Wagner for support.

'Ruslan, we are not welcome at the Kremlin until after victory,' Wagner explained. 'President Lagutov was adamant.'

Of course, thought Yumatov. In case it goes wrong. Lagutov was a snake, which was how he had kept power for so long; voice quiet, fangs everywhere.

'Ask my wife where the children are,' Yumatov instructed Astrid.

Astrid pressed a button. 'This is the farmhouse,' she said. 'Are the children with Dr Yumatov?'

There was a delay as the question was asked. 'They are nearby, and would like to come later,' Astrid reported. 'They look forward to seeing their father.'

Anna would never agree to jeopardizing the children's safety. Meanwhile he needed to buy time to get to the helicopter and get the hell out. 'Dr Yumatov only comes with the children,' he said. 'Not alone.' As Astrid relayed the instruction, he told Nevrosky, 'Get the pilot to the helicopter.'

'Of course. But he's in Petrovice.' Indecision flashed across Nevrosky's face, as though confused about far more than the logistics of summoning a pilot.

'I will fly us,' said Yumatov.

Nevrosky leant against the wall. 'We can't, Ruslan.'

Astrid took Nevrosky's hand, entwining her fingers with his. 'It's over, Colonel,' she said firmly. 'We're not going to do it. Gavril has told me all about your little toy in space. It's best left as a toy.'

Nevrosky's eyes were imploring Yumatov to grasp his point. 'They know we have it,' he said. 'For me, it has always been business.'

Yumatov shed his overt tension and made out he understood and agreed. 'I guess you're right, Gavril,' he said with an understanding smile. 'Seeing Anna so suddenly threw me. Jet lag, all these changes – it's been a confusing time.' He gently touched Astrid on the shoulder. 'Do you mind telling them – of course to search the vehicle thoroughly, like they did with me – then to bring Max and Natasha and come on up?'

Astrid passed on the instruction, and Yumatov opened his arms to embrace his friend. 'You have done so much for me, Gavril.' A hint of a smile returned to Nevrosky's face. He relaxed and stepped close enough for Yumatov to reach up and caress his face in a gesture of apology. 'Yes, we are old friends,' he said softly.

'Old soldiers,' replied Yumatov.

Yumatov slid his hand to Nevrosky's chin, put his left hand behind the German's skull and twisted the head to the right while pushing it hard back. He felt the breaking of the vertebrae and the severing of the spinal cord. As he lowered the convulsing corpse to the floor, he lifted the pistol from Nevrosky's shoulder holster, leveled it at Astrid and asked, 'Who is the shift leader?'

Astrid only stared at Nevrosky's body.

'His name, Astrid?'

'Sven . . . Sven Kolman,' she stammered. She ran at him screaming, thumping him with her fists, shaking erratically. It had been a long time since Yumatov had been so close to another human being, had touched female flesh so intimately.

'It's OK,' he whispered. 'It's OK.'

She weakened and allowed him to steady her in his arms.

'They had him, didn't they?' he said sympathetically

'Yes.'

They must have already seized Nevrosky's assets. Maybe he had cut a deal. The answer gave Yumatov certainty, making Astrid easier to kill. He drew her closer, broke her neck as he had broken Nevrosky's, and dropped her body to the floor beside his.

Immobile behind his workstation, Rudolf Wagner stared down at his well-polished shoes.

'We need the phone,' said Yumatov.

Wagner opened the drawer and brought out the slim black case.

'Thank you, Rudolf.' Yumatov moved toward the shaking old man, took out the satellite phone and unzipped its waterproof case. It was a military-grade Iridium Extreme, one of the lightest, toughest and most powerful on the market. 'You know, you are like a father to me,' soothed Yumatov. 'We make a good team.'

'Yes, yes, we do.' Wagner's eyes flitted to the two bodies on the floor.

'Do you have the codes?'

'Of course.' Wagner nodded. 'We kept it simple, for emergencies like this. The keypad access code is 701991. You can test it by turning it on. The building is sealed. It will not be detected.'

The battery was fully charged. Yumatov entered the code and the screen lit. Wagner stood close to him, as if unafraid, relieved to have something to do. 'Everything is in order, Ruslan, but for a signal we have to go outside.'

'The trigger, Rudolf? Explain again how that works.'

'So simple, although it took years to perfect. Once you have locked on, press 111#. A six-digit code will appear. Enter the code, press Send. The message goes to our server which carries a time-authenticated code to the weapon. The process is completed in microseconds.'

'Press 111# and code 701991,' repeated Yumatov.

'Yes,' said Wagner eagerly. 'Seventy. Nineteen ninety-one. The seventy kilograms of U-235 from Ulba, and the year that we took it.' Wagner wiped down his workstation with a cloth.

'I had to do this, you understand,' said Yumatov. 'Or your work would have gone to waste.'

'Yes, yes, Ruslan. I am grateful.' Wagner gazed resignedly at Yumatov, unaware that he had barely a second to live. Yumatov broke his neck, but without the false smile and embrace he had used for Nevrosky. The brittle vertebrae snapped with very little force. Wagner would have been a liability had he tried to take him along. He laid the body gently on the floor. There was silence, barely a hum. Apart from Astrid's short burst of screaming, everyone had died quietly and comparatively cleanly, no blood, only a little excrement. Yumatov was satisfied that he had not lost his skills. He stepped over the bodies and reopened the line to the guardhouse.

'This is Colonel Yumatov at the farmhouse,' said Yumatov. 'Sven, are you hearing?'

'This is Sven.'

'Keep my wife and Dr Walker in the vehicle.'

'Yes, sir.' A soldier's response, happy with direct orders.

'Bring my children. Detain the driver.'

FORTY-FOUR

Fifteen minutes earlier

There were two guardhouses at the entrance to Nevrosky's property, one on each side of the road, each a dark green metal cabin like those used on building sites. On the left there was a second cabin, just beyond a black metal barrier that was down across the road.

Rake pulled up in front of the barrier. A guard sat behind a sliding window which he opened. Through the door of the cabin opposite, Rake glimpsed a white table, coffee mugs, a water cooler, flak jackets and what looked like Škorpion vz. 61 machine pistols strewn around. That made sense – the Škorpion was Czech-made and standard military issue. Two men lolled with their feet up on the table, eyes on their phones. The drone showed six more in the second cabin further ahead on the left. In front of it stood a long white garden table, like at a customs check post. Behind, wild grassland sloped up toward a copse of trees.

The men came out, carrying pistols. They left automatic weapons on the chairs. One, seemingly in charge, stepped in front of the vehicle. His name tag read Sven. He checked the German plate. Two men took up positions on either side.

Carrie rolled down her window, pointed to Anna sitting silently in the back, and said in English, 'Dr Anna Yumatov and Dr Carrie Walker for Mr Nevrosky.'

'Passports,' asked Sven.

Carrie handed them across. Lucas had run off fakes, hers blue, Anna's red. Sven examined them knowledgeably, found entry stamps into Britain, nothing more. He pointed to Rake.

'Just our driver,' said Carrie.

'His passport or driving license.'

Carrie flipped open the glove box and took out a British driving license with Rake's photograph. Sven handed all the documents to another man who took them to the cabin to scan. He spoke into his headset microphone, Rake presumed to his bosses in the farmhouse. Another man said something in Czech, and the others laughed.

'They're asking why two classy women are with such an ugly driver,' explained Sven. 'It is soldier's talk. Ignore them, but you do need to leave your vehicle for a mandatory search.'

Rake unclipped the hood and got out. Anna and Carrie followed. All four doors and the trunk were opened.

The black canvas bag containing $700,000 bundled in $5,000 plastic-wrapped packs of hundred-dollar bills was at the back of the trunk, with an oil-stained rag draped over it, wedged into the compartment with the spare wheel. The smaller bag with $300,000 was under Rake's driving seat. Neither had yet been taken out. The search was concentrating on the exterior of the vehicle.

A mirror on wheels with a high intensity lamp was pushed under the chassis. A guard patted Carrie everywhere, groin and breasts, Anna too. Anna's purse was put on a table. Next came Carrie's rucksack, scissors, trauma packs, clotting agents, tourniquets, syringes, bandages were laid out. Sven put the passports next to them. He called the farmhouse from inside the cabin. His body language showed that big questions were being asked. He stepped outside, shielding his eyes from the sun, and pointed to Anna. 'What are the names of your children?'

'Max and Natasha,' she answered, folding her arms.

Sven repeated the names, listened to the response, then asked, 'Where are they?'

'Waiting to meet their father.' There was no trace of fear or hesitation in her voice.

Sven repeated and waited for an answer. Anna walked coolly up to the table and took her purse. No one stopped her. She sat sideways on the front passenger seat of the SUV and flipped down the sunshade with its compact mirror. She loosened her hair, let it hang to her shoulders, tried pinning it up, decided it looked better loose and dropped it again. She put on lipstick, rolling her lips to spread it evenly. Rake walked around to join Carrie. Sven said, 'My instructions are that I am not permitted to let you through unless the children are with you.'

Anna faltered. She looked to Rake for an answer, which Sven

noticed: Why consult the driver? Carrie picked up on it and asked Anna, 'What should we do?'

The atmosphere around the checkpoint darkened. The men who had been chatting and joking tensed. Hands went to weapons. They understood how suddenly situations could swing. Rake judged them as similar to those in Uelen: private security, best days behind them, there for the paycheck, professional, doing what they were paid for. But how hard would they fight?

Anna put her hand out for the phone. 'May I speak directly?'

Sven relayed her request. 'Sorry, ma'am, that's a negative.' His expression tightened. 'And they say you have five minutes to decide. After that, you must leave.'

Anna stepped away, her gaze toward rugged, flat grassland and colored wild flowers. Carrie went to her side. By now Sven would have guessed that Rake, Anna and Carrie were part of a more complicated play. Leaning casually against the vehicle, swatting away an imaginary insect, Rake asked outright, 'This a good job?'

'Pays the bills,' answered a guard standing behind the table. The pressure seemed to ease, but the others stayed alert.

'Good pay?' continued Rake. 'See, I'm thinking of ditching driving and doing something like this.'

'Pays more than others,' said the guard. Sven stayed quiet.

The money would have to be shown to Sven first, inside the trunk, out of sight of cameras. If he agreed, there was a chance he could bring the others into line. It was a lot of cash, which was how he had designed it. The dynamics were impossible to judge. Rake ran scenarios through his mind, and the one that came out good was a fast agreement. Sven would stand down the men, lift the barrier and they would drive through. Good scenarios were always the least likely. That didn't mean it wasn't worth the try.

'OK,' Anna said loudly. 'Bring Max and Natasha.'

With a smile exuding a confidence she didn't feel, Carrie hooked her hand around Anna's arm as they walked back. Anna must have judged Yumatov would not harm the children, but if they were there with him, Rake's leverage was diluted.

Anna added, 'But no searches. The children will be frightened.'

No searches meant they would get the weapons through, which

Rake had to read as Anna being on his side. But it did not align with her pledge to make the children's safety her priority. Anna Yumatov remained impossible to read.

Rake held up his hand to delay Sven from passing on the message. Sven walked around to the driver's side, his hand on his holstered pistol, reassessing Rake's role. He would know that drivers hired by foreigners were the ones who cut deals. He would be working out how high up the chain Rake might be. Rake lifted out the small bag from under his seat and unzipped it just enough to show the plastic-wrapped dollar bills. He gave Sven a moment to think. The security guard could share or keep it all. He only needed to lift the barrier and he need never work another shift. In dust on the vehicle door, Rake traced the amount he was offering, $300K, enough for a man to start over, open a bar, get divorced, get married, an amount difficult to turn down. Rake wiped the dust away, zipped up the bag and said, 'The children will be visible in the back seat of a Mercedes Sprinter van.'

Sven spoke to the farmhouse. 'They'll be coming through with the children.' He took the bag, walked over to the guardhouse and placed it on the table. He would share it. Good.

'Mikki, you come up,' Rake instructed through his phone. 'Dave and John, too, but hold back to cover.'

He signaled Carrie and Anna to repack their things. They all got into the SUV. Mikki's Mercedes Sprinter came around the curve in the road. The children were in the middle seats with George Kameroff, Natasha hands clasped, eyes down on the table, Max staring out the other window as if on guard duty.

FORTY-FIVE

Sven spoke to the farmhouse again, and his expression hardened. He signaled two men to step in front of Rake's vehicle, blocking him. Men shifted around to create a cordon on all sides. The barrier began to lift. Sven indicated that Mikki should drive around Rake's SUV to go through. The children were to go in, not Anna and Carrie, which wasn't the deal for $300,000. Sven knew. Rake knew. Sven slapped his hand on the back of the Sprinter for Mikki to start driving.

Mikki didn't move.

Rake opened his window. 'The deal is we all go,' he said.

Sven handed the bag containing $300,000 back through Rake's window and walked to the cabin: It was not enough to risk crossing Gavril Nevrosky or Ruslan Yumatov. The deal had been done and gone bad.

Rake said, 'George, get the kids on the floor.'

'No!' Carrie said sharply.

'Go, Ozenna,' said Anna firmly. 'Ruslan won't harm the children.'

Rake gave it one more chance. He leant out of his window and shouted to the guard at the barrier, 'The children need to see their father. We're going through.'

Which was when Sven brought up his weapon. There was no warning shot. Rake ducked as the round went through the windscreen. Sven died with two shots from Dave Campbell and John Sanger, the Delta Force men, watching from behind the Sprinter. Sven's head jerked up. His legs buckled, and his body crashed down against the side of the cabin.

Sanger let off a burst of automatic fire, deliberately high to give the other men a chance to get out of the way. They didn't. They went for their weapons, a situation of no return. With a marksman's burst of four rounds, Sanger killed the one to the left, tearing out his throat and neck. Campbell, from his driver's open window, took out the one blocking Rake's vehicle with two lethally accurate pistol shots.

Green, next to Mikki, hit the guard behind the sliding window of the cabin. Then unrelenting heavy fire came from behind as Sanger and Campbell, now outside their vehicle, systematically killed any security guard they saw. Two who had taken cover behind the guardhouse spun round as shot by Sanger, while Campbell used a rocket-propelled grenade to obliterate the cabin itself. The road ahead was clear.

As Sanger got back into the driving seat, machine-gun rounds from the top of the slope smashed into the vehicle. Campbell let off another grenade, which exploded high, setting fire to leaves and branches. The machine gun went quiet. Sanger was hit, slumped in his seat, shaking his head to clear it, patting down his torso to his right hip. 'I'm OK,' he said. 'Let's get there.'

'Are you hit?' asked Rake.

'Sanger's good,' said Campbell. 'He's driving, so he better be.'

'I need to treat him.' Carrie's hand was on the door handle.

'No,' said Rake. 'Stay here.'

The barrier was already up. The three vehicles moved through empty twilight-drenched grassland into the darkness of woodland on both sides. There was no communication with Yumatov. They came out of the trees into twilight again and passed a second guard post, no barrier, a single cabin on the right and unmanned. Rake tensed for gunfire. There was none. The road straightened, and the upward slope flattened. In the distance, pillars of sandstone rose out of the landscape, some like mountain canyons, some like needles. The roof of the farmhouse appeared through trees.

The checkpoint violence numbed Rake. It was merciless because it was necessary, which didn't make it moral or good. He struggled to see how it had made things better or worse. Seven, maybe ten, men had died, just to get through a barrier that was already raised. Nothing was resolved. Yumatov and Nevrosky now knew Anna and the children were with a serious military unit. Everything about using kids as leverage gave Rake a bad feeling.

Carrie was quiet, her body language wrapped in protective

cordons. She didn't tell Rake that what had happened was OK, that he had done the right thing. Because it wasn't OK, and maybe he had called it wrong. Carrie had that look written all over her face.

The chances of stopping Yumatov hadn't changed at all. But Rake still had everything to play for. So had Yumatov. Like children in an Iraqi village detonating a roadside bomb, Yumatov could trigger his thermonuclear weapon with just a phone signal.

Rake pulled over. He needed to get Anna back with her children. Kameroff had kept them down, but they had heard the gunfire. Natasha was quivering, sliding up and down on her seat and biting into the arm of a teddy bear. Max stood rigid, hands clasping the tabletop, eyes transfixed through the window. Rake needed to surround them with as much of a sense of security as possible. He kept Kameroff with the children and Anna. He put Tommy Green behind the wheel and Mikki riding shotgun next to him. Rake needed Carrie with him in the lead vehicle. Drone surveillance showed everything was quiet around the farmhouse. It calculated Rake's vehicles were ninety seconds out. Yumatov and Nevrosky would know what had gone down at the checkpoint. Thermal imaging picked up a figure with two dogs walking round from the back yard to the front driveway. The man's height – well over six feet – showed it to be Yumatov, rather than the shorter Gavril Nevrosky, of whom there was no sign. There was no one else outside.

Rake retrieved his HK416 assault rifle, SIG Sauer P226, a Beretta M9 and his two knives. Carrie was checking John Sanger, a flesh wound, painful, to the right upper thigh, muscles torn, not bone, not life threatening. Sanger and Campbell would stay back at this spot where they had pulled up with line of sight to the farmhouse entrance and back down the road to ensure no one could come up.

Rake restored his line to Lucas, who would have seen exactly what happened at the checkpoint. 'We're going in,' said Rake.

Lucas didn't object. 'No visible security,' he said. 'Satellite next in target area 21.00.'

Rake wanted to know more, but had no time to ask. Had the weird Stephen Case broken any of Nevrosky's codes? Had the Kremlin and the White House cut a deal? Was there a plan

B? Had anything good happened at Lucas's end, because on Rake's side things were bad and didn't look like getting better. He got back into the SUV and set off. They had stopped for just over a minute. He took off his cap so that his and Carrie's would be the first faces Yumatov would see.

FORTY-SIX

The rough metal road gave way to loudly crunching gravel. Two large dogs ran toward them, barking excitedly around the vehicles' wheels. Yumatov stepped out alone from the yard of outbuildings to the left of the farmhouse. He wore a dark green shirt, blue cotton heavy-duty pants, a beige waistcoat with pockets and rugged trainers with high ankle protection. He had a pistol in his right hand, lowered, and a slim black metal box in his left which he held above his head. Rake slowed to a crawl. Yumatov pushed a button so the lid of the box fell open. Rake recognized an Iridium satellite phone. Taking the odds face on, Yumatov could easily be overpowered, but not before he had triggered the satellite, and Yumatov couldn't be the only one here.

'An Iridium Extreme. On and connected,' said Harry Lucas in his earpiece. 'Encrypted signal. Cannot yet intercept.'

Satellite phones transmitted and received on two separate frequencies. Jamming them was a matter of matching each frequency with a more powerful signal. The Iridium's encryption was of such a high standard that it was eluding the American government's most sophisticated agencies. They would be able to jam it eventually. The question was when.

Rake stopped and kept the engine running. Yumatov walked confidently toward Carrie.

Why was there no one else? None of Nevrosky's security? No Nevrosky. No civilian payroll staff that Rake could see, no faces at windows. The house and grounds matched the plans Rake had studied. He clocked the kids' slide, swing and pool in the orchard, the small second-floor balcony above the closed front door, the two vehicles parked the far side of the driveway. Through a gap between the outbuildings and trees, a helicopter was visible. Rake didn't like any of it. He particularly didn't like bargaining children for a satellite phone He lowered Carrie's window.

'Hello, Carrie.' Yumatov spoke softly, showing no urgency of a father wanting to be reunited with his children. 'Have you decided to be on Russia's side this time?'

Carrie answered coolly, without hostility, 'Hi, Ruslan. I'm siding with your family. Max and Natasha are behind.'

Disquiet flashed across Yumatov's face. Rake got out. He was fully armed, the Heckler and Koch in his right hand, a holstered pistol, and knives sheathed on his belt. The two men faced each other across the hood of the SUV. Rake asked, 'Where is everyone?'

'You and I, Ozenna. We killed them.' Yumatov wore a sense of triumph, which was good because triumph was emotional, and emotion got soldiers killed.

'Is Nevrosky here?' Rake wasn't sure what he meant by *We killed them.*

'Like I said. And down the road they got your message that this was between us. A lot of corpses back there, Ozenna.' Yumatov set the phone on the hood, close enough for Rake to snatch. Unprompted, Carrie got out. Yumatov had Rake in front of him and Carrie to his right. Yumatov said, 'I'm glad you're here, Carrie. We worked well together before. I thought we could help Rake and work well together again.'

'That would be good.' Carrie avoided looking at Rake and kept her attention on Yumatov, whose right hand stayed with the phone.

'I wanted to say sorry too,' he told Carrie. 'I am not that animal you think I am. In the Diomedes I followed orders. In Russia, what you saw was not me. Not the real me.'

'All of us have our monsters, Ruslan.' Carrie forced a smile. She jerked her thumb behind her. 'Anna and the kids are here.'

Yumatov glanced at the Sprinter. Anna was sitting to the right, head leaning against the window, watching without expression. Natasha rested her head against her mother's shoulder, while Max pressed his face against the window, his hand flat on the glass as if straining to reach his father.

'Did Anna think I was dead?'

'She did.' Carrie kept her reply nonchalant.

'And Max and Natasha?'

'Them too, I guess.'

'Has she got someone else?'

'I don't think so. Why don't you ask her?'

Allowing his composure to slip, Yumatov tilted his head and

said with a mocking sneer, 'Because your Rake Ozenna here wants me to hand over this phone before I see her. How can any soldier sink to such depths?'

Rake had to assume Yumatov would have arranged to trigger in a nanosecond. But that he wanted to speak to Carrie, to play a power game, showed weakness. There was no need. He could have vanished to complete his mission.

'Are you and Ozenna still together?' asked Yumatov.

'Broke up long ago.' Carrie used the same tone, the same disinterest. 'One of those work-life balance situations.'

Yumatov gave a short chuckle. 'You are funny, Carrie. That's why I like you.' He seized the phone and stepped back, his thumb over the send button. Rake could not see a way in. Lucas would have to break the encryption. Yumatov was using Anna and the children as much as Rake was.

'Eric,' said Rake quietly to Wolf in the Sprinter. 'Out of the vehicle and cover the chopper. Mikki outside and cover the kids' playthings and the orchard. Tommy stay at the wheel. George, outside protecting.'

Doors opened. Boots crunched on gravel. Yumatov watched, his gaze moving left and right, which was Rake's intention. Yumatov was alone. He couldn't see everywhere.

'I can press this even with a brain stem shot,' Yumatov said to Rake.

'I know,' replied Rake. The brain stem was at the base where the brain connected to the spinal cord. A shot did not kill instantly, as many thought.

'Once I hand over this phone, I get to see my family?' Yumatov said.

'That's correct.'

'I need to know that Anna is on my side. A wife away from her husband for nearly three years may have a different mind.' Yumatov took a step closer to the Sprinter.

Rake signaled for Carrie to go back and be with the children. He factored two outcomes. The first was that Yumatov needed to know he had his wife's support before surrendering. The second, and most likely, was that Carrie, Anna and Kameroff could shield Max and Natasha from seeing their father die.

Carrie opened the door of the Sprinter. Anna got out.

FORTY-SEVEN

Anna smoothed down her clothes. She steadied herself with one hand on the side of the vehicle, looking closely at the husband she had thought was dead. She showed no trauma, not even nervousness or surprise. Max stood up in the back, yelling, 'Papa, Papa!' and ended up being hugged by Carrie.

'Hello, Anna,' Yumatov said. 'Have you come to tell me to betray my people and surrender to Rake Ozenna?'

'Hello, Ruslan. It's good to see you.' Anna stood back from him, hands loose by her side, relaxed body language. 'I've come to tell you that I love and admire you more than anyone else, that I want to be with you.' She raised her head, eyes welling. 'My God, when they told me you were alive, how my heart sang. I have no idea what you have been through. But for me . . .' She pressed her hand against her chest. 'For me, there has been a dark, black chasm of emptiness. No one to touch. No one to lie with. No one to test ideas with. No one to push back against me. No soul mate. No one to love and be loved as you do. No one to grow old with and give a bright future to our children and grandchildren. That is all you, Ruslan. That is why I am here, because I trust you completely, Ruslan. I always have.'

There were fifteen feet between them, Anna at the side of the Sprinter, Yumatov at the front of the SUV. He relaxed his hold of the Iridium, which was in his left hand as he listened. Rake tried to identify Anna's impact, but Yumatov was difficult to read. He continued to scan around him. He was a man alert for lethal danger. He had not run toward Anna. There was no urge to see the children.

Anna walked toward him, arms outstretched. She had a loving smile, exuding wife, mother, family. During her lecture, Rake recalled her body language that portrayed mentoring and knowledge. She was skilled at turning on a public image. Right now, it was to win her husband's surrender. Yumatov rested the Iridium on the hood, as if to leave it there while he accepted the embrace.

He took his hand away, then confusion creased his face. He picked the phone up again, holding it more securely, stepped toward his wife and stopped again.

'Tommy,' said Rake quietly. 'If it's a no, get the hell out with the kids.'

Yumatov held back, broke into a shy smile and said, 'How is London, Anna? Do you have a nice house?'

'It's compact.' Anna slowed. 'The children love it. They have a good school.'

'We must live in Russia. Max and Natasha are Russians.'

'Of course. London is nothing. It is my dream to do that.' Anna's tone dropped, as if she sensed a breaking of the momentum. She turned her head to check the Sprinter.

'You have to help me, Anna.' Yumatov had a new edge in his voice.

'Yes. I will. I am your wife.' Anna waved playfully to her children, a big smile, to show safety.

'You have to help me do this. With the children.'

Anna turned back. 'Yes, I will, Ruslan. But first, see the children again. Natasha is confused. But Max is so proud of you.'

Weighing up the safety of the children, Anna's warmth projected toward her husband was visibly ebbing away.

'Do you still believe in me, Anna?' Yumatov held the phone high above his head.

'Yes, yes, of course.'

'I know that look you have.' Yumatov shook his head. 'The frustration and disappointment that you married a dreamer who needs to be humored. You get a flatness in your eyes and you squeeze the ends of your lips. I know it so well, Anna, as you tell yourself that you could have married so much better.'

'No. You're wrong.' Anna's whole body hardened. 'They are your children, Ruslan. They are—'

Yumatov's attention was elsewhere. From the house came a woman's scream. The dogs, quiet until now, barked and sped off toward her as she ran out in a blue kitchen apron, yelling in Czech, hands flailing.

Lucas in Rake's earpiece. 'She's saying Yumatov murdered Nevrosky.' Then his voice barked. 'To your left, eight o'clock!'

Rake, Mikki and Yumatov hit the ground as gunfire smashed

into vehicles. It shattered lamps, tore off paint, threw up gravel, shredded leaves, ripped bark off trees, sliced into the paddling pool and toppled the plastic slide. Tommy Green swung the Sprinter around to get Carrie and the children out of there. Anna, exposed by the vehicle moving, was hit and fell.

High-velocity rounds pounded into the Sprinter's tires, not armored enough for the firepower. With two flats, the vehicle was immobile.

Mikki dealt with two men to the housekeeper's right. Rake killed one to the left. The other ran back toward the yard. Rake winged him as he turned inside, then came a shot from Mikki which dropped him.

'Four o'clock,' said Lucas. 'Their targets are your team and Yumatov.'

Nevrosky's men, their colleagues shot to death at the checkpoint, their boss murdered by Yumatov, were emptying their magazines, anger superseding military judgment.

Yumatov, on the ground, took cover behind the front wheels of the SUV. With long-distance accuracy he hit a man running from the orchard. The firing stopped.

The silence meant Nevrosky's men were playing for time, pinning Rake's team down, waiting for reinforcements, reloading. Mikki made the same assessment. He broke out, running erratically across the driveway, a near-impossible small-arms target. He threw a grenade toward the orchard, taking cover behind Nevrosky's black Jeep before it exploded. Drawing their fire, Mikki made himself the primary target, giving a chance for others to reposition.

'Vehicle approaching,' reported Dave Campbell, who was with the wounded John Sanger on the road leading to the farmhouse.

'Take it out.' Rake peered through dimming evening light into the darkness of the orchard.

Yumatov scrambled to his feet. He shot George Kameroff in the face at the Sprinter's side door, opened it and grabbed Max. Carrie tried to hold him back, but Max pushed her away, striking her across the head. He jumped down to his father.

'Hold fire,' Rake instructed.

Yumatov ran with Max to the yard, skirting around bodies, and out toward the helicopter.

'Eric, take out the chopper.' Rake broke his own cover and repeated Mikki's weaving loop, throwing two grenades into the orchard from where the bulk of the enemy fire was coming. Mikki gave covering fire. Rake kept going into the orchard. Two of the enemy were down. One reached for his weapon and Rake shot him through the forehead. From behind him came the crash of Eric Wolf firing a rocket-propelled grenade, and the explosion against the helicopter, then a roar of flame spread like a flashlight into the orchard and faded.

A shadow shifted behind a tree. Rake veered to his left and heard the hissing crack of a round passing inches from his ear. The man was kneeling, changing magazines. Rake pulled his trigger. His magazine was empty too. There was no time to reload. Rake rolled to his left. The man snapped a fresh magazine onto his Škorpion machine pistol. From behind them came another crack and a roar and Dave Campbell's voice in his earpiece. 'Road clear.'

The gunman's name badge read Jiri. Rake's hand reached for his knife. Jiri's lower lip trembled. He looked Rake in the eye. If their roles were reversed he would pull the trigger and be done with it, using as few bullets as necessary. Jiri was younger, probably had no real combat experience. He was facing Rake's certainty and calm, the patience of a hunter raised in the Diomedes. Rake didn't ask for surrender. He said in English, 'There's three hundred thousand dollars under the front seat of my SUV.' Jiri didn't move. Rake judged more fear than uncertainty. He liked the kid. If his time had come, this would be a good death at the hands of a good enemy, until the thought of Carrie butted in, her look that said he had fucked up, a jab of regret that he wouldn't be able to make it good with her before Jiri fired. An impossible dream.

Rake repeated the offer in Russian, which brought a reaction which looked like indecision; temptation was mixing with the fear. For a long moment, Jiri steeled himself to fire. Then came another crack, a pistol shot. Jiri fell forward into the grass. Mikki was there, taking Jiri's weapon and ammunition belt. Blood soaked from Jiri's forehead into the grass. Rake clipped a fresh magazine into his Heckler and Koch. There was no more firing, only the howling of the dogs and the housekeeper whimpering.

As Rake came out of the orchard, he saw Carrie treating
Anna. A single round had gone through the calf on her right leg;
no other injuries, as far as Rake could see, no vital organs hit.
Natasha was curled up on the gravel, rocking back and forth and
crying.

'I'm sorry,' said Anna.

'Thank you for trying,' said Rake.

'We need to go,' said Mikki. 'I have his trail.'

FORTY-EIGHT

Bonn, Germany

As Stephanie walked into her suite on the top floor of the Hilton Hotel in Bonn, her phone lit with a call from an unidentified caller. Only a handful of people had this number.

After much dithering, Kevin Slater had allowed Stephanie to attend the Palais Schaumburg reception. He had been worried about Britain's reputation after all the flip-flopping and U-turning, to which Stephanie had said bluntly, 'We're NATO, Kevin. Europe needs us. We have to be there.' Slater then expressed concern about Stephanie's own safety, to which she countered, 'If it happens it's a power cut, not a bloody bomb. I'll survive.' Technically, she was right. In truth, they both knew she was making light. An electromagnetic pulse attack was far more than a power outage and would ultimately become far more than a single bomb attack. She had flown across in an RAF Airbus Voyager hardened to withstand an EMP attack. If Stephanie had understood the complexities correctly, it would be hardened to 50,000 volts per meter, but unlikely to be for the 200,000 that Brenning had predicted in his death note. She decided not to ask. She answered the call and was not surprised to hear the voice of Sergey Grizlov. 'You're in Bonn, Steph?'

'Just arrived.' No niceties, no jokes, not from Grizlov, not from Stephanie. She had not heard from him since his sudden departure to Moscow. He had not answered messages.

'I'm coming in and need to see you.' Russia had observer status at the summit, but not at Foreign Minister level. The US, Canada and others were sending deputy defense ministers for a nuts-and-bolts meeting starting the next morning.

'Spell it out, Sergey,' she said.

'Needs to be face to face.'

'No.' She felt her disciplined diplomatic rigor slipping.

'Don't screw with me now. By my clock, we've got two hours before—'

'Lagutov knows,' interjected Grizlov.

'Knows what?' Stephanie drew a breath, took off her jacket and dropped it on the bed.

'He controls the satellite. He's made Nevrosky's project his own.'

Grizlov talked her through the information carried by Katia Codic, Lagutov's discovery of Nevrosky's project, his decision to let it happen. Stephanie listened as she kicked off her shoes, undid her skirt that was biting into her, opened the sliding window to get fresh air, took in the Bonn skyline, cathedral spires and office skyscrapers. 'Lagutov could stop it,' finished Grizlov, 'and he's decided not to.'

'Are you saying he has these cryptographic codes?'

'He must have.'

'Then you need to bloody get them, Sergey.'

'I was hoping you would.' Grizlov seemed to slip into their old repartee.

'No,' she snapped. 'This is on you. It's on Russia.'

Stephanie ended the call, sat heavily on the bed's firm mattress and stretched back, splaying out her arms like a cross. An early evening breeze drifted across her, reminding her that her father had been right – the self-effacing, scruffily dressed Lagutov was a snake and the dapper Sergey Grizlov was playing it as straight as he could. That call and the information he gave had risked his life.

She called Bridget England, who was in a smaller room a few floors down, and told her to find the Prime Minister urgently. She called Harry Lucas, gave him a couple of lines of background, and finished by saying, 'It's a Kremlin play. You need to tell the White House.'

'I do, Steph, but I can't,' replied Lucas, 'And there's something—'

'Why the hell not?' interjected Stephanie

'Grizlov might be lying . . .'

'He's not.'

'If Merrow acts on it and he's wrong, his Russian friendship would unravel in its entirety, and if he confronts directly and he's right, Lagutov would deny it.'

'Sergey's not lying.' Stephanie lined her tone with certainty.

'Unless he has the codes, it doesn't matter either way. As an American, it would be unwise for me to tell Merrow. You or the Prime Minister could.'

'OK, I buy your argument.' Stephanie let out a long sigh. 'And you had something else?'

'Yumatov murdered Nevrosky.'

She sat upright. The cool breeze became shivering cold. Lucas explained how the trigger was on an Iridium satellite phone so encrypted that it was impossible to jam; now, as of this moment, Rake Ozenna had no means of stopping Yumatov. A message flashed in – Kevin Slater was on the line. Stephanie hooked him in. Lucas recapped, then Stephanie recounted her call with Grizlov. 'The question, sir, is whether you inform the Americans.'

'Harry, what's your view on the chances of failure of this satellite bomb?' said Slater.

'The most complex is the detonation, and they've had twenty-plus years to work on it. This is not Al-Qaeda and an IED. They would get it as right as can be.'

'If the computer modeling is even close to correct,' said Slater, 'the destruction will be incalculable.'

'But the US is not Britain, with all its secrecy,' said Lucas. 'If the White House knows of Russia's complicity it will get out and Merrow would have to respond proportionately.'

'Severe military retaliation which Britain would have to support, shoulder-to-shoulder manner.' Stephanie had first come across Slater as a young firebrand trade unionist intent on bringing down the capitalist system. As Prime Minister, he was now tasked with upholding it.

'Stephen Case of Future Forecasting has had a minor breakthrough,' said Lucas.

'Then he's got two hours to make it a full one,' said Slater.

FORTY-NINE

Ruslan Yumatov ran, tightly holding Max's hand. Rain clouds were not far away. They would bring more darkness to the summer night. Up ahead there was undergrowth, woodland and weird jagged sandstone pillars, sheer drops into valleys, streams and creeks, enough to keep him hidden, and he only needed two hours.

Having Max by his side – his son, his blood – was the greatest feeling. It was a shame about Anna. He was sure he had read her right. And it was Max who was important. He was legacy. Anna was only a wife.

The vehicle track that ran up from the road, curving around the front lawn of the farmhouse, became a walking trail of treated gravel. For the first few hundred yards, as gunfire was loud, Yumatov and Max jogged. The landscape was open, with rough grass, some bushes and a view across the valley. The gunfire went quiet. With trees to give cover, the trail became an earth footpath trodden down over the years by summer tourists. It followed a narrow slow-running brook upstream through pale green bracken and clumps of undergrowth. Yumatov slowed and looked at his son. 'My goodness, you're strong,' he said. 'You are almost a man.'

In Max's gaze Yumatov read unquestioning loyalty, not like Anna who thought too much, questioned everything, even herself. He had seen her go down and wondered briefly if she had survived. He held Max by the shoulders, resisting the urge to show weakness and embrace him. Max took his grandfather's watch from his pocket, proud that he had kept it with him all this time. Yumatov held it, turning it in his hand. 'I gave it to you, the night you left Moscow – remember?'

'Yes, Papa. And you left us to fight injustice.'

Yumatov felt a welling and nodded.

'Mama said you were dead.'

'They thought I was. I was in prison, but I am free now.' He dropped the watch back into Max's hands. The wind was whipping up, the temperature lower. Rain fell on their faces. 'Come, we must keep moving.'

Max hurriedly put the watch back in his pocket. The woodland path ended, revealing a deep blue summer sky made gray by slabs of rainfall. A mossy earth trail ran alongside rocks glistening in the freshly falling rain, then curved under two massive boulders that formed a sharp triangular arch. Beyond that rose a serrated sandstone canyon wall. Yumatov walked fast, holding Max's hand, careful with his footing on the rock, ducking under the arch to find a cluster of three sandstone pillars rising above the canyon wall. There were steps carved into the side of one pillar. To ensure the strongest signal to the satellite, Yumatov needed a high spot on top of the pillar. He crouched to Max's level. 'We're going up there, Max. Can you climb it?'

'Of course I can.'

'Are you afraid of heights?'

Max shook his head.

'You go first, then.' Yumatov let go his hand and lifted him onto the first step and watched closely while the boy began climbing. Yumatov brushed rain out of his eyes. The location was perfect. The only way to access the pillar was through the triangular arch to which Yumatov would have a line of fire.

Rake and Mikki moved through woodland until the path split three ways, one straight ahead, one curving through trees and one toward a small wooden bridge that crossed a stream. They listened. Rain fell on leaves. Drops splatted on soft ground. Fast-running stream water splashed over rocks. The light was dimming, the descending sun fighting to get through clouds.

Carrie was back at the farmhouse looking after Anna and Natasha with the rest of the team. George Kameroff was dead. An emergency airlift was coming for Anna and John Sanger.

Mikki and Rake had gone after Yumatov because they were the best trackers. Mikki covered while Rake scanned the three trails, looking for disturbances. No animal or human could cross ground without marking their presence. Rake's skill was in reading the signs, which never lied. But just off the path, partly concealed by leaves, Rake spotted an old Soviet watch with stars

and a hammer and sickle on the face. Either it had fallen out of
Max's pocket, or he had deliberately dropped it to be found. Or
Yumatov had left it to mislead.

Rake scoured the immediate ground. It was soft, a mix of soil
and sand. A stone embedded in soil had been turned on its side.
Leaves were pressed and twisted, and he spotted footfall washed
by rain, a heavier print with a lighter one to its left. He crouched,
moving nothing, looking hard, and envisaged an adult and a child
running side by side. He signaled Mikki that this was the direction. Mikki moved parallel, twenty feet from Rake, toward the
edge of the woodland. Soft soil gave way to smooth rock, black-
ened by rainfall. Ahead was a high pointed arch formed by large
square-shaped boulders. If Yumatov were behind it, he would
have full cover and a field of fire. Rake assumed Yumatov had
taken a Škorpion machine pistol, issued to the security guards,
with a range that would reach the woodland, even though its ten
.32 rounds in the magazine did not carry much punch. Yumatov
would also have a pistol, for which Rake would be a distant,
fast-moving target.

Rake and Mikki did not speak. Rake indicated that Mikki
should climb around the edge of the arch while he would make
a run through. Mikki hoisted himself up. His feet slipped on wet
rock, but he found small crevices and reached a slanting, rough
but flat surface of the boulder. He had cover from two trees and
a rock wall that rose vertically. Rake ran, weaving back and forth,
braced for gunfire. Nothing. He took cover against a rock opposite
Mikki, who would judge how next to move forward. He heard
fast-running water, wiped rain off his face and heard Lucas in
his earpiece. 'The Iridium is on, locked onto the satellite.'

Mikki signaled that he had eyes on Yumatov. Lucas sent through
highlighted pixilation of the Russian and his son. Yumatov was
lying flat, with Max beside him, on the top of one of the sandstone pillars. Steps leading up were hewn into the rock. At the
top, the steps came out next to a thick, dark green bush.
The surface was uneven, with small crevices, mounds and
clumps of vegetation. Drone imagery calculated that the flat
area measured 102 feet by 63 feet.

Mikki had a direct line of fire to Yumatov, but he needed a
lethal shot that would separate Yumatov from the Iridium phone.

If anyone could hit that target in this weather it would be Mikki. Rake couldn't see it working. If he missed, or failed to kill instantly, Yumatov could still detonate. He had Max to give him some kind of twisted legitimacy, meaning that Yumatov would not care if his own son died.

Rain gathered at the base of the dark sandstone pillar, mixing with mountain river water to create a swollen frothy whirlpool, splashing back and forth across the path leading to the pillar, covering the lower steps hewn into the rock.

Rake spotted a piton, a steel climbing pin, embedded in the side about ten feet up, and another above it. The tall thin pillar must be used by a rock-climbing school. The pitons ended near the top, underneath a stone lip that jutted out from the plateau. On the edge, a tree-like shrub grew out of the sandstone. Rake could get on at the southern edge of the plateau, opposite to where Yumatov lay with Max.

The drone calculations measured the height of the pillar at 105 feet, equivalent to an eight-story building. Little Diomede, where Rake had grown up, was more than ten times higher, but not as steep. Rake had gone up and down without steps or climbing pins more times than he could remember

When the satellite was over Bonn, Yumatov would have a five-minute window in which to ignite the thermonuclear explosion and hurl the electromagnetic pulse to Earth. After that, it would orbit to the east, taking the attack away from the European power centers of London, Brussels, Paris and Berlin, and risking those cities that were falling into Russia and China's influence.

Rake outlined his plan to Mikki with hand signals. He would scale the pillar to neutralize Yumatov. Mikki would keep Rake covered, with Yumatov in his crosshairs. If he had the opportunity, he would kill him outright. Rake left his pack on a high rock. He strapped the tablet to his chest and kept his assault rifle, SIG Sauer, Beretta and his two knives. According to the drone imagery, Yumatov had not moved. Neither had Max.

Harry Lucas had given Stephen Case a deadline of 21.00. It was just past 19.00, less than two hours. Lucas had set up a couple of laptops on the large coffee table in Case's penthouse office. His screens showed progress from Case's people on the floor below, the drone imagery from over the Elbe Mountains mixed with the carnage on Nevrosky's property, and preparations in Bonn for the treaty signing. A blank screen was reserved for a link to Downing Street or the White House.

Secret Service agents from the US Embassy were all over Case's offices. Case had told Lucas that if this were the price of getting a foothold in America, so be it.

'We're running out of time.' Lucas paced, staring out the window as if taking in the London skyline would deliver a magic wand. Case knew solutions came from data, data and more data, then analysis, analysis and more analysis. Nothing more. Nothing less. He processed a constant flow of information and tasked his people according to their skills.

'We've been lucky twice,' answered Case, picking up his jade green vape pipe and tapping it against the desk. 'Chances of us getting lucky again stand at sixty-forty.'

High and fast computer skills were needed to crack into a network as sophisticated as the one Nevrosky had set up. Simply battering systems with software-cracking programs would not do the business. Success lay with identifying human weakness.

Eighty-nine companies had hired Future Forecasting to manipulate their elections. Each had an executive board. Case now had most of their directors' individual phone numbers. Over the past twelve hours, his people had slipped in key logging applications and were now monitoring every touch. Of the 728 phones intercepted, only forty-six had anti-malware programs strong enough to counter Case's intrusion. He had gathered hundreds of passwords. He repeated the same with accounts linked to Lord Brenning who had designed the satellite, his former employer Compact Space Technologies, the commercial intelligence company Chatham Mayfair, and others. From that came more passwords and accounts, which gave Case's search ballast, but barely scratched the surface of where he needed to go.

Case activated software that analyzed networks, found vulnerable TCP ports and identified IP addresses, that individual signature allocated to every computer. His breakthrough came, not with the chief executives, but with mid-ranking technicians and others. Their weakest elements were their friends, family and children. With tens of millions of data points already accumulated, Case was able to narrow down patterns in specific communities, particularly surrounding anger and drink.

He struck lucky with a phone that had been in Japan at the Uchinoura Space Center when the satellite was launched. It tracked to an account in the Bulgarian capital, Sofia. Case diverted resources to networks around this account which led him to twenty-seven-year-old ornithologist Radka Sarac, working at the Institute of Zoology. She was the daughter of the Bulgarian Defense Minister, Adam Sarac. From keystroke interception, Case's people accessed her cloud which contained files harvested from her father's account. Radka Sarac had been moonlighting for the environmental group Greenpeace, which was investigating Bulgaria's nuclear energy program. The daughter of the defense minister was a perfect part-time employee. Radka may not even have been aware, but one file contained 1,205 blocks of five characters made up of digits and letters. The code began with block 1768A and ended with F2F1D.

'We have the rolling cryptographic code,' Case told Lucas. 'Now we need the time-authenticated access code.'

'Can we stop it or not?' Lucas's face furrowed with the incomprehension of a man fielding too much information at too many different levels.

'We have the base code, but it changes randomly every minute, or every hour, or minutes within the hour. We need to combine the rolling code with the access code to take control of the satellite.'

'What do I tell Rake Ozenna?' Lucas's eyes were red with tiredness.

'To keep going. We don't have it yet.'

FIFTY

'Look.' Yumatov held his arm gently around Max's shoulder. Rain soaked his clothing and he was shivering. Yumatov took no notice. 'See what a beautiful world we live in.'

Max rubbed sandstone grit back and forth with his hand. 'Where is Mama?' he asked.

'It's just you and me, Max. We are so lucky to share this moment together.'

'Where is Natasha?'

Remnants of the slowly setting sun streaked red and orange through the rain-washed sky. All around were the majestic sandstone walls and pillars of the Elbe Valley. 'No one can touch us here, Max.'

Max was making a shape with the grit. His eyes were dimmed, as if he were not even hearing. Yumatov turned the boy's head forcefully toward him. 'Max, you have to pay attention.'

Max's face contorted with fear. Tears mixed with rainwater running down from his wet hair. Of course, thought Yumatov, his mother had made him soft. He showed his son the Iridium satellite phone. 'See this, Max. When the moment comes, you will press the red button. You will be able to tell your children what a wonderful thing we did today to make the world a safer place.' He squeezed Max more tightly. He wiped rain from his cheeks and looked behind him to check they were alone. He must never let down his guard. The night and the weather favored him. Max trembled. It was natural he would be afraid. Yumatov hugged the frightened boy to keep him warm.

Rake tested the first embedded piton with his weight. It loosened, then sprang out, spraying damp crumbling pieces over his head. Soft Elbe Valley sandstone was not the hard granite of Little Diomede. Granite is fused. Sandstone is grains bonded with clay. When wet it becomes weak and unpredictable. With water swirling around his legs, Rake studied the vertical rock face above him. Some places were kept dry by overhangs. Others were exposed, absorbing rain that was heavy and driving.

Rake found a foothold jutting from the pillar. It took his weight and he hauled himself up. Then another, and another, carefully judging whether each was safe or not. The higher he got, the greater the risk of Yumatov hearing the noise of rock breaking. He lost sight of Mikki. He stopped briefly on a ledge to catch his breath. Through rain squalls an evening glow hung over the valley, showing lights on river boats and neat villages with churches. Snow and ice were his friends, summer rain a stranger. He hadn't noticed it falling into his open sleeves and gathering around his elbows. As he stretched up, positioning himself on the ledge for the next level, it fell further, soaking him with damp and cold. The next climbing rod was firm. He gave it all his weight. Testing his muscles to their edge, he pulled up his body, hanging until he found a place firm enough for his feet. Broken chunks of sandstone fell into the rising flood below. Halfway up and closer, he saw a way around the long ledge at the top where the tree clung, one that would get him there out of sight of his enemy.

He found a foothold under the protruding ledge. A cluster of pitons was there, where climbers had picked different spots for this final haul. A blue-and-white-striped nylon rope hung down, left by a climbing team. Rake guessed it was tied around the base of the tree. It tested secure. Rake pushed his feet against the rock to swing out and round past the ledge. A squall blew him back. He propelled himself out again. This time he reached for the tip of the ledge, holding himself in mid-air and using the momentum to swing himself out to where he spotted a crevice for his feet. It brimmed with rainwater. Rake heaved himself to the lip and looked over. He saw Yumatov and Max lying side by side on sodden ground overlooking the valley. Beyond them were clear skies. The rain had only minutes left to fall.

Rake pulled himself up the final ten feet. He found secure rocks for a handhold from which he could lever himself over. The nylon rope bearing his weight lost its tautness. Rake jolted down an inch with a wrenching sound above him. The hold of the tree roots within the sandstone was too weak. With a loud tearing sound, the tree uprooted. Clods of soil and sharp rocks fell on him. Rake tried to hold himself up. Jagged sandstone tore through his gloves. He hauled more of his body over as the trunk of the tree smashed against his face. His boots lost their foothold. He managed to keep one hand on a rock hold and switched the other to the tree branches, easier to grasp.

Mikki broke radio silence. 'He's moving. Straight ahead.'

Yumatov was on his feet, turning to check the noise. His right hand held a pistol and Max's arm, his left held the satellite phone in some kind of glove that made sure it was not dropped. Yumatov let go of Max and levelled the pistol towards the fallen tree.

'That you, Ozenna?' Yumatov asked calmly. If he didn't answer, Yumatov could pre-empt and trigger.

'This is Ozenna,' Rake answered.

FIFTY-ONE

The Palais Schaumburg, Bonn

'Lady Lucas,' beamed the German chancellor as Stephanie reached him in the greeting line. 'We are so delighted the British have finally made up their mind to join us at this historic event, although not, alas, as a signatory.'

'I believe my Prime Minister forwarded his concerns to you.' Stephanie looked into the large palatial room where politicians, lobbyists and industrialists mingled, with a sprinkling of artists and writers. She recognized businessmen who funded political movements that a few years earlier were dismissed as on the lunatic fringe. She spotted three such politicians who now sat in European cabinets.

'Your Prime Minister and I have spoken.' The beam left the chancellor's face, letting her know he knew what she knew. 'Sergey Grizlov is over by the orchestra. I can but wish you luck.'

Stephanie walked past a chamber orchestra playing a Beethoven medley. Bonn was the composer's birthplace. Grizlov stood by a pillar in an empty spot behind the musicians. He stepped forward and gave Stephanie a fulsome wave. He let her weave her way to him. She smiled, saying hello to people, offering congratulations, even one condolence, but never stopping. Gatherings like this moved and dispersed like river water, some parts rushed and loud, others calm and still.

'Hello, stranger,' she began, concealing her tension. 'You buggered off without saying goodbye.'

Grizlov did not match her tone. 'It's worse, Steph.'

'Worse than Lagutov being behind it?'

Grizlov adjusted his cuffs and sleeve, giving him time to check around that they were not being overheard. 'The President plans to bring Yumatov back as his chosen successor.'

All semblance of nuanced diplomacy swept from Stephanie's face. 'Is this you telling me, or are you his messenger?'

'It's me, Steph. That's why it had to be face to face. He knows I'm here. He doesn't know I know about Yumatov.'

She controlled her anger, the destructive type that is bred from impotence, hindsight and regret. What more could she have done? How much more vigilant could she have been? She leant against the pillar, tapping her fingers to yet another orchestral medley of 'Moonlight Sonata' as she calmed her fury at the thought of Ruslan Yumatov controlling the Kremlin.

Grizlov spied the Estonian Foreign Minister approaching and told him, 'A moment, please,' with an expression that read *Fuck off, we're busy.*

'Lagutov sees it as a win-win,' said Grizlov. 'If you stop Yumatov, he'll say you and I met and helped fix it. He will continue his love-in with America. If Yumatov succeeds, Lagutov will ensure Russia-friendly governments win elections in a weakened Europe with the charismatic Yumatov being hailed as our new hero.'

'Does Yumatov know?'

'Yes.'

'Mr Secretary Grizlov?'

'Incoming,' quipped Stephanie.

The overweight and jowl-faced Dutch Foreign Minister weaved toward them. 'Sergey, Sergey. We did not expect the Kremlin to send such a high-ranking envoy. We are delighted. And Baroness . . .' He was about to grasp Stephanie's hand when she waved to an imaginary figure in the throng grouping for the German Chancellor's opening speech.

Stephanie took a caviar canapé from a passing waiter and relayed Grizlov's information to Lucas.

In more than forty European countries, men and women in their governments' security agencies, mostly in their mid-forties and early fifties, mostly in secret jobs which had no public profile, received messages showing a blue square logo against a gray map of Europe with the letters EWS in the top right-hand corner. It was an alert from Europe's Early Warning System against a natural or man-made disaster. The message carried a yellow-black banner, indicating that a man-made attack of the highest level was imminent. Each government graded threats differently – for instance, Britain had five levels, ranging from low to critical, meaning an attack was likely in the near future. This banner specified a situation far beyond a terror attack on a train, an aircraft or in a crowded stadium. It was reserved for a biological, chemical or nuclear attack, at an unspecified level far beyond critical. To give more detail would spread panic, but frontline services were quietly informed to cancel leave, check systems and equipment, stay alert and wait. An attack was imminent.

FIFTY-TWO

'I'm glad it's you.' Yumatov's eyes focused on the source of Rake's voice.

'Let Max go,' said Rake. 'I'll surrender my weapons.'

'Max is here because he wants to be. You cannot separate father and son.'

Rake parted the tree's branches, stepped over the trunk, and came into full view. He stopped forty feet away. The rain was a sweeping drizzle, the wind cold and harsh. The vista cleared like a camera coming into focus. He held out the watch. 'I found this on my way up.'

Like a horse in a starting box, Max began to run forward and was held back by his father's grip on his shoulder. 'Keep it safe, Ozenna. We'll get it from your body when the time comes.' Yumatov adjusted his fingers around the phone and asked, 'How's Anna? She was hit.'

'Carrie's arranging a helicopter to get her to hospital.' Rake half-squatted to meet Max's eye level. 'We're pretty sure your mom's going to make it.'

'Thank you, sir.' Max stared rigidly at Rake as he stood up.

'Is Carrie OK?' Yumatov spoke casually, like one friend asking about another.

'She's good,' replied Rake.

'You're stupid, but not that stupid. You're making conversation while thinking how to defeat me. I haven't even asked you to let go of your weapons because you know as soon as you move to kill, I will press this.'

But you could kill me, thought Rake, and you haven't.

'Carrie's a good Slav. That's why you couldn't keep her. You have no feeling, no emotion. You are barely human. Carrie likes men with passion and vision. She is way out of your league.'

'No progress.' Lucas's voice in his earpiece. 'Negotiate. Deal.'

'You thought you could tell us what to do.' Yumatov tilted his head with a mocking sneer. 'The Slavs are the biggest ethnic group in Europe.'

'We can deal.' Rake tapped his earpiece. 'I'm getting a green light for you and Max to be with Anna and Natasha. A new life. No strings.'

'Bullshit, Ozenna, and you know it.'

Mikki said in his earpiece, 'Clear shot.'

'Family versus mission,' said Yumatov. 'And you Americans fell for it. Max knows, don't you?' He ruffled Max's hair. 'Mission must always come first.'

Rake took another step forward. Yumatov did nothing, as if he preferred Rake being closer.

'The deal's on here.' Rake lifted his tablet. 'Read it. See Anna again.'

'Anna is intelligent and beautiful, but she was lying to me. She betrayed her family and her country.'

Max looked up at his father and rubbed the back of his hand across his eyes. He shifted a step away.

'She didn't have to come,' said Rake. 'She took bullets for you.'

'Satellite orbit thirty minutes out.' Lucas's voice. 'Signature ceremony beginning.'

'Anna's from a family of St Petersburg intellectuals,' said Yumatov. 'I am from a steel town in the Urals. People like you and I, Ozenna, we are used by privileged people like them. They ride through their revolutions like we ride through this little rainstorm. They retreat back to warm clothes and big houses and leave us to clear up the mess.'

'Shit happens and the little people get trodden on.'

'Not anymore.' Yumatov held up the phone again. 'That's about to change.'

Rake unhooked the tablet and held it out with his left hand. 'Take a look at the deal.'

'No.' Yumatov levelled his pistol at Rake.

'They want to know if you have the codes.'

'You are desperate.' Yumatov let out a sharp laugh. 'I don't. Whatever deal I strike here, Ozenna, you would not let me live. You can't. I know you. We are on the same side and you are too blind to see it. It's time for you to surrender those weapons.'

Rake unstrapped the machine pistol and dropped it with a clatter on the ground. He unholstered the Berretta and the SIG Sauer, crouched down and laid them on the damp grit. He pulled up the legs of his pants to show he had no ankle holster and drew back his jacket to show nothing was concealed. He unstrapped the knife tied to his left hip. Each time he surrendered a weapon he edged forward. Twenty-five feet away, maybe twenty . . .

'And the earpiece – take it out. Throw it down.'

As his left hand moved toward his ear, Rake heard a helicopter engine. He signaled to Yumatov and said, 'I'll check that's Anna's medivac.'

As Yumatov glanced skywards, Max barged into him, shoulder into legs like a football player, causing him to stumble. The boy ran blindly, face streaked with rain.

Rake threw himself forward to try to stop him. But Max had gone too far. He thrashed through the branches of the fallen tree.

'No, Max. No!' cried Yumatov.

Max lost his footing, found it again and kept running. Rake grabbed his shirtsleeve, but Max pulled himself free, tripped and fell over the edge. The sandstone peaks echoed to the sound of his cry on the way down.

FIFTY-THREE

Stephanie was seated with a cluster of observers to the right of the long embossed-leather table on which heads of government were signing the European defense force treaty. They sat down in groups of five arranged in alphabetical order, allowing time for photographs and handshakes.

Sergey Grizlov was next to her. On her other side was a Deputy Secretary of State from the US, showing solidarity with Britain for pulling out of the treaty. Stephanie imagined what would happen if the attack was now. Would there be a flash? Would they hear nothing? The lights would go, but the orchestra with their non-electronic instruments would continue. Then what? Televisions and phones wouldn't work. Cars, laden with software, would not start. Minute by minute, hour by hour, the disaster would become apparent. How clever this was! Not 9/11; not Hiroshima; not a physical catastrophic horror, not even blame of a defined foreign enemy. It was the beginning of a drip-feed of decay. People would turn against their governments for not doing enough. Just look at bloody Covid, she thought, and multiply it by a thousand.

'We got it,' said Stephen Case. 'Or we got something.' Strapped across the screen were a string of symbols J!g>2pz_:ydD[G%k S{DVcN~7P>2]47a].

Lucas stood, hands on hips, in front of the screen.

'We followed the trail to a dozen accounts.' Case, next to Lucas, dangled a mineral-water bottle in his hand. 'We've broken into only one so far.'

'That can stop it?' Lucas switched his gaze to the feed from the Palais Schaumburg where the signing had about another twenty minutes to go.

'Technically, yes. And, personally, I am convinced this is the correct code.'

'But?'

'The phone we got into is registered through the Kremlin to the Russian Foreign Minister.'

'Sergey Grizlov?' Lucas turned abruptly to face Case.

'Who's right there.' Case pointed toward the Palais Schaumburg feed. 'Meaning someone wanted us to find it, meaning we might be being set up.'

'So, we use it or not?'

'If one symbol is wrong, we lose it.'

'Meaning?'

'Best case, control of the satellite defaults to the equivalent of factory settings, which we don't have. Worst case, a false access code triggers the weapon. We can't use it, Harry, not until we have corroboration.'

'Then we have fifteen minutes to get it.'

Yumatov stared down from the spot from which Max had fallen. He stood stock still with shock, as Rake unsheathed his seven-inch Fairbairn-Sykes, but too late. Yumatov leapt. Rake heard the crack of Mikki's rifle.

Rake ran to the edge. The eddying pool of water below had risen high up the sandstone pillar. The drop was now only thirty feet, enough for Max to have survived, if he could swim through the frothing currents pushing against each other. He couldn't see Yumatov. Rainfall created a cascade of water, thundering from high ground into the pool, pushing lower through large moss rocks and further into a short white-water river which flattened and calmed into a fast-flowing tributary of the Elbe.

Max was being swept downstream toward a wild pool, where water bubbled and churned as it flowed toward three narrow rock channels which led to descending white-water rapids. Max would either be hurled down or smashed against the rocks. He struggled and clawed in the air, screaming. He careered into a rock which bounced him back into the swirl. Mikki was on the left bank, just ahead. He cut through a clump of branches from a shrub and threw it in, yelling, 'Max, here.' The boy grasped at them with his right hand but couldn't keep his grip. Leaves stripped away. A cascade of water crashed into the pool, tearing the clump away toward a narrow channel in the rocks. Mikki hurled in another, this time ahead of Max. The two clumps of loose undergrowth became wedged in the central channel, blocking it. Max was level-headed enough to seek sanctuary there. He kicked his way toward the rock, letting the water guide him toward the cushion of the undergrowth. Its flow trapped, water in the pool kicked and swirled, sucking Max down. Mikki clipped a rope around a tree on the bank and jumped in next to Max. The boy wrapped his arms around Mikki's neck. Mikki pulled Max out of the water and slid him across a rock streaked with green slime until he was on dry ground. He turned Max on his side, gently hitting his back, making him vomit water from his stomach and cough it from his lungs.

'You OK?' he asked. Max nodded. Mikki sighted his rifle, but Yumatov had gone. From the top of the sandstone pillar, Rake scanned the river. If Mikki had wounded him, Yumatov would have been down there with Max, his body thrown back and forth against the river's rocks. He wasn't. Rake searched more, further down river. He saw him beyond the pool, making his way to the rapids. Rake picked up a pistol and a knife and jumped.

Wind shrieked around his ears. Rain slapped into his face. He fell crookedly, struck the pillar with his shoulder and hit the surface raggedly and hard. The water tasted of rocks and vegetation. The current drew him deep into the pool. He kicked and clawed through, blanking out the pain from his shoulder. Chill cut through like an ice dagger, more brutal than the Bering Strait. His heart pounded in his ears. Water twisted and tore and turned him like driftwood. Lungs squeezed tight, he kicked, until a surge hurled him to the surface, and he glimpsed Yumatov ahead, tossed around, but in control. Rake opened his mouth and gasped for air. A swell of cold water rushed into his mouth. He coughed it out, found a handhold. Ahead, beyond the three channels at the start of the rapids, Yumatov reached for a rock, phone in his left hand, steadying himself against the current.

Rake guided himself to the clear left channel, the widest, with a small drop into another pool before the white water whipped up. Yumatov saw, and let go, turning feet first, protection against rocks as the water narrowed into rapids. Rake judged the rhythm of water swelling, drawing back again, swelling again. He bumped against rock, using his hands to keep control. He felt the drop and he was through. He passed the rock that Yumatov had used as sanctuary. He thought he saw, blurred and fast, a streak of blood above the water line.

In the white water, both men struggled. As the channel narrowed, walls of water streamed up the rock faces and fell back again. Some rolled forward in crests, some sucked back into restless black and green eddies.

Rake was hurled into a wider, shallower river where water settled, splashing lightly around jutting rocks, its flow slowed by vegetation on the riverbed. The water calmed, its color changing from gray-black to a deep smooth blue, ripples instead of waves. At last there was quiet. Ahead, Yumatov rolled, straightened, kept direction, but slowed. He was barely moving. His jacket was ripped. There was a gash on his face. Rake didn't trust the pistol to do the business. Water is eight times denser than air and Yumatov was mostly submerged. The pistol would not have the range or the accuracy. He drew his knife. Yumatov grabbed an overhanging tree branch on the riverbank. As he began to lift himself out of the water, Rake saw his shirt streaked with blood. In his left hand, Yumatov cradled the Iridium phone, secure in its heavy-duty waterproof glove. Rake knew the set-up. He had used them many times in the field. The keypad would still be accessible, but would need a firmer press through the plastic.

'Max is alive,' Rake shouted, wedging himself against a rock. 'Anna is alive.'

'In three minutes, Russia will be reborn,' Yumatov shouted back. Out of the water, blood ran down the left side of his face. His thumb remained unwavering over the button of the phone.

The ceremony was running slightly ahead of schedule because the United Kingdom, which would have been last, was no longer a signatory. The leaders of Sweden and Ukraine posed for photographs, then moved away. Next, the Bulgarian Defense Minister Adam Sarac, standing to the left with the German Chancellor, would be signed in as the European defense force commander. Like Nevrosky, Sarac had skillfully wrapped his political and business dealings into impenetrable knots. They knew what he was doing. They couldn't prove it.

A message came through from Lucas. 'Trigger code tracked to Grizlov's phone.' Grizlov was sitting close to Stephanie. He seemed deeply pensive, cradling his phone. Surely not Sergey, she thought. Her own instinct, her father's story telling her that precisely because of flashy clothes and ostentatious wealth she could broadly trust him. The small things, yes. He might try to screw her. But not this big. She reached across to tap his arm and pointed along the row. They squeezed out, heads turning toward the disruption, which was good because she gave the German Chancellor a firm right-hand halt signal to delay the proceedings. He nodded an acknowledgment. If Lucas knew, the German and British intelligence services would, too. She took refuge behind the same pillar, pointed to Grizlov's phone.

'I know.' Grizlov showed her the screen with a red cross on it saying Access Denied in Russian.

'You're being set up.' Stephanie scrolled her phone to the direct number to Lagutov's office and handed it to him. 'Call your boss, now, and tell him don't even think about it. It's game over for him and one more step wrong, for Russia.'

From his eddy against the rock, Rake assessed Yumatov's position. The Russian clung to an overhanging branch, water above his waist, arms above the surface, his feet seeming firm on the soft muddy riverbed. He kept his eyes on Rake. They were shielded on both sides by trees and undergrowth. In the quiet came a boy's scream – 'Papa! Papa!' Yumatov's gaze shifted to somewhere behind Rake, who drew his Fairbairn-Sykes and dived under the water, kicking forward through the reeds. Visibility, though blurred, was enough to make out Yumatov's left leg, which he grabbed, dragging him down. The Iridium knocked against Rake's left cheek. Rake held it, followed the cord, pulling it taught against Yumatov's wrist, and cut it.

Yumatov's fist cracked against the side of Rake's head. With another blow he knocked the phone from Rake's hand. Mindful of Max out there with Mikki, Rake kept the knife blade under the water, hoping the boy would not see him kill his father. But Yumatov was hurt more than Rake had seen.

His eyes quivered and rolled upward. His strength was draining. Rake need do nothing except wait.

'It's on a timer.' Yumatov coughed blood. The phone didn't need activation. In a few minutes it would do so itself.

Rake dived down again. He ran his hands along the silt, feeling through reeds and pushing away driftwood. The phone was caught between two rocks. Rake clutched it in both hands and brought it up. The encasing waterproof glove could easily withstand the knocks and the water. Its signal was transmitting to the satellite 253 miles almost directly above.

Yumatov leant against a rock. He was alive but dying. Despite the cold water, blood trailed into a still pool underneath the overhanging branch. The Iridium was switched on, with a clock in the top right corner, and a number indicating which satellite it was locked onto. Nothing else. It would be programmed to detonate on the single press of a key or, as Yumatov had warned, on a timer which would be set for around now.

'Max worships you, Ruslan,' appealed Rake. 'For God's sake what is the code?'

'Fuck you, Ozenna.' Yumatov slipped. He began to keep himself up but had no strength. Rake let him slide into the water.

One minute, five minutes, it didn't much matter. He slit open the glove with his knife and had no idea if he was about to trigger or neutralize. He took the phone out. At the top, next to the stubby antenna, he pressed the Off button and kept it down until the screen went black.

Yumatov's body bumped against him in the sluggish current. He held up the Iridium and ran his finger across his throat to signal to Mikki that Yumatov was dead. Rake hauled the corpse onto the bank.

Two hundred and fifty-three miles above northern Europe, a pale yellow-colored oblong metallic satellite, weighing 210 kilograms and the size of a household refrigerator, sped at 17,500 miles an hour over the city of Bonn. It carried a thermonuclear warhead designed to paralyze everything below. The unnamed satellite received no instruction to do anything except continue its orbit.

Rake tested his earpiece and mic. Lucas was there. Mikki crouched, hair dripping, his jacket around Max's shoulders to give him warmth, holding him close in comfort. The boy stared at Rake and his father's body.

'Thank you, Major,' said Lucas. 'And Stephen Case came through. We now have control of the satellite.'

'How's Carrie? And Anna?'

'Carrie's fine. Anna will pull through,' answered Lucas impatiently. 'This was Lagutov's game and he needs to pay.'

Rake heard Lucas asking him to keep Yumatov alive because he was needed as a witness against the Kremlin. He smelled river vegetation. Slime and algae ran down his face. His boots sucked into silt and mud, and cold eased its way through his body. His shoulder, where he had hit the sandstone pillar, hurt like hell.

'Yumatov's dead,' he said. 'It's best that way.'

FIFTY-FOUR

Harry Lucas met Rake at the White House entrance and took him up to the sitting room attached to the famous Lincoln bedroom in the President's private quarters. Merrow was alone, anxious, relieved to see them. Lucas opened the line to Downing Street where Kevin Slater and Stephanie appeared at a small mahogany table with a portrait of Winston Churchill on the wall behind them. Merrow asked Lucas to speak first.

'We have separated the polonium-210 initiator from the thermonuclear warhead. No detonation is now possible,' he said. 'At some stage we will find a way to bring it safely to Earth. Until then we monitor.'

'We have a wider challenge,' said Merrow. 'There is still sixty-five kilograms missing from the Ulba plant theft, enough for five to seven more warheads of a similar size. In the past three years, three hundred and twenty-six satellites have been launched, of which only fifty-three would be too small to carry the charge needed for such an attack. Having designed one, we should expect them to build more. We need to know who has them, and who holds the triggers. I've asked Harry Lucas to oversee a world hunt to secure the missing material and we need new protocols to cover weapons in space. The 1967 Outer Space Treaty needs updating.'

'There are already well-established systems to track black-market supply chains of nuclear material,' said Lucas. 'That's how we stopped Iran. We'll keep closer watch on private satellite launches.'

'What do the Europeans say about rolling up Nevrosky's networks?' asked Merrow.

'Not that easy, Mr President,' said Stephanie. 'Most haven't done anything illegal. Elections to the organizations he controlled are seen as part of our democratic process.'

'Stephen Case will be working for us on that,' said Lucas.

Stephanie said, 'We've got a similar problem with Ariga, which funded the whole operation. The Japanese are shielding them, throwing up threats and excuses.'

'Lagutov needs to go.' Merrow frowned, pushing his tongue against his lower lip. 'That was my fault. I trusted him too much.'

'And we owe Sergey Grizlov,' said Stephanie.

'Can Stephen Case get Grizlov into the Kremlin?' said Merrow. No one answered. No one objected.

A restlessness swept through Rake. He listened, but he had nothing to contribute. The red velvet chairs, the expensively upholstered yellow sofa, the old dark wood writing desk – it was all like out of a museum. None of it matched his mood.

'Major Ozenna,' said Merrow. 'Since you know the background, I would like you to help Harry set up this world search.'

'Yes, sir.' If the President asked, there was no question of Rake saying anything else. For a blink, he thought about Yumatov's accusation that he had no feeling, no vision. Maybe the Russian was right. Maybe he was the guy who does what's asked, good at following orders.

As they were being shown out, Lucas said, 'I followed up on the Chukchi boatman you asked about from Uelen.'

'You found him?'

'He didn't make it. That first gunfire you heard from Big Diomede. That would have been him getting shot. Katia was fast enough to get away. Or try.'

They walked onto Pennsylvania Avenue. Rake turned down Lucas's offer of a lift. It was late evening, with a full summer night sky and only a mile or so's walk. He enjoyed the humid city air, the sidewalks with people spilling out from restaurants, the stuff going through his mind that was both good and bad.

He called Mickael Korav, the Chukchi leader from Uelen who had saved his life. Rake relayed Lucas's information, saying, 'Vanya didn't make it. I'm sorry.'

'Thank you.' Korav was on the beach and Rake could hear sea and birds. 'Are you Rake Ozenna from Krusenstern?' Krusenstern was one of the Russian names for Little Diomede. Rake said he was.

'I knew your father.'

Rake was at a green pedestrian light on H Street. He ignored it, stepped back from the curb into Lafayette Square where it was quieter, his stomach churning. 'You knew him?'

'I did.'

'Where is he?'

'I was going to ask you. We were friends. One day, he disappeared. He's a good man. A very good man.'

Rake heard the beep of the traffic signal. He watched the green walking figure and stayed where he was. Korav talked about the Arctic research station being sealed off again. Moscow agencies were all over it. 'When the shit's died down, come across and see us again. My grandfather, he came from your Little Diomede.'

Rake walked up Pennsylvania to Washington Circle and headed down New Hampshire. Rake thought of his blood family, or lack of it, his island family and his work. It all made sense. None made sense. Except he would use Lucas, Merrow, whatever it took, to go across again and spend an evening with Mickael Korav.

From his jacket pocket, he brought out the keys Carrie had given him for her apartment. She had flown in from London, where she had settled Anna back with the children and the nanny. Anna's leg wound would need physiotherapy but she would be fine. The children would take longer to heal.

Rake let himself into the building, rode the elevator to the eighth floor and walked along the corridor. He put the key in the lock, but Carrie opened it first. She was fresh out of the shower, wearing a white towel robe, barefoot, hair wet and dripping. 'We'll never be good together,' she said. 'You need to know that.'

'I know,' answered Rake as she pulled him inside and kissed him.

'We will not talk about the future.' She kicked the door shut and pulled at his shirt. He slid his hand under her robe and kissed her shoulder, drawing her closer to him.

His phone in the top pocket of his untucked shirt vibrated. It was less than thirty minutes since Rake had left the White House, and Lucas was calling. Rake read the message and showed Carrie, who eased the phone from his hand and dropped it onto a chair.

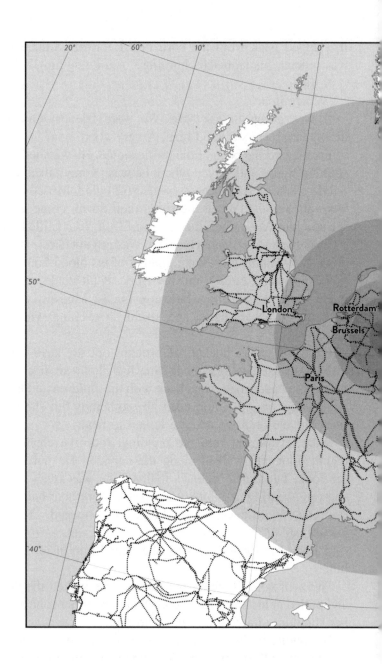

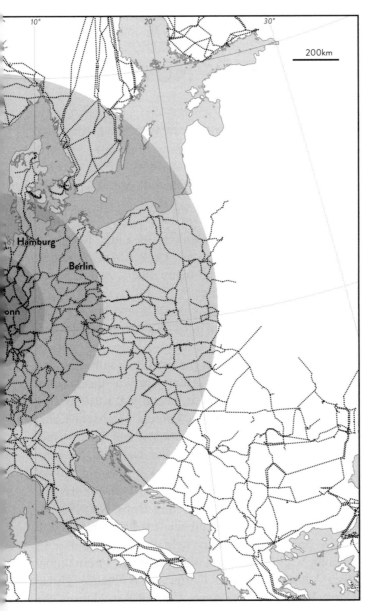

An estimate of the impact of a super electromagnetic pulse 253 miles above
Bonn. The serrated lines show the intensity of Europe's electrical grid.

AUTHOR'S NOTE

A multitude of thanks to all those who gave time and insight in helping with *Man on Fire*. Many asked to stay anonymous because of the sensitivity of the issues, whether electromagnetic pulse, organized crime, political manipulation or matters of the heart.

But for the others:

I am forever grateful for the islanders of Little Diomede, including Frances Ozenna (no relation), Opik Ahkinga, Robert Soolook, Henry and Jo Ahkaluk and many others, and in Nome to Sue Steinacher and Jim Stimphle.

Thanks to the government of Kazakhstan for inviting my BBC team to the Ulba Metallurgical Plant in Ust Kamenogorsk. Project Sapphire did happen as described without, I hope, the theft of the weapons-grade uranium used on the satellite bomb. Zhulduz Baizakova and Ambassador Kairat Abbusseitov at the London Kazhakh Embassy helped fix up the visit. Anatoliy A. Kuchkovskiy and his team showed us around Ulba. Foreign Ministers Kanat Saudabaev and Erlan Idrissov provided context and background, and Thomas Blanton and his team at the National Security Archives in Washington, DC did much work on getting Project Sapphire declassified. For those interested to know more, the details can be found in the NSA's Briefing Book No. 491. Dr Togzhan Kassenova's insight on both nuclear proliferation and Kazakhstan has been of enormous help, as have interviews and conversations with Tariq Rauf, then with the International Atomic Energy Authority, Charles Curtis of the Nuclear Threat Initiative, Daryl Kimball at the Arms Control Association, the late Senator Richard Lugar who, with Senator Sam Nunn, pioneered the Cooperative Threat Reduction Program against nuclear proliferation and, at a more personal level, to Fred Scott, my long-time friend and camera operator who came with me to Ust Kamenogorsk.

R. James Wolsey Jr, CIA director 1993–95, first brought the threat of an electromagnetic pulse attack to my attention. Thanks to Dr Peter Pry of the US Congressional Electromagnetic Pulse Commission, for giving his time to explain the science and impact and for looking through my drafts on EMP. I drew heavily on Dr Pry's *The Long Sunday, The Power and the Light* and other work. At the time of writing, North Korea had satellites in space on a southern polar trajectory orbiting the United States that remain of concern to intelligence agencies. Dr Sally Leivesley of Newrisk Ltd was especially generous with her time, experience and ideas as we speculated how such a weapon might be constructed. Sally referred me to work by Richard Garwin, Edward Teller, Lowell Wood, John Organek of the Electrical Infrastructure Council and others.

The manipulation of elections and the future of Europe has become an enveloping issue in recent years. I am grateful to many for their time and guidance on this issue and more. They include Duncan Bartlett, Ian Bond, Lesley Downer, Shihoko Goto, Matthew Henderson, Christopher Hill, Ian Kearns, ShaRon Kedar, Karin Landgren, Jacques Marion, Robin Marsh, Tom McDevitt, Max Moskalov, Jim Murphy, Alexander Nekrassov, Yo Osumi, Charles Parton, Vladimir Petrovsky, Victor Razbegin, Paul Reynolds, Adam Thompson, Martin Turner, Mark Valladares, Tom Walsh, Irina von Wiese, Adam Williams, Austin Williams, Robert Woodthorpe Browne, Alexander Yakovenko, Alexander Zhebin and Peter Zoehrer.

Much has been written about electoral interference and populism. Carole Cadwalladr's boundary-breaking work for the *Guardian* newspaper after Britain's Brexit referendum lay much of the ground together with numerous investigations and books. Among the more accessible are Malcolm Nance's *The Plot to Hack America*; *This Is Not Propaganda: Adventures in the War Against Reality* by Peter Pomerantsev; *The Light That Failed: Why the West Is Losing the Fight for Democracy* by Ivan Krastev and Stephen Holmes and *Deer Hunting with Jesus: Dispatches from America's Class War* by Joe Bageant.

Jane Brown, David Gammon, Kasim Javed and Roger Whittaker took me along the contours of codes, artificial intelligence, programming and encryption; and Benedict Mills and Carrie Roller guided me through Carrie Walker's trauma surgery and battlefield first-aid.

Sven and Petra Cazastka of Enthusia and Daniel Mourek, Lucie Druckerova and Katarina Hobbs of the Czech Tourism Authority guided me through the hazards and wonders of the Elbe Sandstone Mountains. To those familiar with this beautiful part of Europe, you may have noticed my taking liberty for the purpose of storytelling with the geography, and exact locations of rivers, trails and waterfalls.

In London, I used the lovely house of my friends Cherry and Charlie Parton to describe Stephanie's Clapham home, which included a similar chess set whose pieces were molded by Cherry. In Washington, DC, I borrowed the apartment of Nancy Langston in Virginia Avenue, opposite the Watergate Complex, to describe where Carrie lived, and Nancy kindly lent her name to the farm where Yumatov was being held.

An author is never the sole writer of any book. My thanks to Liz Jensen, Don Weise and Mary Sandys for helping to streamline sprawling early drafts, to Kasim Javid, Ammar Nazir and the team at Creative Video Solutions for their Rake Ozenna social media and videos, to Kate Lyall Grant, Michelle Duff, Natasha Bell and all in the efficiently professional team at Severn House and Canongate, and to my long-time agent, David Grossman, who enthusiastically supported the Rake Ozenna series from the beginning.